TARNISHED BEGINNINGS & TARNISHED LEGACY

SOUL DANCE BOOKS 1 AND 2

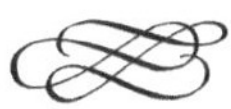

ANN GIMPEL

Edited by
ANGELA KELLY
Edited by
DIANE EAGLE

CONTENTS

TARNISHED BEGINNINGS

A PREQUEL

Soul Dance, Book One
Historical Shifter Fantasy
By Ann Gimpel

Tarnished Beginnings

1700s Egypt is a haven for magic-wielders of all kinds. Vampires hold court, staying one step ahead of the priests and priestesses who want them dead. Gypsy caravans roam the Nile from north to south and back again, plying their wares, telling fortunes, casting Tarot cards, and stealing from the gadjos.

Tairin Jabari was born in a caravan and has always believed she's Romani. Why wouldn't she? Her mother and father never suggested otherwise. The Rom have harsh rules. When Tairin's first shift catches her unaware at thirteen, her father disappears, and the elders move with deadly speed to punish her mother for mating outside the blood.

Hurt, lost, confused, and fearing for her own life, Tairin runs away, leaving her mother's smoking funeral pyre behind. If she could only find her father, he'd welcome her. He's always loved her, hasn't he? Only problem is he's in a shifter settlement. With her mixed blood, they won't welcome her any more warmly than the Romani. It doesn't take long before Tairin discovers how desperately unprepared she is for life outside her protected caravan. With her survival on the line every single day, she and her wolf have some hard choices to make.

CHAPTER 1

*E*gypt 1740

"Tairin. Get moving! The water buckets are still empty," her mother shouted. Long black hair hung in two braids behind her shoulders, and her dark eyes snapped dangerously. She stood over Tairin with her hands on her hips, staring down at her. Dressed in long, colorful skirts and a red, patchwork tunic, she dug her bare feet into loose sand. Beads and bracelets clanked against each other when she moved, and rings circled all her fingers and several of her toes.

"Yes, Mother. Sorry, Mother."

Tairin rose from where she crouched on the shady side of one of the wagons in their Gypsy caravan. Midday sun beat down on her, making her dizzy and nauseated. She hadn't felt right for days. A wolf—the same one that had haunted her dreams for years—was making its presence known with greater and greater frequency. Every time she closed her eyes, the creature was there, and she wondered if she was losing her mind. The thing was actually talking with her.

Urging.

Pushing.

Exhorting.

Appealing.

Shouting.

She'd always seen the animal as a special imaginary friend who visited her in the dream world, but it wasn't content to remain in the shadows any longer. It was angry, fury evident in its snarls and raised hackles, and Tairin was frightened. She'd tried to talk with her mother, but Aneksi curved two fingers in the Romani sigil against evil and told her to throw herself on the goddess's mercy.

Confused and wondering what any of the goddesses had to do with her problem, Tairin had asked which one to petition, but her mother shook her head. "You cannot talk about such things, even with me. They are forbidden. For the sake of all that's sacred, do not mention these visions to anyone else. They'll think you mad."

Tairin pushed the unsettling exchange with her mother aside. It had happened a few days ago, but it still haunted her. Snatching up two buckets fashioned from goat hide, she trudged toward the Nile River. It ran fast and muddy not far from their encampment. Their caravan had just left Cairo where they'd done well telling fortunes and entertaining wealthy patrons with dancing girls and tarot spreads. Tomorrow or the next day, they'd head for Giza. They plied the settlements up and down the Nile, along with several other caravans. The elders set a schedule so not more than one group was in any given city at a time.

Her head spun and she shook it to clear black spots swimming in front of her eyes. What was wrong with her? She'd always been healthy, but she'd just turned thirteen. On the heels of her birthday had come blood and cramping pain in her lower abdomen. An uncomfortable bundle of rags bunched between her legs made it impossible to ignore her body's betrayal. She wasn't bleeding as much as she'd been a couple of days earlier, but this would happen every month. Forever.

Would she always feel this bad?

Tairin hoped not. Her body was changing, and she'd have to get used to the awkwardness of breasts and blood. It wasn't as if she could alter anything. Kneeling, she dipped her buckets in the brown, murky waters of the Nile. Their weight made her stagger as she headed back to drop them off and get two more. Ten buckets twice a day provided enough water for her mother's wagon. Tairin longed for brothers and sisters to share the chores, but no such luck. Her grandparents were too feeble to do anything requiring much effort, and her father wasn't always around. Even if he were, men didn't dirty their hands with menial tasks like carting water.

Not for the first time, she wished she'd been born a male. No blood. No breasts. No hucking water. She'd enjoy sitting in circles with the other men, drinking, smoking, and cracking jokes. And she liked taking care of the horses and goats, chores traditionally done by men.

May as well demand the moon on a platter.

Partway back, raised voices drew her to a halt. Her mother and father were arguing. They'd done more and more of that of late, but they always shut up fast when she drew close. Maybe this time, she'd actually hear something.

Tairin dropped to her belly in tall marsh grass that grew thickly in the Nile's delta and shrouded herself in magic. She might earn a session with the whip for not delivering the water faster, but she wanted to hear what was wrong. Her father had left for a long time the previous month. He'd been gone so long, she'd been afraid she'd never see him again. Even though he'd returned, things between him and her mother had remained tense. The usual sounds of their lovemaking conspicuously absent.

Their voices vanished abruptly, but Tairin wasn't fooled, nor did it deter her. They'd summoned a spell to hide their words. Not wanting to miss anything critical that might shed light on what was wrong between them, she snaked a tendril of magic outward and drilled through the ward enveloping her parents. She was careful to intrude near ground level to lessen the odds of her mother or father noticing.

"We must leave the caravan, Aneksi. There's no choice."

"I refuse to penalize my parents for my bad decisions, Jamal."

"So leave them the wagon. I'll secure another for us. I found an oasis to shelter us. It's what I was doing last month: hunting for a place we might settle. No one need know—"

"Maybe it won't happen." Her mother's voice shrilled. "And we will have turned our lives inside out for nothing."

"It will. Nothing you or I can do will stop it. Not only will it happen, it's close. Closer than you imagine. I see it in her eyes, and my wolf walks with hers in the place where the animals all roam together. I must talk with Tairin. Prepare her—"

"It's forbidden. You'll do no such thing."

"It's not fair to her. Whether she wills it or no, her first shift will catch her unaware if I say nothing. None of us are ever quite ready. If it happens in the midst of the caravan..." Her father's voice trailed off.

Tairin swallowed hard. First shift? What on earth was her father talking about? Did he and her mother have another child? One she didn't know about? Tairin muted her racing thoughts and focused on her mother's next words.

"We must make certain that first shift never comes to pass." Aneksi's normally low, musical voice was strident, strained.

"You can't stop it. Nor can I, which is why we must leave," her father argued. "You and I were selfish indulging in a love we should have been strong enough to resist. When you became pregnant and decided to keep the child, we didn't think it through. We've offered our daughter nothing but tarnished beginnings. At least if we steal away together, we can be a family who lives out truth, not falsehood—"

"I'm not going, and that's final. Find another way."

"Aneksi. Be reasonable. I'm your husband. I could order you to leave with me, but I don't want to have to do that."

"I wouldn't go. I'd divorce you first. I'd have grounds. I could tell the elders you tricked me, obscured your shifter roots with magic. My home is with my people."

"You should've thought of that before you became my wife." Jamal's words held a harsh, bitter edge.

Tairin choked back fear that made her throat so thick she couldn't breathe. Like a macabre puzzle that suddenly yielded to persistent efforts to solve it, understanding slammed into her. And she wished she'd left well enough alone. Wished she'd never eavesdropped.

Wished she'd never been born.

Her father was a shifter. He had to be since he'd mentioned his wolf and her mother had thrown his shifter blood in his face. Tairin was half shifter, which meant she was unclean. Once the Romani discovered that, they'd cast her from their caravans. Or worse. She'd seen the Rom burn their own for lesser offenses. Drawing her knees up, she wrapped her arms around them and stuffed a hand into her mouth, so she wouldn't give her presence away with whimpers and moans.

How could her parents have been so stupid? Romani didn't mate outside their blood, and they sure as hell didn't mate with shapeshifters. The Rom saw shifters the same way they viewed vampires, as abominations.

Tairin held onto herself tighter, afraid if she let go, she'd shatter into a million pieces. She was a shifter. Half a shifter, anyway. That was what the wolf in her head was about, and it was tired of waiting.

Her mother and father were still conversing in tense, stilted tones, but Tairin had stopped listening. She hated them. They'd been selfish and ruined her life.

They ruined their lives too, a small voice insisted.

Maybe not. I'm the one with mixed blood. The one who's unclean. Forbidden.

Tears burned behind her eyes, but she refused to give in to

them. She was old enough to be on her own. Children half her age roamed Cairo's streets, living on scraps they begged from strangers. If they could do it, so could she.

Brave words, but the specter of leaving the caravan tore at her. This was her home. She had friends here. She'd learned to ferret out truths from the gadjos who paid them, and her fortunes and tarot readings were in high demand. Because she was quick, one of the elders had begun grooming her in the finer points of pilfering—

"Tairin!" Her mother's voice was edged with steel. "Where've you gotten yourself off to? The horses need water."

She bit her lower lip hard enough to draw blood, dragged herself to her feet, and picked up the heavy buckets. Once she was close to the wagon, she dropped them and picked up two more before her mother could grill her about why the first buckets took so long.

Tairin snuck a glance at her father before heading back toward the Nile. He looked sad, with lines carved into his high forehead and eyes pinched at the corners. His brown-gold hair and dark eyes were just like hers, and she'd always loved him.

Until now.

She traipsed back and forth again and again, grateful to have something to do. It didn't quiet her mind or her fears, but at least she could pretend her life was still normal.

Not for much longer.

Tairin positioned the last two buckets, keeping them out of direct sunlight so her hard work wouldn't evaporate, drawn into the dry, baked air of northern Egypt. The heat was worse in the south, but this was the only place she'd ever lived. The only life she'd known.

Her magic told her that her grandparents slumbered in the back of their wagon. Her mother and father were nowhere to be found. Maybe they'd left the area to continue their argument about her. She abandoned the circle of wagons and the scent of cook fires and headed back toward the Nile. A glance at the sky told her she should light their own fire and get tonight's grains softening in boiling water, but she kept walking.

The river was shallow here, and she made her way across rocks and sandbars to a small island, rucking up her skirts to keep them dry. Like most of her kinsmen, her feet were bare. They only wore shoes when they went into towns with their open sewers and garbage pits. No need out here.

She unwound the rags between her legs, inspecting them. What had been a flow was now spots. Maybe her moon cycle was done for now. She returned to the water and rinsed out the rags, hanging them from clumps of vegetation. Not having the bulky strips of cloth bound to her body made her feel more like herself.

She sat on a low, flat rock and watched the river flowing by. It held a timeless aspect that drew her, soothed her. The Nile had always been here, and it always would be. People came and went, but the river endured.

"I should leave."

The words surprised her, but she'd said them out loud for a reason. Maybe to focus her wandering attention. Where would she go? Would she end up a beggar? Or maybe worse. She was old enough to marry, which meant she was old enough for what men and women did behind curtains in the dark of night. Without the caravan to bargain for a husband for her, though, and pay a dowry, she'd never secure a husband. No man would want a woman who came to him penniless without a wedding gift.

No man would want a woman with mixed blood like mine. Not to marry, anyway.

The thought made her wince and pounded a few more nails into the coffin her future had become. Just because she wasn't marriage material didn't mean men wouldn't want her for the hidden mysteries of her body, though. As a woman alone, she'd be vulnerable to every passing male with an itch in his private parts.

It wasn't cold, but Tairin shivered and wrapped her arms around herself.

Maybe her mother was right and she'd never shift. So far, she'd been stronger than the wolf. She'd kept the upper hand. If she were vigilant, she could keep the creature hidden. Force it to remain in the shadows of her mind. Even a few years would make a huge difference. She'd be far stronger at sixteen than she was right now. Her magic had been expanding by leaps and bounds, and she expected that to continue.

"Tairin! What are you doing here?"

She snapped her head up at the sound of Calista's voice. "Nothing. Thinking. Why are you here?"

The other woman looked away, clearly uncomfortable.

Tairin's stomach twisted into a hard, painful knot. Maybe her father and mother's argument had become public, and something unspeakable had happened.

Stop. I'm jumpy as a scalded cat. Calista was surprised I was here, which means she wasn't hunting for me.

Tairin pushed her anxiety aside, waiting.

*C*alista made her way to where Tairin sat, color high on her dark-skinned face. A few years older than Tairin, she had neither wagon nor family. She remained with the caravan out of the kindness of its members, who allowed her to drift from wagon to wagon. Her fine, dark hair was wound into a bun and secured at the nape of her neck with bone pins. Dark eyes skimmed the ground, and she shook out her long, black skirt. It had been bunched in both hands to keep it out of the water.

"I'm meeting someone," Calista mumbled, "but I can tell him we need to pick a different place."

Tairin gazed across the river, but didn't see anyone else. Calista must have an assignation with one of the men. Maybe one of the married ones, which could get uncomfortable fast. "I can leave. It's all right. I don't need privacy."

"Thank you." Gratitude flared from the other woman.

Tairin sensed it with her magic. She rose and gathered her bunch of rags. The incessant sun had nearly dried them. To lessen the odds of running into whomever was on their way to meet Calista, Tairin walked to the far end of the island before crossing the river. It was deeper here, and her skirts got wet even though she held them higher than before.

She wasn't ready to return to her wagon. Wasn't ready to see her mother and pretend she hadn't overhead her earlier. The safest path for everyone was if she left the caravan. Maybe after they got to Giza, she could fade into its ancient, crowded streets. Isis and Anat had temples there. If she threw herself on their mercy, they might take her in, allow her to work in exchange for shelter and food.

It was as good a plan as any.

Sorrow threatened to spill from her eyes, and she blinked back tears. The only way she could pull this off would be if she pretended nothing had changed. She was Aneksi and Jamal's dutiful daughter, a loving granddaughter to Aneksi's parents, and a devoted caravan member who turned all the money she made over to the caravan elders.

An uncomfortable rolling sensation deep in her gut made saliva pool in the back of her mouth. Was she about to be sick?

"You failed to factor me into your plans." A familiar voice pushed words into her mind.

The wolf.

Tairin sank to her knees in a clump of rosin cress studded with sweet marjoram. She plucked the marjoram, stuffing it into a pocket for the drying rack. Years ago, the wolf had been a playmate, a friend. They'd never talked about anything serious, and she'd enjoyed its company.

An idea formed.

"You want me to be your friend, right?" Tairin sucked in a breath. Would her gambit work?

"We are more than friends."

"I—I don't understand. I used to like you, but I don't anymore. Not very much, anyway." Strategy frittered through her fingers as she opted for truth.

A low, rumbling growl filled her belly. Some of it spilled from her mouth before she choked the unnerving sound off at its roots. She'd sounded like a wild animal, and it worried her even more than having the wolf in her mind talking with her.

"You have to let me out. It's time. We bonded long ago when you were still a child. The rules state that once you become a woman, you shift and I run free."

"Rules?" Shock stiffened her spine, and she curled her hands into tight fists. *"What rules? Who made them? Where can I find them?"* The last question was sheer bravado. She didn't read well enough to decipher Coptic, but the wolf couldn't know that. Or could it?

"Teaching you was your father's job. He failed you. I've had this discussion with Jamal's wolf."

Tairin flashed back to her father's words from earlier that day. *"Not only will it happen, it's close. Closer than you imagine. I see it in her eyes, and my wolf walks with hers in the place where the animals all roam together. I must talk with Tairin. Prepare her—"*

Before her world fragmented around her and turned into something alien, foreign, she drew herself together. *"I don't want you. I don't want to shift. Not now. Not ever. I'm done with that part of things. Go away. Leave me alone."*

Sorrow deeper than her fear sluiced through her. Tears overflowed, and the place her heart sat behind her breastbone ached as if someone had died.

"What's happening to me?" she moaned, not expecting an answer. The shape she was in, she would have been horrified if anyone came upon her.

"Let me help you," the wolf said, its voice gentle. *"You're frightened. You don't really want me to leave. If you order me from you, break our bond, I'll have to comply, but you'll be less than half a person then. I'm an elemental part of who you are. Without me, your life will be bleak, black, empty."*

"I know what I want—" she began, but the place the wolf had been in her mind was blank, and she knew it had left.

"Damn it." She pounded a fist into the hot sand beneath her. "It left before I could banish it."

Maybe it left to save me from making the worst mistake of my life.

Her thoughts sobered her. Giza wouldn't be for a few days. If her father hadn't left again, she'd find a way to draw him aside and ask him point blank about wolves and shifting. Her mother wouldn't tell her, but maybe he would. The wolf inferred she could rid herself of it. She needed to know the ramifications if she did. Was what it had said true? The part about her life turning bleak, black, and empty?

A shudder racked her, followed by several more, and she pushed to her feet. Could her life possibly become any worse? Any bleaker, blacker, or emptier than it already was?

Preoccupied and apprehensive—because so many loose ends mocked her—Tairin made her way back to her wagon. She'd catch grief for not starting dinner an hour ago, but with all the other problems facing her, that one was laughable.

The evening meal was long since over, and Tairin couldn't put off rolling herself into her blanket for much longer. She was too keyed up to sleep, but she didn't want to do anything that drew attention to herself. Her mother had been quiet through supper, but her grandparents chatted up a storm. Either they were oblivious to the tension in the air, or they were compensating for it by pretending it didn't exist.

Tairin finished cleaning and drying the last of the pots and utensils they used at every meal. "Do you know where Father went?" she asked Aneksi, trying for a casual tone.

"Why?" Her mother latched her discerning gaze onto Tairin's face.

She shrugged. "No reason. He was here earlier. I felt his magic."

"He has business interests to address. They often draw him away from us." Aneksi's words were stilted, tense.

Tairin sent what she hoped was a subtle thread of magic to delve beneath her mother's message, but Aneksi screwed her face into a frown.

"None of that, young woman. Show some respect."

The stress of the day caught up with her, and Tairin's temper—never her long suit—snapped. She rounded on her mother and crossed her arms beneath her breasts. "You never show me respect. I'm having a hard time, and you won't tell me anything about—"

Her mother moved faster than Tairin had ever seen her. Hooking an arm around Tairin's waist, she dragged her away from the circle of wagons. Tairin squirmed, trying to escape, but her mother's grip was too strong to break. Once they'd covered some distance from the flickering lights of the caravan, Aneksi stopped, but didn't let go.

She moved in front of Tairin and dropped a hand on each shoulder. "I will not have our business publicized for the entire caravan, nor do I want my parents upset. Do you understand me?"

"Perfectly." The word choked her, stuck in her throat. "Let go of me. All I asked was where Father is." Tairin buried a desire to throw herself into her mother's arms. Once upon a time, Aneksi had been a source of comfort.

Not anymore.

"He and I had a difference of opinion. I don't expect him to return." Aneksi shook her head hard enough her hoop earrings jangled. "We don't need him. The caravan will provide for us."

"But he can't not return. I have things to ask him."

Aneksi narrowed her eyes to slits. "Things you have no need to know." She lowered her voice. "You must fight this other part of you. Do not let it grow or gain ascendency. If the Romani discover the truth, they'll banish you, and young women on their own face many…complications. Problems the caravan shields you from."

Something else rode beneath her mother's words. Tairin didn't see where she had much else to lose, so she probed. "And what will they do to you? Last I checked, marrying outside our blood-lines was forbidden. You deceived everyone—including me."

Her mother let go of one of her shoulders long enough to slap her hard across the face.

"Do not let her get away with that." The wolf, who'd vanished earlier, was back.

Tairin didn't need much goading, she'd had enough of her mother for one day. Pouring magic into a casting, she jerked free from her mother's grip and wove wards around herself. "There," she taunted. "You can't hurt me anymore."

Aneksi reached for her. Sparks flew where her hand connected with Tairin's ward. Fury contorted her features, and she skinned her lips back from her teeth as she called power of her own.

Here it comes, Tairin thought.

She'd suspected she'd grown stronger than her mother. Was it true? Power battered her wards, turning the night blue-white where the two magics collided. Tairin reached deep into the earth that nourished her. Earth and fire were her preferred elements. She was fairly proficient with air. Water ran a poor fourth.

"Don't just protect yourself," the wolf urged. *"Hurt her. She drove your father away."*

The wolf's emotions cascaded through her. Primitive, harsh. They dragged her back to her senses. Tempting as it was to take her pain out on Aneksi, if she alienated her mother, she'd seal her fate. Thinking about leaving the caravan, versus being forced to because her mother threw her out, were two entirely different things.

Tairin straightened and began reeling in her magic. "Mother. I'm sorry. I don't want a war with you."

The glowing nimbus around Aneksi receded as she sheathed her power. "Glad you've come to your senses, daughter, but some things cannot be undone. This is one of them. Get to bed. It's late." Turning on her heel, Aneksi stalked into the night.

Tairin watched her go, nursing an empty place inside her. Father was gone. Mother didn't care anymore. Or maybe she was worried about her own hide. It was easy to believe you'd never have to pay the piper for your sins. Tairin had done enough sketchy things, only to get caught later, to understand that dynamic.

Jamal was a beautiful man. Tairin understood how her mother could have fallen hard for him, ignoring what he was. Who knew? Maybe he'd hidden his true nature until there was no turning back. If they'd never had her, though, her mother might have dodged retribution for her sins.

Forever.

Tairin turned it over in her mind. She hadn't actually shifted yet, so her mother might still escape justice. Maybe the wolf was more controllable than she thought. It was gone again. She'd come to recognize its presence within her. Feeling sad, desolate, she trudged back to the wagon. Her grandparents would be asleep, so she wouldn't have to explain where she'd been. Goddess knew when her mother would return.

Tairin stopped at one of the water buckets to throw water on her face and swish some around her mouth as she scrubbed scum off her teeth with a particularly hardy variety of marsh grass. She crept into the wagon and spread her blanket on the floor in the corner where she'd slept since she was old enough to sleep alone.

The blanket and corner smelled familiar, soothing, but she wasn't fooled. Her life teetered on the edge of a major change. Whether she took to the streets in Giza, or her mother booted her from the caravan before they got there, made little difference. Aneksi was done with her. Tairin had recognized dismissal in her mother's face before she strode off into the night. It was like blowing out a lamp that had once shone bright, but was now dark and cold.

What had she done wrong? All children grew up. Surely, her mother hadn't expected her to remain a baby forever.

Her heart hurt, and her throat was thick with unshed tears. Babies didn't shift. That ability—or curse—came with maturity. Aneksi had told her to fight it, and maybe she could, but her mother hadn't offered any help. Hadn't said she'd stand behind her. Hadn't opened her arms so they could make up after their fight.

What she'd said was, "Some things cannot be undone. This is one of them."

No Mother. No Father. Just her.

"And me." The wolf was back.

Tairin shut her eyes. The last place she wanted comfort from was the wolf. It was why her mother and father were no longer together. It was why her mother hated her. If it would go away, her life could be normal again.

"It's not how the world works, Tairin. You're tired. It's been a difficult day. Sleep now. I will watch over you and see that nothing harms you while you rest."

The wolf's words were so kind, she stuffed a hand into her mouth to stifle her sobs. Confusion made it impossible to think. How could the thing that was responsible for her plight provide comfort? It made no sense.

She should hate the wolf, but she couldn't summon the energy.

Her lids felt heavy, and she shut eyes that swam with tears. Tairin hadn't expected to sleep, but the descent into blackness happened so fast, she suspected maybe the wolf had magic of its own and had spelled her to sleep.

CHAPTER 4

Gray light pushing through slats in the wagon's sides woke her. At first, the morning felt welcome. She'd always taken pleasure in the beginning of a new day, but reality cascaded through her bringing memories of yesterday. Her muscles clenched, and she probed with magic. Her grandparents were still sleeping, which wasn't anything new. They were almost fifty. Old by anyone's standards.

Being careful, she hunted for Aneksi but didn't find her.

What exactly did her mother's absence mean? She might be done with Tairin, but surely she wouldn't walk away from her parents. She was their only child, and she cared for them now that they were too old to provide for themselves. It was the Romani way. Tairin's eyes widened. If her mother banished her, who would provide for her once she grew old?

Not my problem. I have plenty of my own without worrying about someone who doesn't care about me anymore.

She folded her blanket and stowed it in its place in a simple wooden chest, taking pains not to wake her grandparents. That done, she let herself outside and built up their cook fire to get the morning meal going. Aneksi might be gone, but that didn't mean her parents wouldn't want to break their fast.

The grain gruel studded with nuts and dates was almost done when the rustle of skirts and her mother's scent drove Tairin to her feet. She spun to face Aneksi, unsure what to say.

Her mother saved her the trouble. She looked like she hadn't slept. Dark circles ringed her eyes, and her normally well-groomed hair was a mass of tangles. "Thank you for preparing the morning meal." Her tone and words were formal.

"You're welcome." Tairin wanted to ask where her mother had been, but it wasn't the kind of question a child asked a parent.

"We'll get through this, somehow," Aneksi muttered.

Tairin didn't see how if they couldn't talk about it, but she bit back the words. Her mother looked defeated, her shoulders slumped and her eyes glazed and dull. Nothing like her usual, forthright self.

Aneksi knocked on one side of the wagon to let her parents know a meal was ready. Picking up a bowl, she scooped some of the mixture into it and began to eat. Tairin wasn't hungry, but she did the same. For once, her grandparents weren't overly chatty while they crouched in the dirt eating, alongside Tairin and Aneksi.

Tairin scanned them with magic, keeping it very subtle. The dark place in her grandfather was growing larger, and the spots where her grandmother's mind was unraveling were bigger as well. Before the year was out, her grandfather would be dead and her grandmother not much different from a very young child.

Not comforting, but impossible to put a better face on.

She felt her mother's gaze on her. When Tairin glanced her way, Aneksi shook her head. The meaning was clear. She'd divined what Tairin was doing and expected her to keep her mouth shut.

Tairin trained her eyes on her empty dish. Had her mother rethought last night? Could they be a family again, after all?

Maybe Aneksi's ill temper had been over Jamal never returning, and she'd taken her frustration out on Tairin.

She stood and held out a hand for her mother's bowl, piling them in a corner until everything was ready for washing. Half the buckets were empty, so she picked up two and headed for the Nile. If her mother were willing to give them one more chance as a family, Tairin was determined to do her part.

On her second trip back with sloshing buckets, the wolf flashed into her mind.

"Not now. The morning's been going so well. Go away," she pleaded.

"It's time." The wolf's voice in her head was implacable, ruthless, relentless.

Before she could launch arguments about it not being time at all, her body began to tingle and burn. The sensation began in her toes and moved slowly upward. Tairin dropped the buckets and shambled back toward the river, determined to hide somewhere. Maybe the island.

Surely once the wolf had its way, she'd be able to shift back. If nobody noticed, she might get away with it.

Maybe if she were strong enough, it wouldn't go that far. She pulled magic like a madwoman, winding it around herself, but the pain jabbing her with a million knifepoints only grew worse, almost as if it fed on her power.

She reached the Nile. Heedless of her skirts, mostly because her hands and fingers had moved beyond her control, she plowed through the water and pitched up on the island. Walking wasn't working, so she crawled, dragging herself up damp sand to where bushes grew thickly. Assuming she reached them, she'd hide there.

"This hurts," she wailed.

"The first time always hurts the most," the wolf informed her. *"But it's worse because you're fighting me. I control your first shift, but once it's done, you'll control all the others."*

"I can't give in. I don't want this." She curled into a ball, surprised

her body still looked the same even though it felt foreign, alien, like something that belonged to someone else.

"You have no choice," the wolf repeated. *"If you don't shift, you'll die. It's the way things work for our kind."*

Death might be welcome—if it meant the pain stopped. Her head pounded mercilessly. Even her teeth and eyes ached.

"Death is not welcome." The wolf bit off each word. *"If you die, you'll drag me down with you. I did not bond with you to have you kill us. What happened to the girl who romped with me? She'd embrace this change."*

"She doesn't exist anymore," Tairin said dully. *"She grew up."*

The ripping, tearing sensation intensified. When she dragged her eyes open, her perspective had shifted, as if she viewed the world through poorly blown glass. Her torso was growing shorter, and fur sprouted on her limbs. Where she'd had nails, claws formed.

She wanted to shriek, to howl, but if she did someone would hear and come running. The last thing she needed was a witness to her humiliation. Her mother's punishments paled in comparison to what the Rom elders would do to her. They'd banish her not only from this caravan, but also from every caravan. Word traveled fast in gypsy circles. Before a fortnight had passed, she'd be relegated to the shadowy world of beggars and street urchins.

Agony shot through her, turning every nerve into a red-hot coal of misery. Somewhere in the midst of it, she ended up standing on all four legs with a tail swishing behind her. As quickly as it had risen, the pain ceased. Scents bombarded her, and she licked her nose. The world came alive through her snout and ears. When she angled her head, she was certain she heard insects burrowing in the sand. The chittering of small rodents made saliva gather and flow from her lolling jaws.

"There. It is done. You survived, and so did I." Her wolf sounded relieved—and pleased.

Tairin fell back on her haunches, the unfamiliar form clumsy and awkward to control. *"How can I change back? No one can find out about this. No one."*

"Ssht. Take a few deep breaths. Enjoy your dual nature. There are so many advantages—"

"I don't care about them. I don't want to enjoy this. How can I change back? So far we got lucky, but that can't last."

"I want to run."

Pressure built in her body, but Tairin resisted it. *"And I want to change back. I can't be stuck this way. My father had a human form."*

"If we run and you get used to me, it won't hurt so much next time." The wolf's voice was softly seductive, hard to ignore. Even harder to refuse.

"You're using magic on me."

"Of course. You can do the same. Your power will become ever so much stronger because of me. It's one of those advantages I alluded to. The ones you didn't want to hear about."

Tairin felt herself relaxing, considering potential benefits hidden within her new abilities. She put the brakes on hard. *"You have to tell me how to change back."*

"Don't you want to hunt first? I hear fat mice. They'd be easy to catch."

"No. I want to know how to be human again. Tell me now or...or I'll banish you. Even if it kills us both." She sucked in a tense breath. She didn't really want to resort to breaking the bond with the wolf. In a very small corner of herself, she was enjoying the experience of having another form. That appreciation could grow given time, but not if she felt trapped.

"Ah. I see how it is. I live in your mind, so I'm privy to all your thoughts. If you need the keys to shifting back in order to be comfortable with your new ability, all you need do is visualize your human form. It's the same way you find my form. Summon the particular magic you felt earlier and visualize either human or wolf. If you let the power flow freely, it will happen as easily as breathing."

"Will it hurt?" Tairin grimaced—although her wolf's features

must have skewed it beyond recognition—and rebuked herself for cowardice. So what if it hurt? She'd have welcomed the tortures of the damned to be human again.

"Not as much or for as long. Go ahead," the wolf invited. *"Try it. Next time you shift, we can pick a more private place so we can run and hunt and feel the wind in our fur."*

Tairin focused power and held a picture in her mind of what she looked like as a human. The same grating, tearing sensation pulsed through her, but this time, she didn't fight it. Her backbone lengthened and her limbs spread from their position beneath her. Her vision took on its usual aspect. Just as she was inspecting the scraps that had been her clothing, but had ripped during her shift, a muted scream, followed by the unmistakable sound of a slap, drove her to her feet.

Calista hunkered a few feet away, her eyes so wide the whites showed all around. A reddened spot on her cheekbone told its own tale. The man next to her was turned so Tairin couldn't see his face, but she knew his scent: sweat and stale liquor. It was even more distinctive to her newly enhanced senses. Nehi, with his ten children and browbeaten wife, was a chronic philanderer. His wife was close to term with their next child, which explained the dalliance with Calista, but didn't excuse it.

"I know it's you," Tairin growled. "You needn't hide your face. You should be ashamed—"

Nehi spun so fast, dark, greasy hair fell across his face. "Ashamed? Of what? You're the abomination. The unclean one. Wait until I let the elders know. You'll be out of this caravan so fast, it'll make your head spin, sister. And that mother of yours is nothing better than a whore."

"How'd you sneak up on me?" Tairin demanded, rattled by his presence.

"I'm Rom, or did you forget? I have magic that allows me to mask my presence same as the rest of us." An unpleasant light kindled deep in his dark eyes and he moved toward her, his body lithe and corded with muscle. He held out his hands. "Maybe you and I can come to an…understanding. I'll keep my mouth shut if you'll pleasure me. Haven't had a virgin in a long time."

He leered unpleasantly.

"What makes you think I wouldn't tell?" Calista said sullenly. "I thought you wanted me, but now you want her."

Nehi snaked out a hand and slapped Calista again.

She yelped and clutched her face.

"You'll hold silence if I tell you to, bitch," Nehi snapped. "I was with you last night and today, and I'll say you're raving, that you must've helped yourself to the liquor again."

"You'll reveal yourself as an adulterer," Tairin countered. Calista might be afraid of him, but she wasn't.

"So what? Men understand these things." Nehi sidled closer. "What about it, sister?"

Tairin didn't need an assist from her wolf nattering from the sidelines. She bared her teeth and snarled. "No. I'd rather be dead than accept your offer."

Fury contorted his face into an ugly mass of wrinkles. He drew back a fist, but Tairin snarled again. "You'll be sorry. I'll summon my wolf, and—"

Nehi shoved Calista toward the Nile. "Back to the caravan. Now." He splashed into the water after her.

Tairin stared after them. She couldn't believe she'd threatened to send for her wolf.

But I did.

The sense of power rocketing through her was hot, bright, and welcome.

"See?" The wolf sounded insufferably smug. *"We'll be fine. We don't need your Romani kin."*

"I wouldn't be so quick to assume that," Tairin shot back. *"We may have won a battle, but this is just the beginning of a long war."*

She glanced at the remains of her clothes one last time. No way around it, she'd have to walk back to the wagon naked. If she hadn't entered womanhood, no one would've looked twice. As things stood, she might be branded a harlot.

None of that mattered. By the time she returned, Nehi would've spewed his poison, and Calista—eager to remain in his good graces—would validate every word. A long, rustling sigh escaped. If she were very lucky, the elders would allow her to cover herself before they kicked her out of the only life she'd ever known.

"We could run," the wolf piped up. *"No pressing reason for you to go back now. Or ever."*

"We'll run later," she told it. *"I need to face up to whatever's waiting for me."*

"You're an us now. Not a me."

Tairin ignored the wolf and picked her way across the Nile. The confrontation with her people wouldn't get any easier if she put it off.

CHAPTER 5

*H*er mother's screams trumped the rush of the Nile long before Tairin crossed the water's wide expanse. She wanted to run, find out what was happening, but prudence won out. Tairin summoned magic to shroud herself. The invisibility spell jumped to her bidding far faster than she expected. It made traversing the expanse between river and wagon easy.

No one stopped her because no one saw or sensed her.

She let herself into the wagon and dressed hurriedly, grateful her grandparents weren't there. Likely, they were wherever Aneksi was pleading for whoever was hurting her to stop. Figuring this might be her last chance, Tairin stuffed what she could of her belongings into a cloth sack and swung it over her body so the strap crossed her chest and one shoulder.

All the while Aneksi's shrieks continued, sometimes louder, sometimes mere whimpers. What the hell were the elders doing to her? Or was it more than the elders? Tairin could make herself invisible, but not her cloth bag. When she stepped from the wagon, she loosed her spell. No reason to squander magic for nothing.

She made her way toward her mother's voice, stopping at the

outskirts of a circle. No wonder she hadn't passed anyone on her way. Everyone was here, chanting in Coptic, goading, urging the elders to spill Aneksi's blood.

Nooooo.

They couldn't kill her mother. Aneksi hadn't done anything wrong, except falling in love.

"She did." The wolf was back. *"She slept with a shifter. It's forbidden. If Jamal's people knew, they'd penalize him as well."*

"They'd kill him?" Tairin asked, aghast.

"They probably wouldn't go that far, but they might cast him out. Wolves are pack animals. Your mother never appreciated how much Jamal's offer to take them far away from everyone cost him. It wouldn't be unlike death for him to lose his pack."

Tairin started to push her way through the wall of bodies to the center of the circle, but stopped before she'd actually touched anyone. Drawing attention to herself was a bad idea.

A very bad idea. So far, no one had noticed her.

What should I do?

She hadn't asked it, but the wolf answered anyway. *"We should leave. This is not something you want stamped into your memories."*

"Tairin. Are you close enough to hear me?" Aneksi's mind voice was thick with strain.

"Yes, Mother. Is there anything I can do?"

"Not for me. They're preparing a bier to burn me alive. Find Jamal. His people live in the hills above Cairo. They may help you, but don't be surprised if they don't. I'm sorry, daughter. So terribly sorry."

Tairin choked back a wail. Tears spilled, but at least they didn't make any noise. *"I want to kiss you goodbye."*

"No. You must leave. The elders won't kill you, but they will banish you. Leave before they mark your forehead so all will know you're an outcast. I love you, Tairin. Now go."

"It's good advice," the wolf said. *"We should follow it."*

The crowd was so high on bloodlust, no one had looked her way. She slipped back a few yards, and then a few more until a wagon masked her from the circle of cheering, shouting gypsies eager for her mother's blood.

"I love you too, Mother. I'm leaving. Use your magic to withdraw to where they can't hurt you."

Aneksi didn't answer.

Tairin returned to the wagon one last time for her shoes. She'd forgotten them when she was getting dressed, and she'd need them if she were going to walk far. She thought about taking one of the horses, but if she stole what the caravan considered its property, she'd meet her mother's fate. Gypsies might be thieves at heart, but they stole from the gadjo, not each other.

She stopped at the door and turned to look at everything in the familiar wagon one last time. She'd been born here, had never known any other home. She wanted to bring everything in the wagon with her. Wanted to never have to leave, but it was a little late for that.

"A head start isn't a bad thing," the wolf commented.

Its words had a steadying effect. She pushed her grief deep. She'd have plenty of time to mourn once she left. A quick scan with her power told her the yard outside the wagon was still empty. She opened the door and put one foot ahead of the other. Walking away from everything she'd ever known was the hardest thing she'd ever done.

Smoke wafted through the hot, still air. Smoke thick with the scent of cooking flesh.

Not meat. It's Mother's body, burning. I can never forget that. Not ever. The Romani aren't my friends. They murdered my mother.

"They're just enforcing their rules. This one hurt you, but it doesn't make a society that lives within its laws bad," the wolf commented. For once, its voice was empty of inflection.

"Say more."

Tairin broke into an easy lope as she left the circle of wagons and her mother's immolation behind. She headed north for Cairo.

It had taken the wagons two days to reach their current location, which meant it might take her double that on foot.

"Laws protect. Long ago, Romani and shifters decreed mating was dangerous—"

"Do you know why?" she broke in.

"No. But it was one area of agreement among two peoples who agree on little else." The wolf hesitated. *"Jamal and your mother were fool-hardy. They thought they could rise above the odds, but that never ends well, and your mother paid the price for their hubris."*

"I'm paying a price too." Tairin pointed out. She stopped shy of saying if the wolf hadn't been so pushy about her shifting, her mother would still be alive.

"Yes, you are. I told you on the island that I can hear your thoughts. You had no choice. If you didn't shift when you did, you'd have died. I wasn't willing to sacrifice us, no matter what the consequences were."

Tairin reached the main road and turned north. Maybe it wasn't a good idea to travel on the main thoroughfare, but the journey to Cairo would take forever if she left the well-beaten track for either the delta to her right or the trail-less desert to her left. Bitterness warred with sorrow. The wolf had spelled things out. They'd traded their existence for her mother's. If Tairin had died rather than shifting, Aneksi would still be alive.

"Some choices have no good outcomes," the wolf observed, its voice gentle.

"Did you know the elders would kill Mother?"

"Not for certain. No."

"But did you suspect it might happen?" she persisted.

"Yes. I will never lie to you. Bondmates don't do such things."

"I have a lot to learn, don't I?"

"That you do, but you need time to move past mourning your losses."

Something sat beneath the wolf's words. *"You don't think Father's people will take us, either, do you?"*

The wolf was silent so long, she gave up on it answering.

Finally, it said, *"It would surprise me if they did. It's not the shifter way to accept mixed blood kinfolk."*

"What will happen to us?" The words burst from her. Sorrow, anger, and confusion vied with wanting to lie down and give up. Why even try? She was only thirteen. Never mind she was a woman in the eyes of the world. She felt too young to be cast adrift on her own.

"You have ample reason, but feeling sorry for yourself won't help you."

"Shut up. Just shut up." Pain sluiced through her. Her heart ached, and smoke from her mother's funeral pyre still burned her nostrils. Maybe that last was only her imagination, but her thoughts spiraled downward into a bottomless pit.

She kept walking because she didn't have anything better to do. At least Cairo was a city. If the shifters refused her, she'd figure something out.

"A caravan is coming," the wolf noted. *"We need to get off the road."*

Tairin sprinted east toward the Nile. She could hide herself within the lush vegetation growing by the water, so long as the caravan didn't pick this exact spot to rest their horses and goats.

"What do you think will happen if another caravan sees us?" she asked.

"Today, nothing. Word will travel, though. Your caravan will discover that you're missing very soon. Word will go out, and they'll make a token effort to find you. Better if no one sees you who can report back and document your location."

"They may as well have branded me." Bitterness filled her.

"You're not thinking. By next year, you'll be yesterday's chatter. No one will be thinking about Tairin Jabari. You can call yourself by a different name and make a life for us somewhere."

Tairin had her doubts, but she kept them to herself. The wolf didn't know the elders from her caravan like she did. Two men, brothers, they were old and vindictive as hell. They'd take it as a personal affront that she hadn't stuck around for them to brand her as tainted. Hunting her would be at the top of their priorities —until they died.

She focused magic to listen. The *clip-clop* of hooves was fading behind them, and she trotted back toward the road. Sun beat down, hot and without mercy. She'd be well served to wait out the heat of the day near the river. Another hour of walking, and she'd take a break.

"We can shift and hunt."

The wolf sounded so hopeful, she didn't have it in her to tell it the last thing she wanted was to do either one of those things.

CHAPTER 6

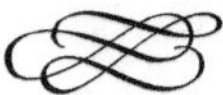

*U*nused to the confinement of shoes, her feet began to ache. Toughened from years of running barefoot, her soles were fine, but spots on the sides and tops of both feet burned where leather rubbed against them. She slipped the shoes off and tucked them in the cloth sack still slung around her body. Sweat ran into her eyes, making them sting, and she pulled the loose neck of her tunic over her head to shield her from the sun's harsh rays.

She kept track of time by watching the sun and forced her mind to blankness. If she replayed the morning, it would flatten her, demoralize her, make it hard to keep moving. When the sun was close to overhead, she angled toward the river and hunted for high marsh grass that would shield her from anyone who happened by. That particular danger would increase as she drew closer to Cairo. The odds of discovery were minimal where she was.

It took a while before she found a good hiding place. No islands in this stretch of river, but the Nile fanned out as it moved north, creating hundreds of spots where she could lose herself. She walked into the water, enjoying its coolness on her tired feet.

"How far have we come do you think?" she asked the wolf.

"We have a long way to go."

"Mother said to look for Father in the hills above Cairo. That could take a long time."

Tairin trudged into a thicket of marsh grass and sat. She unwound the cloth sack's straps from her body and placed it beside her. Not moving felt like a blessing. Daughter of gypsies, she'd traveled on horseback and in wagons. The farthest she'd ever walked before was back and forth to the river for water.

"Won't take long to find your father once we're there," the wolf replied.

Tairin drew her brows together. *"You know where he is, don't you?"*

"Of course. I can locate him through his wolf."

"We have time," Tairin said. *"Tell me how that works."*

"I propose a bargain."

Tairin's nostrils flared. She'd had a bellyful of bargains from watching Romani parley with the gadjo. *"What kind of bargain? Usually that means no one gets what they want."*

A low whuffle that might have passed for laughter rang in her mind. *"It means everyone gets some of what they want. Entirely different slant."*

"You still haven't told me what you have in mind."

"We shift and hunt. I'm hungry. You must be too. Once we've caught four mice, we'll shift back and I'll tell you a story about how bond animals came to be."

Four mice weren't very many. Tairin didn't see how it could possibly satisfy the wolf, but maybe its needs were different than normal animals. She lurched back to her feet, wincing as she weighted them, and stripped out of her clothes, tucking them beneath her cloth sack.

"You're on."

She visualized her wolf form, black and gray fur, large, shaggy paws, elongated snout. Because she had no idea what its eyes looked like, she assumed they'd be like hers, dark with amber centers. The transition was uncomfortable, but the sharp pain from her first shift didn't materialize.

Lifting her muzzle, she scented the air and her jaws parted in the lupine equivalent of a smile. Mice were everywhere. Even better, her feet didn't hurt anymore. She broke into a lope, heading for what felt like a mother lode of mice. Squeals teased her ears. They knew she was coming. The stupid little things were running every which way. Gathering her haunches beneath her, she sprang and snapped her jaws over a particularly fat white and gray mouse.

Its blood spurted hot and rich as she bit into it, chewing and swallowing while she ran after its brothers, sisters, and cousins. Her powerful jaws made short work of fragile bones, and she scooped up another mouse as soon as her mouth was empty.

Tairin stopped thinking. She lived in the wolf's body, saw the world through its senses, embraced the simple joy of killing and eating. She didn't bother counting mice. She killed and ate until her belly was full. Standing in water up to her belly, she drank deep and let the Nile sluice mouse blood from her muzzle and bits of bone and gristle from her teeth.

Contentment—an emotion she'd thought would elude her forever—spilled from her head to her paws. She made her way to where she'd left her clothes, visualized her body, and found her human form. The physical parts of shifting were getting easier. So much easier, she could look toward a day when it would become second nature.

Tairin slipped back into her skirt and tunic. Once she was covered, she positioned herself on her back in a thick clump of marsh grass with her clothing sack for a pillow.

"That was wonderful." If the wolf had been a cat, it would have been purring. *"Thank you."*

"No. Thank you for pushing me. It got me away from my troubles for

a little while. Guess we won't have to worry about me stealing food from the street vendors in Cairo."

"Only if you get tired of mice and other small game." Whuffling laughter that followed the wolf's words warmed her.

"You owe me a story." Tairin closed her eyes and waited.

"So I do." The wolf paused for long moments. *"In a very long ago time when the world was young, shifters were born from the sun and the waters of the Nile. Animals were important to the mythology and religions of ancient Egypt, far more important than we are today. Some of us were sacred to the gods, others designated as their living embodiments.*

"The Egyptians believed a god could inhabit the body of a particular animal. Because I am a wolf, it's the mythology I was taught. We are linked to Anubis. As such, we guide the newly dead. Tales and legends depict us lurking in places tombs are usually built."

"What does that have to do with shifters?" Tairin asked. She was full and sleepy, but rest could wait until the wolf was done.

"It's background. Since we're viewed as sanctified by the gods, it was natural men with magic would want to bond with us. A small group cast strong magic and lured a wolf, a lion, a cat, a vulture, and a raven from the otherworld where they lived. The same powerful magic snared each animal as it appeared, and the sorcerer who'd summoned the creature absorbed its power.

"According to some myths, the animals were furious, but soon came to see advantages to their newly conferred dual natures. Mankind might be brash, rude, and overbearing, but they were generous too. They were willing to share their power, and so the animals' magic became stronger."

"So did the men's," Tairin pointed out.

"So it did. In truth, this was one of those bargains where everyone benefitted." The wolf hesitated before continuing. *"Over the years since the first shifters were tricked into crossing the veil, men discovered easier ways of creating the shifter bond. The current method where young shifters dream their bondmates while they're children has stuck."*

"Like I dreamed you."

"Exactly. I knew you were different, that your blood was mixed, but I

was drawn to your energy. It's pure and strong, so I gave in to the pull of the shifter bond."

"*You make it sound like falling in love.*" Tairin clapped a hand over her mouth, the gesture automatic even though she was conversing in mind speech. "*Sorry, I misspoke.*"

"*No, you didn't. What bondmates share is a type of love. It's not sexual, but our spirits, our essences call to one another, share an attraction. It's not unlike having a sister or brother you care deeply for and would protect with your dying breath.*"

Tairin turned the information over, sifting through it. Her father must have known she'd bonded with a wolf. She played his words back, and they broke her heart. "*Not only will it happen, it's close. Closer than you imagine. I see it in her eyes, and my wolf walks with hers in the place where the animals all roam together.*"

"*How could father underestimate the strength of your bond to me?*" Tairin demanded. "*He of all people should have known.*"

"*I don't believe he underestimated it. He began planning far too late, though. His people don't know about you. He never told them about his Romani wife or his mixed-race child.*"

The implications shot pins and needles from her sore feet to her tired mind. He'd kept her existence secret, so when she came knocking on the shifters' doors, they might well not believe her.

No. They'd have to know I speak the truth. They can scan me with magic to verify my story.

"*Do you know if Father has another family? A shifter one?*" Tairin sucked down a ragged breath. Such things weren't unheard of in caravans where men sometimes kept women stashed in several different ones, rotating between them like a debauched male whore.

"*No. Jamal might be a coward, but he's not dishonorable in that way. He kept his wedding vows.*"

The knowledge didn't bring relief, only a sick certainty that Jamal was ashamed of his weakness where Aneksi was concerned, of his marriage, and of his daughter. If he hadn't been, he'd have stood tall and acknowledged his family. Her mother hadn't been much better. She'd hidden what Jamal was and tried her damnedest to conceal her daughter's true nature.

"When we play to deceive," the wolf chimed in, *"it always catches up with us in the end."*

"Father found a place for Mother and me," she said. *"I heard him, but Mother refused to go."*

"Aneksi was a fool, but your father's attempts to fix the unfixable should have begun years ago." A mournful howl rose within her. *"We cannot change the past."*

"Is it a mistake to try to find Father and his kin?"

"Since you have no one else, it's not a mistake. Just don't hope for too much."

Tairin closed her eyes again. The sleepy, satiated place she'd found after eating had fled, but she should rest anyway. Later this afternoon, they'd get moving again. She offered a small prayer to Bast, a goddess who protected children, to see her through this.

It was all she could do. She turned on her side and tucked a hand beneath her cheek, drawing her knees up until she was curled into a ball. She felt weak, vulnerable, weary, but none of those had any place in her heart or mind.

Only the strong survived in this world.

"Yes, bondmate. We will be strong. I will help you."

"Someday," she gritted out not bothering with mind speech, "I'll grow into my own power. Then we can protect each other. I refuse to be a burden to you forever."

Big words. Would she make good on them?

I have to. There's no choice. None at all.

The sun was well on its way to the western horizon when she woke. Tairin bolted upright, startled she'd slept at all, never mind so long.

"Why didn't you wake me?" she asked the wolf.

"*You needed rest,*" it replied.

"You can hear me if I talk this way?"

"*Of course. Don't waste magic on mind speech when you don't have to. I hear you fine either way.*"

Tairin scrambled to a standing position, still shaking sleep out of her eyes and mind. She slung her cloth bag around her body and started for the road, leaving her shoes in her sack. Her feet had raw places from her last stint wearing them.

"*Not so fast,*" the wolf cautioned.

"What? We're late. I should've been walking at least two hours ago."

"*You're still alive. It's better for me if you remain so. You must scan with magic before you set out. The world isn't a friendly place. You could blunder into something far worse than having slept longer than you might have wished.*"

She stopped dead. The wolf was right. She wasn't thinking. So far, it hadn't cost her anything, but her luck might not hold forever.

Luck? What luck? she thought bitterly. *Mother is dead, Father's a coward. I've been banished from my caravan—*

"We escaped the caravan. No one has come after us. At least not yet. We've eaten, rested. The heat of the day is passing. Depends how you define luck."

"Stay out of my mind," she bristled.

"It's where I live—most of the time. You'll get used to it."

Tairin swallowed her annoyance and sent power zinging wide, searching. She sensed the abundant varieties of wildlife that made the Nile Delta their home, but no people. Determined to put as much distance as she could between herself and her old caravan, she broke into an easy lope.

As she ran, she sifted through what the wolf had told her earlier. "What happens to you when I die?" she asked. "Even if no one kills me, ends my life sooner than the fifty or so years I expect, I will fade and die. Will you continue? Bond with another? How does that work?"

"Many questions. Good ones, though." An appreciative bark punctuated the wolf's words. *"Shifters live long lives. You'll last at least five hundred years, perhaps much longer than that. Bondmates choose their fate when their human passes. We might die with you, or request that you release us."*

Breath whooshed from her lungs, and she slowed. "Five hundred years?" she repeated, disbelieving. "How can that be?"

"A few of the first shifters are still among us. They're millennia old."

"Oh." She wasn't sure what to say. If felt as if she'd fallen head-first into one of the old tales, except this one was real.

She forced herself into the same lope that ate up distance. Her feet ached, but standing still didn't help. "You just said something that contradicts what you told me earlier."

"What was that?"

She could almost visualize the wolf, sitting on its haunches, ears pricked forward with interest. "You said I had to shift or we'd both die. How does that square up with me releasing you at my death?"

"Easy enough. Shifter law doesn't allow unconsummated bonds. Your first shift seals our compact with one another, makes us bondmates."

"So I could release you now without damaging you or causing you harm?" Tairin wanted to make certain she understood.

"You could, and I wouldn't fade into the otherworld, but I would be very sad. You just opened yourself to our bond. We have so much ahead of us. A whole life to get to know one another."

Tairin opened her mouth to respond, but before she could get any words out, the wolf continued. *"Had you been raised by shifters, we'd have spent far more time in the dream world—and during your waking spells as well—getting to know one another. Because you had no idea you were a shifter, I trod gently, made you believe I was less than I am so as not to frighten you."*

The wolf's words touched her heart. "You've cared about me for a long time."

"I have."

"I feel…ungrateful." She stumbled over the word.

"Better to focus on what's ahead of us rather than what's behind."

Tairin nodded. The wolf might have been the catalyst in her current plight, but it was also her only friend. A thought rocked her. "My father, is he one of the old ones? You said millennia. That's a thousand years."

"No. Only the first shifters are that old, and not all of them are still with us. I'm not sure of Jamal's exact age. If I had to guess, I'd say maybe a hundred years, give or take a few."

The air was changing around her, ripe with the scent of a late afternoon thunderstorm building to the north of them. She'd loved to curl up in the wagon during rainstorms and listen to water pelt its roof. Once she grew older, though, her task when it rained was to make sure every single bucket was in a spot where the sky could fill it. Rain was infrequent enough, the gypsies took full advantage of it. Rainwater held power, and they used it to craft amulets and talismans for the gadjo—and themselves.

She inhaled, loving the crispness, the tang of the approaching storm. Something smelled off, though. Or maybe she was nervous since she was alone. Flash floods sometimes rolled through the delta. If the storm was severe, she might drown if she were swept into the Nile.

"We need to keep moving."

"I know," Tairin replied. "Weather's blowing in."

"Not that. Don't you smell the other? The putrid, death smell? It shouldn't be here, and it bodes ill for anyone close to it."

CHAPTER 8

airin tipped her head back, inhaling until her lungs burned. Her sense of smell was sharper, or she might have missed it entirely, but the wrongness that had pricked her radiated menace. She'd smelled it before in crowded cities, but couldn't quite place what it was.

Maybe she'd never known.

"Whatever it is, we're getting closer." She kept her voice low. "What is that? It smells dead."

"They are dead in a manner of speaking. They're vampires. We're approaching a nest, and they grow much stronger at night."

Tairin shrouded herself, hiding her power. Not much she could do about the cloth sack, which would look as if it were walking down the road suspended in the air.

"Should we stop?" she whispered.

"No. If we do, we'll be stuck sitting out the storm far too close to their nest."

"Why do you call it a nest? It's not as if they're birds." She racked her mind for what she knew about vampires. Creatures who'd cheated death, or died and been reborn, they lived on the blood of others and could make new vampires by force-feeding

"

their blood to humans. She might not have gotten everything right, but the thought of a confrontation with them made her heart pound and her legs shake. Romani viewed vampires as pure evil and avoided them at almost any cost.

"What their dwelling places are called isn't important. Move toward the delta. We'll shift and stay off the road until we're well past them."

"But what about my clothes, my sack?"

"My vision is better than yours. So is my ability to travel, sticking to the shadows. I hadn't considered your need for clothing. We can try hanging the sack around my neck, but..."

Tairin understood and melted into gathering mist and clouds that thickened as they moved toward the Nile. The first raindrops drizzled down, growing into a punishing deluge so fast it shocked her. Surely the weather would deter vampires—or anyone else.

"Maybe," the wolf answered her thoughts. *"Can you follow the riverbank in your own form?"*

"I—I think so."

"Open your mind to me. I will make your senses nearly as sharp as mine."

Tairin experimented with her magic until something shifted in her head. The night, which had grown increasingly murky, developed depth and contrast again. The cries of panicked birds and animals, running before the storm's fury, pummeled her. She ignored them. She might be running from bigger predators than the storm, but her plight wasn't any different.

With the wolf's augmented senses pulsing through her, the charnel pit rot smell intensified until her stomach twisted in rebellion and she was afraid she'd be sick. Tairin kept moving. She didn't have time to stop and vomit.

"They're closer." She reverted to mind speech, afraid vampires might have sharp enough ears to hear her.

"Not really. Their nest is on the other side of the road. We've drawn abreast of it, and now we're past."

"What do they look like? I've never seen one."

"Do you want to?"

The question intrigued and startled her. *"Isn't it dangerous?"*

"Not in my form." The wolf hesitated. *"The more I think on it, the more I believe you should see what they look like. They're beautiful and terrible and very hard to resist. You will need my body, though."*

"Won't they recognize you as a shifter?"

"Unlikely. They're mostly sensitive to humans. This is up to you, but there is much evil in the world. You've seen very little of it." The wolf stopped shy of saying the faster she learned, the better she could guard herself, but it didn't have to.

Lightning flashed, turning the blackened sky brilliant. Thunder followed on its heels. Her hair was plastered against her head, and her clothes were soaked. *"I could leave my things here."* She ran to a pile of good-sized rocks high enough off the ground to be safe from flooding and stuffed her sack into a hole between two of them. Her tunic and skirt followed.

Fear lent sharp edges to the shift magic when she called it, and her wolf form took shape. Maybe because she was so wet, the pain was minimal. Or maybe this would continue to get easier the more she did it. The wolf had inferred that might be the case. She'd have to ask for more details, but not now.

"Hold silence until we return here," the wolf cautioned. *"Do nothing that could draw their attention. Vampires aren't unduly sensitive to expended magic. They've sat at the top of the magical food chain so long, they've gotten sloppy. Still, no need to take chances."*

"Got it. Let's go."

Adrenaline pounded through her as she ran. The wolf's sleek gait made short work of the distance between them and the nest. She ceded control of their shared body to the wolf, trusting it would know how best to approach the unnatural creatures.

The stench worsened until she almost couldn't stand to breathe, but not breathing wasn't a choice. The wolf circled around the bad smell, approaching it from the far side. Lanterns illuminated a rough clearing. If she'd been human, Tairin's eyes would have been wide as twin moons. Eighteen vampires milled about the tamped down earth. Water streamed down them, but it didn't dampen their unearthly beauty.

Everything about them glowed—from their perfect hair to their perfect features. Some of the creatures were female, which surprised her. The wolf dropped to its belly at the top of a small knoll, giving her an unobstructed view of the tableau. One of the males wore soaked, cream-colored robes. Golden hair spilled past his waist, and he opened his arms to the sides as if invoking a ritual.

"I am ready for tonight's festivities." Laughter followed his words, so melodic and lovely it could have charmed snakes from their dens.

Another of the vampires approached. This one was female with red tresses, her figure outlined beneath her sodden black dress. "I hear, master, and I obey."

Tairin waited, barely breathing, as the woman retreated to where two other vampires stood, holding a man between them. He had to be human because he wasn't radiant like the vampires. Fear oozed from his pores. His head was shaved, and he wore an unadorned black robe sashed with crimson.

"Come now, my pretty," the woman cooed.

As if in trance, the man followed, but the fear stench didn't abate.

Had the vampires hypnotized him? Tairin added it to her list of questions to ask once they were safely away.

The vampire the woman had called master angled his head to one side, his attention riveted on the man being dragged toward him. "It's been a long time, Masud," the vampire said in clear, ringing tones.

"Not nearly long enough." Masud sneered, showing a mouthful of half-decayed teeth. "My brothers know you captured me. They'll be along soon enough."

The vampire quirked one well-shaped, tawny brow. "And here

I was going to offer you a gift. I should kill you for what you and the other monks did to my last nest."

Masud spat at the vampire, but his spittle was driven into the dirt by the pouring rain. "I pick death over gifts from you."

"Is that so?" The vampire closed the distance to the man, who didn't make any move to run away despite no one holding onto him. Why wasn't he making an effort to flee?

"You're toying with me," Masud growled, sounding like a caged animal. "Get it over with."

The pleasant expression on the vampire's face vanished, replaced by something harsh and forbidding. It was as if the creature had two temperaments, or maybe what showed now was what it really was, and the other had been nothing but showmanship. The Rom were like that. They had pretty faces they wore to woo as much coin as possible out of the gadjo, but their nice sides rarely made an appearance in the caravan. The same men who charmed the gadjo had burned her mother alive.

Tairin tried to shake her head, but the wolf forced their shared body to remain still. She wanted to apologize for being careless, but piling a second mistake—breaking their silence—atop the one she'd just made would be stupid.

"I'm going to enjoy this," the vampire purred, his tone lethal, but edged with velvet. Grasping the man's shoulder with one hand, he twisted his neck with the other and bent his head, closing fangs into flesh that gave way without the slightest resistance.

The air filled with the rich, metallic scent of blood, and Tairin watched the vampire's throat as he swallowed again and again, fast and efficient. Color left Masud's face, and he sagged in the vampire's grasp. When he developed the ashen pallor she associated with death, the vampire lifted his head. Blood fell in crimson streams from his elongated incisors, and he raised his own wrist to his mouth, ripping a hole in it that pulsed with blood so hot, it steamed in the humid night air.

At first, Masud took the wrist the vampire held to his mouth, sucking like a starving infant offered a teat, but then his rheumy dark eyes snapped open and he tore his mouth from the stream of blood.

"No," he wheezed. "Never." He spat blood from his mouth, and then spat again, tilting his head back to rinse his mouth with rainwater.

"Too late," the vampire pronounced, looking pleased with himself. "You drank enough."

"Noooooo," Masud shrieked and tore at his robe, shredding it. "Noooooo."

Tairin's heart hurt for him. He'd just become something he hated. Would he kill himself? Was such a move possible for vampires, or was he stuck with his new existence?

The wolf slithered backward through thick mud, still on its belly. It stopped when only its eyes were above the level of the tussock sheltering them. She wanted to ask if they were leaving, but didn't want anyone to discover their presence. Since she couldn't talk, she used nose and ears to search for clues. The distant *clop* of horse hooves mingled with the scent of incense.

Must be priests coming to reclaim their brother. No one else would venture out on a night such as this. Tairin had thought it bravado, but Masud told the truth about that part. She eyed the vampires. They'd gathered around Masud, taunting him, cutting more wrists open and spraying him with blood when he refused to drink from them.

The female with the red hair tore Masud's robes open and grappled with his cock, taking it into her mouth. She worked him until his member grew engorged. Dragging it from her mouth, she cast a spurious smile at the vampire who'd turned Masud.

"Different paths for different men." She licked her full lips before taking Masud's erect cock back into her mouth and sucking hungrily.

Masud groaned and drove himself into the vampire's mouth.

His life had just turned to crap. He was a vampire now, but all he cared about was sexual release.

Men. Slaves to their desires.

Women too, an insidious inner voice suggested. *Look what happened to Mother.*

Tairin and other gypsy children had hidden themselves and watched couples have sex enough times, she understood the dynamics. What was playing out a few yards away was such a perversion of human lovemaking, though, that she felt ill.

Masud grunted, and his cock jerked in the vampire's grasp. She pumped her hand faster and swallowed. The salt tang of semen joined all the other scents permeating the air.

From out of nowhere, fifty men on horseback swept into the clearing swinging long-handled sabers. The vampires fought back, but their heads rolled from their bodies faster than they dealt death to the group of priests savaging them. At least blood stench trumped the rotten death smell of the vampires. The priests killed mechanically, efficiently, as if they'd done this hundreds of times before.

Who knew? Perhaps they had.

Lightning flashed. Thunder rumbled until the air thickened with electricity and stank of ozone. All the vampires were dead. The only one still standing in the mud was Masud. One of the priests galloped to his side and extended a hand. "Ride with me, brother. I'll see you home."

Masud shook his head. "You must kill me. I drank from one of the abominations when I was weak."

"How much?" the priest on horseback asked in a deep, gravelly voice.

"Two mouthfuls, but enough for it to turn me. I already feel the change rooting itself into my body."

Spewing curses in Coptic, the priest leapt from his horse and held Masud's head between his hands. Tairin assumed he was using magic to test the extent of his brother's contamination.

The stark planes of the man's face yielded to a hopeful expression. "Thank all the blessed gods, we are not too late." He barked a command. Ten men, all dressed in identical black robes, jumped down from their horses and ran to where he stood. They drove Masud into the mud, chanting over him in a language Tairin didn't recognize.

It sounded like Coptic, but a far more ancient version. Drawing sharp-bladed dirks from waist belts, the priests fell to their knees and made a series of cuts in Masud's arms and legs. Blood flowed, but not for long. The cuts healed almost as soon as they formed.

Masud's head lolled to one side as consciousness left him. Made sense. He couldn't have much blood left, not after all the vampire had drunk from him.

The priest who'd said it wasn't too late bolted to his feet and hoisted Masud over one shoulder. Staggering under his weight, he walked to his mount and placed Masud facedown across the animal's back.

The other men had gotten back on their horses. One trotted next to the priest who'd given his horse to Masud and offered him a hand up so they could ride double. The priest clucked to his horse carrying Masud, and it fell into line with the others.

"Will he live?" the man he rode with asked.

"I hope so. He's one of our strongest. It's why he was able to stop after only drinking a little."

"Did we drive out the demon presence?"

"That we did," the priest replied. "If Masud dies, it will be a clean death and his ashes can hold a place of honor in our temple."

The wolf waited until the sound of hoof beats faded before rising to its feet. After a head to tail shake, it took off at a run for where they'd left her clothing.

"Two things to remember," the wolf said. *"Vampires mesmerize their victims. It's why Masud didn't run away. He couldn't. Sometimes they use sex to immobilize their victims, sometimes a form of mind control.*

Shifters are immune from both. Vampires can still kill us, but they can't immobilize us to make it easy for them."

"The priests seemed awfully proficient."

"They are. That sect exists to annihilate vampires."

Tairin considered it. *"Are there that many vampires?"*

"Oh my, yes. You saw how easy it is for them to replicate themselves. Thousands roam through Egypt. Many temples have dedicated themselves to eradicating vampires. If they didn't, vampires would be a much worse problem than they already are."

"Are the newly formed ones as powerful?"

"Not for a number of years." The wolf woofed softly. *"That was an excellent question."*

It stopped next to where she'd left her clothing. The rain was abating and night had fallen. *"Before we shift, can we hunt a few more mice?"* she asked.

The wolf made a snorting noise. *"Watching death is hungry business. Of course, we can hunt."*

Tairin followed the wolf's lead. The vampires were dead. Masud was an honorable man who'd done the right thing. Still, seeing the deadly creatures ply their trade had been a brutal lesson.

The world is full of evil, just like the wolf said.

I'd better get used to it because no one will step in to shield me from any of it.

She stopped thinking as they closed their jaws around a succulent young otter, displaced from the swollen river. By the time they'd fed on it and a dozen mice, she was ready to find her human form, dress, and close her eyes for a short time.

If the goddess were with her, vampires wouldn't haunt her dreams.

"I will watch over you," the wolf said. *"Now and always. It's what bondmates do."*

They arrived at the outskirts of Cairo near evening two days later. After the one vampire nest, nothing else unusual had materialized to slow them down. They'd taken to the wolf's form after discovering her cloth sack fit nicely around its neck, and they'd made good time sticking close to the banks of the Nile. No people had seen them, so they'd avoided impossible-to-answer questions.

At least so far, no one from the caravan had come after them, or if they had, they'd headed south rather than north.

After a midday break, she'd reverted to her human form and returned to the road. It became much more crowded as they neared the ancient city, but she blended in with the ragtag masses surging toward Cairo. Cities offered work, remunerative begging, and food. Rich people threw scraps away, scraps that could be scavenged.

"Where will we find Father?" she asked the wolf.

"We must pass through the city to its far side. Once we're past the walls, we will climb west into the hills."

"Why not go around instead of through? Wouldn't it be faster?"

"No. Not faster. Undesirables who've been kicked out of the city mill

about its borders and set up camps outside town. You've never been here without your caravan. It provided a measure of safety."

"You know a lot. How did you come by your knowledge?" Tairin had grown bolder. It seemed the wolf knew almost everything about her, yet she knew next to nothing about it.

"I have been alive for a long time. You are not my first bondmate."

"What happened to the others?" Tairin chided herself. Curiosity was one thing, but that was an extremely personal question, akin to asking a lover about who else had shared their bed. *"Never mind. Not my business."*

For once, the wolf didn't answer.

Tairin kept moving. People jostled her from both sides, but all she had were a few clothing items in her sack. It hung from her neck, making it difficult to steal. The sixth time someone bumped into her, supposedly by accident, she grinned. Romani were accomplished thieves. Hard to pull one over on someone like her who'd been trained by the best.

The city's mudbrick walls came into view, and she quickened her pace. They'd close the gates at sundown. It was still possible to enter—and leave—but not without talking to a guard. She had no bona fide reason for being in the city, but the majority of the stream of humanity pushing forward on all sides of her probably didn't, either.

A name.

She needed a different name. Just in case. Tairin tried out and discarded several, settling on Eshe. It meant life, and she hoped she'd still have one when the dust cleared. Last names were trickier. If she had a last name, it would mean she had a father who'd claimed paternity. Better to stick with Eshe. If one of the guards questioned her, she'd say she had no idea who'd fathered her.

She swept beneath a high, arched gateway. The actual gate was constructed of rusted metal staves. Currently it folded back flat against the mudbrick wall, suspended from several massive hinges. The choking tide of humanity drew her along with it.

Cairo was enormous. The only part she was familiar with was the old town center where her caravan had set up its wagons. She started for it to help gain her bearings.

"Bad idea," the wolf spoke up.

"Why?"

"Another caravan will be there. Someone might recognize you."

She breathed a silent thank you to the wolf and set as straight a line as she could manage through crowded, twisting byways. Vendors called to her, offering wares from foodstuffs to clothing to charms guaranteed to make the man of her dreams wed her.

The food carts smelled delicious. She hadn't had anything to eat as a human since fleeing from her caravan, and she missed bread and cheese and dates and sweetmeats. Tairin eyed the wares, considering how to swipe something and run.

"Don't do it."

Tairin exhaled briskly. She'd gotten used to the wolf being a permanent resident in her head, but sometimes its suggestions annoyed her. *"Why not? See those roasted nuts? The vendor went around a corner. He'd never notice."*

"If you're caught, they'll chop off your hand."

Breath caught in her throat. She wanted to argue she was just a child, but maybe that part didn't matter. Besides, she wasn't. Not really. Lost in thought, not paying attention, she heard the wolf's warning just before someone closed a strong hand over her shoulder and pulled her into a deserted byway that stank of stale urine.

"You're a ripe one," the man said in accented Coptic. "New here, eh? I haven't seen you before. Not in this sector of the city."

She writhed against his grasp, but couldn't break free. Twisting, she saw a man of perhaps thirty with strands of silver mixed into his long, black hair. Naked from the waist up, he wore loose fitting trousers that had once been tan but were covered with grease spots. His feet were bare, and he had Hindu markings painted on his forehead. Vertical stripes suggested he'd once followed Vishnu, but they'd faded with time.

"Let go of me." She struggled harder, hissing and spitting.

"What's in the bag?" The man stared at it and at her chest.

"Clothes."

"What's your name?" His tone was mild, but she read danger with her magic. He meant to hurt her, use her.

Of course he does. Why else would he have dragged me back here?

"I don't have to tell you anything. Let go of me or I'll start screaming."

"Go ahead. I'll tell whomever shows up that you're my daughter. I dragged you away from the married man you were fucking and you're not happy about it. Speaking of sex—" he leered at her "—you'd be a juicy addition for my business. Girl like you, young and clean, you'd be worth quite a bit to one of the temples or a rich patron with a taste for virgins."

"How do you know I'm a virgin?" She leered back.

He shrugged. "I don't, but you look like one. It's good enough."

"Shifting is a last resort," the wolf said, *"but if this goes much further, we won't have any other options."*

"Yes, we do," she replied. *"Even if he drags me somewhere else, it will take him time to find someone to sell me to. While he's gone, we'll escape. I could kill him, but that might land me in the dungeons if anyone showed up at the wrong time."*

The man narrowed his black eyes to slits and drew his thick eyebrows together over a hawk-like nose. "What was that? Who are you talking to? I have power, I do."

Ha! Not enough to light a candle.

"Let go of me," Tairin repeated through clenched teeth. "Bruised merchandise won't bring so fine a price." She bared a mouthful of teeth. She should be frightened, but this joker was more of a nuisance than anything else. She thought again about flattening him with magic, but then she'd have to answer to the authorities—if they found out. People with magic had to register when they entered Cairo. She knew that from the caravan. It was something the elders had handled.

The man fished a length of rope from one of his trouser pockets and tied an untidy knot around one of her wrists. Satisfied she was trapped, he took off at a fast trot for the crowded square he'd abducted her from.

She followed along, pretending to be cowed, docile.

He'd make the mistake of believing her tractable, and then she'd escape.

*T*airin waited until they were in the midst of a crowd. No one would look twice at a man leading a woman roped to him. They'd believe she was his slave. She took stock of her options. No reason to delay escape until he locked her into a cage—or whatever he had in mind. He didn't look as if he had enough coin to have access to an actual room to leave her in. Maybe he planned on a goat pen or a chicken coop.

She'd be gone long before then.

Once she found what she was looking for, she sent a quick jolt of magic toward the knot, suggesting the ends release each other. When it fell from her wrist, she ducked through an open doorway into a crumbling hovel, pushed her clothing sack into a dark corner, and cloaked herself in invisibility, barely breathing.

The man wasn't very sharp, but he'd figure out soon enough she'd escaped and he'd return to look for her.

"Excellent. I'm impressed," the wolf said.

"We're not safe yet. Quiet."

Her words weren't exactly prophetic, but she heard an outraged shriek, even over the noisy marketplace. It suggested her absence had been discovered. She crouched in the corner where she'd shoved her cloth sack, shielding it from view with her body. Someone with strong magic would see through her spell. The man didn't worry her, but maybe he had associates in his brothel business. She hadn't felt afraid before, but she did now. Her heart thudded hard, and saliva pooled in her mouth. If he found her, he'd punish her. Fury would drive him; the same emotion had seen her mother tossed on a pyre and burned alive.

If he hurt her, she'd have to kill him. If it came to that, and killing was all that was left, she prayed to every deity she could think of that there'd be no witnesses around to drag her before the authorities.

Heated cries drew closer. The man was asking—no demanding —her return. Someone had stolen his property. His slave. He demanded her return. Immediately, or he'd summon the king's guard. He had an in with them, he did. Whoever had tricked him would pay…

At first, he received a sympathetic response from the merchants and townspeople, but when everyone looked and no one found the woman he claimed to have lost, their patience wore thin.

"She's given you the slip," a male voice said, followed by a hearty slapping noise. "Best move on. Female slaves come cheap. Go get yourself another and give up on this one."

"But I wanted her," he wailed. "She was mine."

"Move along," a woman cried. "You're driving away business. I haven't sold a thing this whole time you've been kicking up a fuss."

A chorus of *move alongs* followed, and Tairin began to breathe easier.

"We can't leave yet," the wolf said. *"Unless you abandon your sack and remain invisible."*

"We could leave my things here."

"If you do that, they're as good as gone," the wolf cautioned.

Tairin was loathe to abandon her sack. It was all she had left of her old life. It was hard to sit still, wondering whose hovel she'd stumbled into and when they'd return. She gave it an hour. The noise from the marketplace was dying down when she squared her shoulders and emerged from the alcove where she'd sheltered. She had no idea who lived there, but the goddess had been good to her because no one disturbed her hiding place.

The first few minutes were tense, but when she'd traveled a hundred paces without incident, she began to hope she'd make it to the town gates without problems. She'd have to convince the guard to let her out, but that shouldn't be a problem. Getting in afterhours had to be harder than leaving.

Another ten minutes brought her to the edge of a part of town she knew. The old square was to her right. She recognized landmarks. Shops and restaurants lined streets that were wider than they'd been where she'd taken refuge. True to the wolf's prediction, a caravan spread out at the far end of the square, and she stayed as far from it as she could.

Safely past the square, she figured she'd made good on her escape. Beggars on every corner mingled with gypsies who sang or played a variety of handmade instruments. She whistled a tune her mother used to sing, but it made her sad so she stopped.

Tairin caught glimpses of the gate and tried to hurry, but people clogged the main road. Some were going her direction; others just arriving. Night had fallen while she crouched in the grotto, and lanterns bloomed, lighting the darkness. People jostled her on both sides. She built a small perimeter with magic, but it didn't help much.

"Ha! There you are!" rang from right next to her.

The man. How had he snuck up on her?

Easy. I dropped my guard and wasn't paying attention.

She feinted away, but there was nowhere to go. The crowd was thick around her. Tairin shrieked, tried to get away, but the man screamed louder. She was his slave. She'd escaped. A good beating was in her future. Her immediate future, and if she didn't want to make it worse, she'd come along.

The crowd did part then, making sympathetic noises, but not for her. Everyone was happy the man had recovered his property.

"See?" he hissed right next to her ear. "You got no rights, girlie." He dragged her down a side street, through heaps of stinking garbage until the path ended against an imposing wall.

Tairin glanced about. No one was near enough to help her. Not that anyone would. Women had no standing in the eyes of the law. She gathered her magic, ready to fight back. Maybe the lack of people close by was the goddess's way of answering her earlier plea.

The man jammed her flat against the wall. She felt the bulge of an erection press into her buttocks, and he grappled with her skirt, lifting it out of the way. "Tried to do things nice," he grunted, breathing harder. "But no. You didn't want nice. Guess I'll find out if you're a virgin right now. Before I auction you off to the highest bidder."

Lust rolled off him in thick, nauseating waves. Rancid breath curdled her stomach. He pressed a hand against her back, holding her flat to the wall. She figured he was using his other hand to free his cock from his trousers. No time to shift, but plenty to destroy him with magic. It was fast, easy, clean, and a whole lot less work than fighting his superior strength so she could claw his eyes out.

In addition to her native power, she called on the earth beneath her feet, letting its magic stream into her. His hardness pressed between her legs, seeking entry, but she was ready. Focusing her ability, she sent a jolt into his heart. Nothing happened for long, tense moments while he continued prodding her with his erection.

Tairin readied herself to send more power after her first blast. She had it captured, formed, and was ready to loose it when the man's hold on her dropped away. He fell to his knees behind her, clasping his body and moaning.

"*Finish it,*" the wolf instructed.

"*More magic?*"

"*No. Your knife.*"

She'd never killed anything that wasn't slated for food, but she didn't stop to consider things. Drawing her dirk, she plunged it into one of the man's eyes and beyond into his brain, twisting the weapon for maximum damage. No one had been there to witness her attack, which worked out well for the nameless man. Now it gave her the advantage since no one had seen her commit murder.

Not waiting for her luck to change, she sprinted toward the gate, taking a different route than the man had. A stream of raw sewage running down the last lane before she merged back into the throng of humanity provided opportunity to rinse the blood off her dirk. The method she'd used to kill meant she'd avoided being covered with his blood.

In case any of the people who'd parted to let the man lead her away in disgrace were still around, Tairin wove a glamour to disguise herself. Last thing she needed was for someone to recognize her and start asking a bunch of questions. Like what happened to her master? It wouldn't take a genius to locate the body and tie his murder to her.

The gates were closed, which was why the crowd moved so slowly. A guard asked each of them a question or two before letting them out of Cairo.

Her turn came after a long wait. "Your name?" the official barked.

"Eshe."

"Why were you in Cairo, Eshe?"

She cast her gaze downward. "I am a traveler, sir. Just passing through."

"Why not go around the city, then, if you had no business here?"

She wrapped her arms around herself and shuddered. It wasn't hard to look scared. "I did. It's not a good place for a woman alone." Tairin snuck a glance upward at the man and saw him frown.

"I thought we'd cleaned that up. Thank you for the information, Eshe. You're free to go. Open fires and safe journeys to you."

Tairin bowed her head. "Thank you, sir." She scurried through the gate and broke into a lope, anxious to put distance between herself and her crime.

Murder. I killed someone. Worse, I used magic to do it.

There were stern prohibitions against raising power to harm another. She wasn't certain if Romani law would absolve her since she was in the process of being raped, but she didn't want to find out.

"You had no choice," the wolf said. *"I'm proud of you."*

She tried to glom onto some semblance of justification for her actions, but all she felt was a dull ache behind her breastbone. Was this what her life would be like? Men viewing her as fair game for their lust?

"Life on the road isn't easy for a woman alone." The wolf must have been inside her head. *"Turn left at the next junction. The wolf pack your father calls home isn't far from here."*

"What happens if they refuse us?" She reverted to talking out loud since no one was close enough to hear her.

"I don't know. We'll figure things out as we have to."

She inhaled sharply, blew it out, and did it again. Some aspects of life in the caravan had rankled, but it was paradise compared with what she'd traded it for.

I didn't trade anything. They'd have forced me out if I hadn't run.

Tairin balled her hands into tight fists. Damn her mother and Jamal to everlasting fire. She replayed the conversation she'd horned in on—the one where Jamal tried to get Aneksi to leave—but stopped midstream. It didn't matter who was to blame.

The only thing that mattered was that she was on her own

with pathetically few resources. She needed a crash course in practicalities and survival. The time to react to the man grabbing her would have been right when it happened. Once he had her shackled to him, she was his in the eyes of the world.

"*We learn as we go, eh?*" the wolf commented. "*Turn here. You almost missed it.*"

CHAPTER 11

airin trudged uphill. She did her best to keep her mind blank, but every time she dropped her guard, she relived driving her blade into the man's brain. He was scum and didn't deserve to live, and he'd backed her into a corner, but her heart hurt for the life she'd taken. She'd stolen from the gadjo, but this felt worse.

Much worse.

Taking from someone who had so much they'd never miss the coin was in a whole different universe from murder.

"He would have raped you and sold you into slavery to a place where men use women," the wolf said, sounding stern. *"It was him or you."*

"Easy to say. Hard to believe. How much farther?"

"The distance we've come from Cairo one more time."

Tairin glanced at the moon and stars. By the wolf's estimate, it would be midnight before they came to the shifter settlement. "Will anyone be awake?"

"Of course. Shifters hunt at night."

Tairin squeezed her eyes shut, opening them when she stumbled over a rock. Everything was different. Nothing was left of the life she'd known. Nothing at all.

Better get used to it.

Feeling sorry for herself, or worse hoping someone would drop out of the sky to take care of her and save her from the lonely existence stretching before her, weren't options.

"Thanks for sticking by me," she told the wolf. "This would be much harder if you weren't here."

"It's what bondmates do. There's a spring off to your right. Do you want to stop for a bit? Have some water and pull yourself together?"

Tairin tilted her head, nostrils flared to locate the cool dampness of a spring. Jamal had said he'd found an isolated oasis. Maybe he'd be willing to go there with her—at least until she was a little older and better prepared to take on the world by herself.

The spring was the merest trickle, but water was water, and she unwrapped the sack from her body and knelt next to it. Cupping the tepid liquid, she sluiced it over her face and drank her fill. She wished for the Nile to immerse herself and wash the stench of the man from her.

Later. Once the next part played itself out.

She scrubbed her hands, making certain to eradicate any traces of the man's blood. It might not matter to the shifters, but it did to her. Tairin rose to her feet and draped her sack over one shoulder. She stood straight and marched back to the trail, heading upward.

The wolf was silent until they came to several steep cliff faces blocking the way. *"Stop here."*

"Doesn't look as if I have any choice." Tairin's tone was surly, but this looked like a dead end.

"They know we're here. Someone will come."

"What? They live in these cliffs?"

"Something like that. I can't divulge anything further."

Tairin rocked from foot to foot, waiting. The night wasn't cold, but she would have liked to curl up in her blanket and sleep. Except she'd left the blanket behind. It was too bulky to cart with her.

Yeah, wrapped in my blanket in my corner of the wagon. I need to forget that life ever existed.

Wary after what had happened in Cairo, she deployed her power settling it around her like a net. No one would catch her by surprise a second time. Time slowed to a crawl before magic kindled, alerting her, and she turned to face whomever approached.

A tall man with golden brown hair, a stern face, and green eyes moved toward her. He was dressed in form-fitting leather garments and knee-high lace-up boots.

"State your business here."

"I'm hunting for my father, Jamal Jabari."

The man's eyes widened, but he wiped the surprise from his face fast. "Father, you say?"

"Yes. Use magic to check if you need to." Tairin held herself straight.

Perhaps because she'd given permission, she felt a shock as what she now recognized as shifter magic probed her.

"Humph. I see," the man muttered. "Your name?"

"Tairin." She hesitated before adding, "Jabari." No reason not to. It wasn't as if Jamal had ducked out from beneath his role as her father. At least with the Romani.

"And who is your mother, Tairin?"

She opened her mouth, but before she could speak, the wolf cut in, *"That is for Jamal to reveal to his people."*

"I heard that," the man said. "It appears the bond with your animal has been consummated."

Tairin nodded, hoping the man might look more favorably on her. She wanted to ask his name, but if he wanted her to know, he'd have told her. She was on shaky enough ground. Better to keep her mouth shut.

"Wait here," the man said. Spinning on his heel, he broke into a lope.

Tairin settled on a flat rock. "What happens next?" she asked the wolf.

"Rafa probably went to confer with some of the elders. He'll return with one or more of them."

"At least I know his name now. Interesting. They have elders too. Will Jamal come now that he knows I'm here?"

"There's a chance they won't tell him." The wolf hesitated. *"There's an equally good chance they won't allow him to see you."*

"They're as powerful as the Rom elders."

Tairin set her lips in a tight line. Of course, they would be. Maybe more so since their magic was stronger. Rather than say something else stupid, she clasped her hands in her lap beneath her sack and waited.

Time dripped by, maybe over an hour. Tairin was close to chalking this up as wasted effort when she felt shifter magic drawing near. Scrambling to her feet, she stood straight to face what approached. Rafa was there, but so were three other men.

Jamal wasn't among them.

Once they got close enough to hear her, she asked, "Where is my father?"

"Not here," a man with black hair and dark brown eyes replied. "What is it you want with him?"

The question took her aback. "What any child would from a parent." She stammered over the words.

"True enough." Another man with red hair examined her through discerning green eyes. "But you're scarcely a child in need of her father."

The black-haired man stepped closer to her. "You may be a shifter, but your blood is not pure. We only allow shifters with untainted bloodlines to live in our settlements."

"You're sending me away without seeing my father?" After everything she'd gone through to get here, Tairin hadn't expected much, but she'd at least expected to lay eyes on her father one last time.

"It's not as if you're not fully grown," the man pointed out.

"Your wolf will provide and protect," Rafa added.

Her eyes pricked with the hot bite of tears just before they spilled over. She stuffed a fist in her mouth and bit down hard, but it didn't stem the tide of her sorrow.

"If you wish, you can wait out what remains of the dark hours here," Rafa said. "Our magic will shield you at least for tonight."

Before she could craft a reply, spit in their faces, and tell them to shove their pity up their asses, the men left as quickly as they'd come. She and her wolf were alone with cliffs ringing them on three sides.

"They didn't have to offer anything," the wolf spoke up.

"I don't want scraps from their table," she muttered, still trying to stop crying.

"There's a place for pride, but it's not here. We should remain until sunrise."

"Is there any chance they'll change their minds? That Jamal will come for me?" Tairin hated herself for the hope in her question and her voice.

"No, bondmate. No chance. They offered a respite from our struggles. No more, no less."

She let herself down heavily on the flat rock where she'd waited for the four shifters to quash her last hopes. Would the shifter elders kill Jamal for breaking their laws, like the Rom had done to her mother?

"Jamal will be censured, but his kin won't take his life."

Relief spilled through her, and she didn't understand why. She should hate both her parents. They'd brought this on themselves —and her—but she didn't have any hatred left. Maybe when she was through mourning, she could hate, but that wouldn't happen for a while.

Her eyes were hot, gritty, weary, but sleep was out of the question. She needed to be gone from this place before dawn. She didn't want that quartet of hatchet-faced men to show up again and punish her for taking advantage of what they likely viewed as a generous concession.

"Rest. I will see you're up in time to leave."

Tairin was weary and discouraged. Between watching vampires' wickedness and being set upon just walking through Cairo, she didn't hold much hope for any kind of future. Because she didn't have a better idea, Tairin curled up on the flat stone and closed her eyes. The wolf must have spun its magic because she dropped into blackness almost at once.

CHAPTER 12

The wolf was as good as its word, and Tairin made her way down the mountainside as night's dregs yielded to a pearlescent dawn. The sky came alive with color, but the dead places inside her couldn't appreciate the beauty. She did what she could to kick herself into a better mental state, but reasons not to give into hopelessness eluded her.

No mother. No father. No caravan. No one who cared if she lived or died—except the wolf, and it had survived the loss of other bondmates.

Had Jamal known she was within arm's reach and chosen not to see her? Or had his kin conveniently neglected to tell him until she was gone? Tairin had questions she never expected to find answers for.

Which way should she go? If she kept traveling north, there was an enormous sea and a busy port with ships that traveled the world. Maybe she could find work on one of them. Did women even go to sea? She suspected the answer was no.

"I have to do something," she mumbled.

"For now, let's head toward the big river. Hunting is plentiful there, and I'm hungry."

Tairin was too, but she was tired of game, eaten raw. She shuttered her thoughts, burying them deep. The wolf had been kind to her, and she didn't want to hurt its feelings.

They crossed the main road and moved deep into the Nile Delta. It was busier here than downriver where her caravan was camped. After her near miss with the man yesterday, she skirted encampments. Beyond folk who obviously lived here, other groups had gathered on the river's banks fishing or collecting water or washing clothes. Some cut vegetation to add to their cookpots.

She undressed behind two boulders, stuffing her skirt and tunic in her bag. Hurrying before anyone happened on her, she left her clothing sack in a crevice between the boulders that sheltered her. A small spell would hide its presence. Tairin marked the location in her mind. Once she wasn't encumbered with the bag, she shrouded herself with invisibility and picked her way across side streams until she reached a spot she could shift and not run into anyone.

When she'd withdrawn her attention from the past and the future, her attitude improved. *One thing at a time*, she told herself. *I'll do one thing, and then I'll do the next.*

It was a far different mindset than the one she'd grown up with, where everything was planned out, but that life was gone.

The shift magic took her. It was a relief to cede her fragile body to the wolf with its fangs and claws and fur. Its joy at being free warmed her, and when it rocked onto its haunches and howled, other wolves howled back.

Family. They could be my family, stand in for the one I lost.

Tairin shut down that line of thought fast. She was human. She'd lost almost everything, but she couldn't lose that. If she did, she'd… Her mind stumbled to a halt. She had no idea what would happen if she remained a wolf for long, but she was certain it was the wrong thing to do.

The wolf hunted with her along for the ride. They caught,

chewed, and swallowed so many mice and rabbits, her belly grew distended.

"It's enough," she told the wolf. *"We shouldn't be greedy."*

Instead of answering, the wolf padded to the water's edge and drank deep. *"Do you want to rest or return to your things?"* it asked.

The answer should have risen quickly, but it didn't. She wasn't anxious to be human again, not when she became prey, rather like the rodents they'd consumed.

"You don't have to—" the wolf began.

She cut it off. *"Yes, I do. We must return to my things. It's one thing to be in your form to feed ourselves, but it's not right to stay that way."*

She'd expected arguments, but the wolf padded back the way they'd come. It located the boulders without any help from her. Moving through shadows, they skirted several groups of people, but no one looked twice. The wolf must have ways of shielding its presence the same way she could.

A scan told her no one was close enough to bother them, so she visualized her body and let the shift take her. Before, she'd been relieved to be back in her own body, but not today. With her humanness came pain and worry and apprehension.

When she understood why today was different, sadness filled her. Even though she'd told herself it was unlikely, she'd pinned her hopes on her father. He loved her. Surely he wouldn't desert her.

But he had. By now, he knew she'd been there, and he hadn't tried to track her. With his shifter senses, finding his own blood would be a simple matter.

Stay in the present. I'll drive myself mad if I don't.

"Why aren't you saying anything?" she asked the wolf. "I know you hear my thoughts."

"This is one path you must tread alone. I can't humor you out of your grief or your losses. They're real. The pain will fade, but it will take time. I respect you too much to pretend your anguish isn't real."

"I wish we could both have bodies." She snuffled a little, but didn't cry. "Because then I could hug you."

"I'd like that. I could lick your chin."

She dressed and slung her sack around her neck, but wasn't in a rush to leave the protection the boulders offered. The world had tilted on its axis. Everyone had ulterior motives and was a potential threat. She had to keep that front and center if she was to survive.

Tairin waited until no one was close enough to see her emerge from her hiding place. Setting a fast pace, she headed north. The delta spread on both sides of the road now and vegetation grew thickly, replacing more arid terrain. Avoiding people became impossible, so she settled for sprinkling magic to lessen the odds of anyone approaching her. Her spell suggested she was insignificant, not worth anyone's time or trouble.

"So long as you don't start believing that, we'll be fine," the wolf growled.

Its protectiveness touched her, but caring about anyone or anything was the source of why she hurt now. Easier to build walls around her mind and heart. Walls no one could penetrate.

Would Alexandria, where she was headed, be any less dangerous than Cairo? Both cities were ruled by the Ottoman Empire. She'd learned that much from her limited schooling in the caravan. She culled through her memory for what else she knew about both cities. She'd spent time in them with the Romani, but her experiences with kinfolk surrounding her weren't relevant to a young woman traveling alone with all her possessions in a bag around her neck.

"Do you know anything about Alexandria?" she asked the wolf, pitching her voice very low. Her bondmate was a rich source of knowledge, but maybe not about cities.

"Vampires lurk there and a sickness fatal to humans, but not to shifters, sweeps through every once in a while."

Tairin knew about the plague, an illness that made people

bleed to death from the inside. Interesting—and a piece of welcome news—that she couldn't fall prey to it anymore. The caravan had been in Alexandria during an outbreak, and they'd left as soon as word of the first deaths reached them.

Before the city herded everyone with symptoms outside and sealed its gates.

"Why would vampires pick Alexandria?" she asked, wanting to know more.

"They cull humans fresh off the ships and turn them. The city you call Alexandria hosts multitudes of temples dedicated to managing the vampire infestation. Still, it's never been enough to wipe them out."

She could see why. Vampires could add to their ranks in the blink of an eye. "I asked this before, but once they're made, exactly how long does it take for new vampires to become a threat?"

"Many seasons must pass for them to come into their full power, but they're a threat after they recover from being turned. Perhaps a single transit of the moon."

Tairin shivered. Her run-in with vampires had been enough to convince her killing them was a worthy goal. Maybe one of those temples would take her on as an acolyte—if they accepted women. Isis, Bastet, and Nephthys had shrines in Alexandria, which suggested someone tended them. The host who'd ridden to Masud's aide had all been men, but that didn't mean women couldn't be warriors too.

I have to find a place I can fit in. Somewhere I can do something besides running away and hiding.

She waited to hear what the wolf thought, but it remained silent. What had it said earlier? *"This is one path you must tread alone. I can't humor you out of your grief or your losses. They're real. The pain will fade, but it will take time. I respect you too much to pretend your anguish isn't real."*

"You have a good memory," the wolf murmured. *"None of that has changed."*

They walked in silence until the midday sun beat down on

Tairin's head. She longed for an actual shawl to throw over herself, but it wasn't one of the items in her clothing sack. Besides, her *ignore me* spell was working, and she didn't want to do anything to disturb it—like stopping to paw through her bag. Something like that would alert people—if anyone happened to be watching—that she did, indeed, have a few possessions.

A child's enraged squalls rang from not far away. Tairin kept walking. The world was full of unhappy children, and she had problems of her own. The child's wails grew in intensity, punctuated by the sound of an open hand slapping flesh. Once. Twice. Three times.

Move past.

Not my business.

Nothing I can do.

Tairin tried not to look as she drew closer, but the little one's grief tugged at her heartstrings. The Romani may have broken many laws, but they treated children well—at least when they were small. Gypsy babies were fussed over and treated like little kings and queens by the entire caravan. The Rom viewed children as gifts from the goddess. They ensured the Romani people would be strong and continue.

The road wended between waterways in the delta, its lazy curves following the riverbank. She trotted around a corner and came to a halt, heartsick and disbelieving. A man swathed in nomad's robes held a child of perhaps five by his feet. Suspended upside down, the child squalled. Red marks coated his small, naked body, and tears and snot streaked his face.

While Tairin stood staring, the man struck the boy again. "You stole from me," the man thundered.

Between sobs, the little boy choked out that he hadn't.

Others dressed similarly to the man milled about. Tairin counted six women and one more man. A group of naked children cowered behind the women, who were bunched to one side.

Was this a harem? One of those arrangements where men took

multiple wives? She'd heard of such things, but never seen one before. At least according to other Romani, women in harems were hidden from public view.

The man slapped the child again.

"We need to move past before someone notices us," the wolf prodded.

Sound advice, but Tairin stepped toward the tableau and dispersed her spell. "Excuse me." She cleared her throat and kept her gaze downcast. Men didn't like it if you looked directly at them.

The man holding the child trained harsh, dark eyes on her. "If you're looking for coin, move on."

The other man angled his head to look at her. "On the other hand, if you're offering yourself for coin, I might take you up on it. One copper. Take it or leave it. I'm not interested in haggling."

Tairin took a ragged breath. This was a huge mistake, but she couldn't hold herself back. "I didn't stop to beg." She closed her teeth over her lower lip so hard she tasted blood. "I heard the child crying and wanted to help. I could take him with me. Get him off your hands if he's such a problem."

Both men broke out laughing. The women all looked away.

"It's a good offer," Tairin insisted.

"How much will you give us?" The man holding the child cast a different kind of speculative glance her way.

Heat rose from her chest. Money. Of course. She was being stupid, and she'd put herself at risk for nothing. They could always put the boy up for auction at the slave market. He'd stopped wailing and had turned liquid dark eyes full of pleading her way.

"Sorry," Tairin mumbled, looking away from the supplication in the child's gaze. It tore her already damaged heart to tatters. "Sorry. I have nothing. I'll be on my way."

"Please," the child cried. "Please, kind lady."

Tairin plodded on to the sound of another slap. The last thing she needed was another mouth to feed, one that couldn't live on fresh game like her and the wolf.

As if thinking about it drew it out, the wolf said, *"Admirable, but ill-advised."*

At least it wasn't berating her for sheer idiocy.

She faded off the main road, wanting to sit for a spell and gather her wits. Maybe it would save her from any more well-meaning but foolhardy acts. It didn't take her shifter senses to alert her to someone following her.

Maybe they're just heading for the water like me.

"This isn't good," the wolf said. *"We should shift."*

"No. Too many people to see us."

She zigged and zagged, but the same energy remained behind her. Finally, Tairin spun, summoning magic to deal with whomever was back there. The nomad who'd held the child smiled with a mouthful of teeth. His predatory expression didn't bode anything good.

"I told you I was sorry—" she began just before pain exploded at the base of her skull. Must be the other man wielding a club. She twisted to see who'd hit her, but her vision blurred. Tairin tried to form more words, but he hit her again and her knees crumpled beneath her. Consciousness wavered and then faded away.

airin opened her eyes to the night sky. Her head pounded and throbbed, and nausea made her gut clench from the pain.

"You're awake!" Relief streamed from the wolf. *"I tried and tried to reach you, but you were sunk so deep, I couldn't rouse you."*

Groaning, she rolled onto her side and vomited bile from her empty stomach. The spasms stole her breath and made her light-headed. Lying flat wasn't helping. Tairin gathered her knees beneath her and straightened her upper body. Her head spun crazily, and she waited for it to settle before trying to stand. Her sack was gone, but the men had left the clothes on her back.

"Small things," she muttered, gagging at the bitter taste coating her mouth and tongue.

Tairin staggered upright and made her way to the nearest stream. It wasn't far, not more than twenty steps. Once there, she bent and splashed water on her face, swishing it around her mouth. When she probed with her fingers, she found a huge lump at the base of her skull. It was so big, she was surprised the blow hadn't killed her.

"Did you see what happened after I blacked out?" she asked.

"Of course."

"Why didn't they kill me?"

"They would have raped you, but I intervened." The wolf growled, low and menacing until it reverberated through her.

Tairin dropped her aching head into her hands and sluiced more water over herself. "I don't see bodies. What'd you do?"

"Separated enough to hover above you as you lay in the dirt. It scared the hell out of them, and they ran like cowardly puppies, invoking Allah's protection." Another snarl. *"If I'd been able to speak, I'd have told them Allah wouldn't go out of His way to spit on such as them."*

"You can do that? Take your form while I still have mine?" Tairin rocked back on her heels. Her headache had moved from impossible to harsh but livable.

"Not fully, but I can cast an outline of myself. If they'd challenged the vision, they'd have been able to punch their hands right through me."

"What happens to your magic when I'm unconscious?"

"It's diluted. I can do a few things, like project that image of myself to try to protect you, but not much else."

"What would you have done if I'd died?" Tairin felt torn. Part of her selfishly wanted the wolf to follow her into death, but another more sensible part hoped it would keep on living. Find a bondmate worthy of it, not someone like her who knew nothing and was mostly a liability.

"It didn't come anywhere close to that," the wolf snapped off the words. *"Do not talk of dying. It tempts fate in bad ways."*

The distant howl of wolves rang from the south and was immediately answered from the other three directions. Tairin rubbed the back of her head gingerly. The lump was still there, but it seemed to be growing smaller.

"It is smaller," the wolf said gruffly. *"I'm helping you heal yourself so we can get moving. You'll miss the things in that bag, but not having it will make our lives easier."*

Tairin smiled grimly. Nothing left to lose. It did simplify things. A lot. One thing was certain. A woman on her own would have a hard go—of everything. Should she keep to her original plan and head for Alexandria, hoping one of the temples would offer her a place to live in exchange for work?

The most logical solution for her would be as a servant in a Romani caravan. She understood their ways and their traditions. That might work for a short time, but eventually word of a missing female about her age would leak out. Someone would scan her with magic, discover her secrets, and she'd have to leave. Better not to put down roots in one more place, only to have them ripped out from under her.

She hunted for her earlier sadness, but couldn't find it. Not exactly. Mostly, she felt empty inside. As if she'd been stripped of everything and kicked aside, left for worthless.

The wolves howled again. It had to be past midnight judging from the position of the moon and stars. "Should we shift?" she asked the wolf. The thought of eating made her stomach knot up, but maybe the wolf was hungry and would welcome the chance to hunt.

"*You must be more healed before we shift.*"

"Why? So my injuries don't weaken you?"

"*Not at all,*" the wolf replied. "*I want to make certain you're feeling more yourself. This is new magic for you. You're still exploring how you and it fit together. You should be stronger before we shift again.*"

She pushed herself to think, to figure out what to do next. Fear rode just beneath the surface. Daylight would increase the chance of discovery, of people, none of whom cared if she lived or died.

"*If we could locate a safe spot, one where we could wait out the next day or two, would you like that?*" The wolf's voice was gentle.

Tairin nodded numbly. It seemed like too much to ask for, though. "Does someplace like that even exist?"

"*I believe so. This delta is riddled with caves. People have lived here for a very long time. I will lend you my senses so you can smell the remains of fires and settlements.*"

The same mind-bending alteration she'd experienced last time the wolf opened its nose and ears to her shot from her feet to her head. Her skull throbbed, but not much worse than it had before. Multicolored lights flashed, and her nostrils flared at an array of scents. Rich loam. Crushed vegetation. Rodents busy hunting for food. Fish splashing as they ran from predators, intent on catching them.

She lurched upright from where she'd knelt next to the water, her senses on full alert. Because she wasn't used to tracking with her nose, she wasted time on several false starts before she picked up the undeniable scent of a place humans had gathered. The scents were faded, faint, which meant people no longer lived there. Had the smells been stronger, she'd have run the other way. People meant trouble, and she didn't want any more confrontations.

The last one was my own fault.

Yeah well, I learned something. Compassion is an indulgence and a dead end street.

The hours of moving had helped her headache. It was almost gone when she clawed her way through a rubble pile next to a tiny creek almost lost in a tumble of vegetation. Exultation raced through her when she slithered through the hole she'd made into an underground dwelling. No one had been here for a long time, but it was dry and unlikely to be discovered.

To be on the safe side, she pushed dirt to cover the hole she'd come through. Did she have enough magic to summon a light?

I don't need one. I'm safe. For now.

"Excellent choice," the wolf said.

Tairin crawled into a corner and propped herself against a wall. Shutting her eyes, she blanked her mind, not wanting to relive anything about the last few hours. Not the poor little boy, or the men who'd robbed her. If it hadn't been for the wolf, she'd have lost a whole lot more than her possessions. She'd have been raped and maybe even murdered.

Daylight came and went twice—filtering through thin places in the dirt she'd shoved over the hole—before she felt ready to do anything but hide. She and the wolf had come out for water and to hunt, but never for very long. Night had fallen a few hours ago, and she leaned against the spot she'd claimed when she first found the cave.

"This isn't any kind of life," she told the wolf.

"*No, but you had to decide that. Me telling you wouldn't have worked.*"

"I'll live a long time, right?"

"*Yes, you will.*"

"This isn't a workable world for me as a human. Let's take your form and wait out fifty years or so. It's possible things might improve for a woman by herself if we wait things out."

"*We can take my form,*" the wolf spoke slowly, thoughtfully, "*but that's too long a time. If you remain in my body too long, you'll never find your own again.*"

"Fine. So we can shift every few years for a short while. Just to test the waters. If nothing's gotten better, back to wolves we go."

The more she talked about it, the more feasible it felt. No more hiding in shadows. No more cringing every time someone looked at her. No more smothering her kindheartedness over someone like the little boy who was being beaten.

"*Easy to say now,*" the wolf cautioned. "*Harder to do. The longer you're a wolf, the less you'll want to be human again, and the impetus for the shift must come from you, not me.*"

"What is it you're not saying?" She leaned forward and wrapped her arms around her knees.

"*You must promise me you won't abandon your human parts.*"

"What if I don't?"

"*Then I shall request to be released from our bond.*"

The wolf's response felt like a kick in her guts. "You'd leave me? Over me wanting to be a wolf?"

"*Stop reacting and start listening.*" The wolf's voice was stern.

"What I said was you had to give me your word you'd not relinquish your humanity. Can you do that? Only a few days ago, it was precious to you."

Tairin unclasped her arms and slumped against the wall. "Yes, I can do that. Why is it so important? Important enough you'd sever our bond."

"Shifter law is quite clear. A human cannot take on the animal's form indefinitely. It alters the natural order of things and will eventually impact all shifters adversely."

The wolf sounded as if it was quoting from memorized lessons. "Do something for me, please."

"If it's within my power."

"While we're in your body, tell me more about shifters. I know next to nothing."

"I will try. The longer we're wolves, though, the less time we'll spend talking about esoteric topics. They don't come easily to the animal part of our shared nature."

"It's a fair answer."

"I will do the best I can."

"That's all I can ask for."

Wolf song rose outside the cave dwelling. Tairin took it as an omen she'd chosen the right path. She sent magic spiraling wide. No one was about, so she crawled out the grotto where she'd sheltered.

"Ready when you are," she told the wolf.

"Remember your promise."

"I will."

"Then I'm ready. Call the shift magic."

Tairin slipped out of her skirt and tunic, hanging them over a nearby bush. Maybe a passing woman could use them. She visualized the wolf and felt the change take her, relieved to have found a way out of the cruel and arbitrary world of men. Not forever, but for now.

Once she had fur and fangs and claws, she broke into an easy lope, heading for the nearest group of wolves. They might chase her away, but they might not.

"Let's tell them we're on our way." The wolf stopped and tossed its muzzle back to howl.

Other wolves howled back, and Tairin ran to meet them.

YOU'VE REACHED the end of *Tarnished Beginnings*, the prequel to the *Soul Dance* series. The next book, *Tarnished Legacy*, jumps forward two hundred years. Tairin welched on her promise and spent half that time as a wolf. By the time her wolf forced her to shift, she almost couldn't find her human body, and she'd forgotten how to talk.

TARNISHED LEGACY

SOUL DANCE, BOOK TWO

Shifter Paranormal Romance
By Ann Gimpel

Tarnished Legacy

Germany, 1940

Half Romani, Tairin's no stranger to hiding her mixed blood from gypsy caravans. What she can't hide is her perpetual youth, courtesy of her shifter heritage. Every few years, she drops out of sight, resurfacing in a new country to join a caravan where no one knows her. She's overstayed her welcome where she is, but Germany is at war, and travel has become all but impossible for everyone targeted by the Reich.

Elliott's clairvoyance is strong, even for a Romani. Seer for all the caravans in Germany, he catches Tairin eavesdropping outside their leader's wagon one night. He should turn her in, but it would mean her execution, and he can't bring himself to do that. Instead, he interrogates her. Her magic is different, but he can't figure out quite what she is.

Any association between Romani and shifters is forbidden, and Tairin shields herself from Elliott's probing. She should leave right now, tonight. It would be easy enough. Shift to her wolf form and run, keeping out of hunters' gunsights. She's on the edge of flight when Elliott suggests a covert task to prove her loyalty.

Tairin agrees immediately, kicking herself for being weak where he's concerned. Shifters and Romani have no future together. Zero. Zilch.

She should be smart about this and vanish into the night—before he discovers what she is and destroys her.

PROLOGUE

January 1940
Munich, Germany

ELLIOTT BREND MOVED his hands in a circular pattern over three lit candles, the stench of wax made from sheep fat sharp in his nostrils. Patterns danced like mad creatures on the walls of his grotto, and he chanted faster to bring his casting to life.

Darkness swirled, surrounding him. The candles guttered and died, their wicks drowning in pools of grease. Elliott bolted to his feet, hands extended, still working the spell he'd summoned. Fear thickened his tongue, but he couldn't stop now. Partially cast spells would make it possible for the demon he'd apparently conjured to drag him back to Hell with it. Usually this casting brought visions, not an actual entity.

The temperature in the grotto plummeted until ice crystals formed in the air. Wind wailed, thin and menacing. Shudders racked him.

"Why have you freed me? Not that I'm complaining, mind

you." The words echoed around Elliott, chilling him further. "Speak, human. While you still can."

Elliott tried. Instead of words, a breathy croak emerged. He swallowed around his dry-as-dust throat. "F-future," he stammered. "What will happen? Many of the Rom have been captured."

Unholy laughter drove into Elliott's brain like overheated nails. It took all his self-control not to clap his hands over his ears, but if he did that, he'd be lost. His spell would falter, as would his tenuous hold on the demon. He'd be damned if he'd cede the upper hand to it.

Who am I kidding? It already has all the power it needs.

"You scarcely require me for future-telling," the disembodied voice said. At least the profane laughter had stopped. After the briefest pause, it added, "Flee while you can. Or the Rom will die out—here and elsewhere."

"Why do you care?" The words tore out of Elliott before he could stop himself.

"About your people? I don't, but magical energy will keep me on this side of Hell. Along with death. Fear helps too." A low, menacing chuckle punctuated the demon's words. "It's a perfect mix. You can blame the Nazis for my freedom. They provided an ideal medium. Coupled with your drawing spell, it allowed me to pierce the veil."

Elliott gathered power, letting it surge through him. The demon may have ridden in on the coattails of his earlier spell, but he couldn't allow it to remain. Too much evil was running unchecked as it was. Sparks crackled from his fingertips, burning him until his flesh smoked. The incantation, a surefire way to banish Hell's minions, crashed to the rotting wooden floor in a shower of glowing embers.

"Don't waste your magic, human."

"It's not a waste to return you to your proper place," Elliott snarled, wishing he could see the fucking thing.

"Try that last trick again, and you're a dead man."

Elliott sucked in a frustrated breath. He'd suspected the Rom were in serious danger. Signs they'd soon be targeted *en masse*, right along with the Jews, were impossible to ignore. All he'd sought this night was corroboration—and now he had it. He changed the cadence and timbre of his chant, hoping for an end to his spell, the hideous cold, and the abomination that scared the shit out of him. All he wanted now was for it to leave since returning it to Hell was beyond his ability.

"I am not leaving yet," the voice informed him. "You have no power over me, but you've already figured that out. Evil has risen. Rampant. Ubiquitous. As I noted earlier, it feeds me, right along with your magic."

Elliott clamped his jaws together to stop his teeth from chattering. What had he loosed on the world? "You must return at some point." He infused compulsion into his words. "If not today, or tomorrow, then surely soon. The dynamic balance between worlds will fail if you remain on Earth."

Laughter again. This time, it was even more loathsome and obnoxious.

"You haven't been paying attention, *human*. That dynamic balance? It's on its way out." Still laughing, the thing's foul presence receded.

Elliott sank into a crouch, mostly because his legs shook too badly to hold him upright. He wrapped his arms around himself and rekindled the candles with a jot of magic, welcoming their pools of light. Because it was easier than reconstructing what had just happened—and the wickedness now free because of him—he shuffled through options.

The demon's advice—if demons even handed out such things —had been to flee. But where? Austria, Poland, and Czechoslovakia were out of the question. Austria was a German ally. Both Poland and Czechoslovakia had fallen to German occupation a few months earlier. France would soon be under German rule. While his seer skills weren't absolute, he'd seen that particular event clearly.

Even if they could find a favorable location, how would they move the entire Romani population out of Germany? They still favored wagons, so any kind of stealth exodus was out of the question.

He rose to his feet and shambled to a window, gazing out at a moonless night. The elders from all the Rom groups in Germany had assembled a few days earlier, and they were waiting for him to return. Though they dealt in magic, his particular affinity for the darker side of the spirit world unnerved many of his kin.

Should he confess what he'd done?

He'd loosed wickedness eager to sign on with the blood-soaked Nazi regime, but how much worse could things get? He knew what the work camps really were, and so did the other Rom. None of his people fit the Aryan model of perfection, and their nomadic lifestyle was an affront to neat rows of impeccable houses where blonde wives raised blonde children in perfect obedience to the Reich's precepts.

Not much leeway for the Roms' brightly colored wagons or their sturdy horses. Their children who didn't go to school, or the canvas tents where they revealed futures, healed the sick, and fixed whatever was broken.

Bile splashed the back of his throat; he swallowed it down, and it burned all the way to his knotted belly. He still didn't understand how the Reich had mired Germany in such a chokehold, but it didn't matter. What did was ensuring Rom magic survived. It may have provided fodder for the newly released demon, but it also ensured the natural world would continue.

The traveling folk were tied to the world's beginnings in ways that had faded out of time and memory. They'd been run out of countries before and always endured, retooling themselves and keeping their magic under wraps as the world grew more modern.

If leaving Germany were impossible, they'd have to find a way to conceal themselves. The more he thought about it, the more the idea appealed to him. They faced evil, the likes of which the world had never seen. Evil that believed it could kill whomever it wished under the guise of cleansing the gene pool and producing a master race.

It would take gargantuan effort, but he and his kin could leverage magic to sabotage the Reich. Maybe even free the poor sods in those abominable camps. And make damn good and sure Germany went down in flames it would never recover from. Elliott had no idea if the elders would agree, but he'd float his idea. See if their philosophy, *Opré Roma*—Roma arise—was more than empty words.

Even if they don't agree, there's nothing that says I can't gather a few handpicked companions...

He curved his hands into fists until his nails cut into his palms. The more he rolled it around in his mind, the better he liked the idea of small vigilante groups that struck fast and hard, while remaining invisible to the *SchutzStaffel*, Germany's elite corps of political soldiers.

Determination straightened his spine. He dug a warm cloak out of the clothing chest leaning against one wall and wrapped it around himself before striding out of his well-hidden grotto located beneath the city. Part of a deteriorating tunnel system under a crumbling castle, his hideaway dated back to Roman times. He'd titrate what he told the elders until he saw which way the wind blew. Once he had a sense of that, he could make better plans.

Since none of them had stronger power than he did to banish the demon, probably no reason to mention it at all…

He shook his head. Secrecy was a bad idea. He had to live with himself, which meant full disclosure. No matter how much shit he got for his folly.

airin Jabari prowled from one end of a clearing to the other in a forested glen. Her Rom family group had established a temporary camp here after local authorities ousted them from their previous location inside Munich's city limits. More than a dozen wagons fanned out in a circle, and horses were hobbled off to one side where grass grew thickly. Cars might be faster, but the smoky, noisy contraptions that always required repair had never appealed to Romani sensibilities.

She rolled her shoulders back to quell the creature sharing her skin. Her wolf wanted out, but it was too dangerous. For all their magic, power they scattered about like so much faerie dust, the Romani were superstitious about shapeshifters.

Worse than superstitious. They hated them.

She pulled her thick, black wool cloak tighter around herself and buried her hands in its thick folds. Her leather boots were soaked through, but it was winter. Short days and wet ground meant they never dried completely. Reaching within, she soothed her wolf, agreed its lush double coat and furred paws were far better suited to damp and cold than their current arrangement.

"Promise me," the wolf spoke into her mind.

"Anything, heart of mine."

"Find us an hour when I can run."

Tairin closed her teeth over her lower lip, not wanting false words to fall between her and her bondmate. *I'll do my best.* Whether *her best* would yield the privacy required remained to be seen.

Something mollified the wolf. Maybe her words. Maybe her honesty. It withdrew to the place where it lived when it wasn't front and center in her mind.

She'd managed to hide what she was from the group she traveled with for the better part of twenty years. Soon it would be time to fade away—to find another country and maybe more Romani traveling companions. As it was, several of the women had made snippy comments about her perpetual youth. Tairin led them to believe she employed a glamour, but no one had the kind of magic to keep something like that going all day, every day, for years.

The sounds of male laughter, boasts, and glasses slapping a tabletop rose from the leader's wagon. He played host to eleven other elders this week. They'd gathered to discuss the evil that had descended on Germany. Elliott, the group's seer, was off doing goddess only knew what. Maybe he'd actually have a vision that would galvanize the Rom into something beyond business as usual.

Not a moment too soon, her inner voice muttered sourly.

If the disaster she suspected were imminent fell out the sky and onto their heads, they'd be rounded up. Herded into the death camps sprouting like cancers across what used to be the Prussian empire.

And that would be that.

She'd find a way through. Her wolf form would see to it. She could join one of many packs that howled their way through Germany's thick forests. But she'd become fond of the Romani after a rocky start. That and shared blood was why she'd traveled with several of their family groups for the past hundred years.

She wove her way into a thick evergreen grove where she wouldn't have to hide the anger that still filled her whenever she remembered how her people had kicked her out. Looking back was a dead end, yet once she'd begun, it took time to redirect her energy.

She was different from other shifters. And other Romani. Born of a forbidden coupling between a wolf shifter father and a Romani mother, she hadn't been welcome in either camp once her powers blossomed. Her moon blood presaged her first shift, and her life had turned to warmed over crap right afterward. Shifters might have had more tolerance for how strong her magic was if her blood were pure, but it wasn't.

That she could shift at all meant the Rom wanted nothing to do with her.

Tairin took to her wolf form after being rejected by both sides of her kinfolk. She'd lived with local packs in northern Egypt for her first hundred years, give or take a few. Some alphas accepted her; others drove her away. She'd been between packs when a caravan of Romani wagons passing through attracted her attention, alerted her it was time to be human again. As a wolf, she was used to following her instincts without overthinking things. After so long, her animal nature was firmly entrenched.

So firmly entrenched, her first shift back to her human body took days to finesse. A Romani fortuneteller with Runic markings on her face and hands had found Tairin with her arms wrapped around her naked body, crying. After so long as a wolf, speech didn't come easily, so she'd had a ready excuse not to reveal that her tears were relief she still had a human form. Over the days she'd languished part wolf, part human, she'd been petrified she'd never find the purity of either body again.

The woman who rescued her moved her into the back of her wagon. As Tairin regained her very rusty ability to speak, she discovered the Romani group was on the move, traveling through Pakistan, Persia, and Turkey on their way to Romania. The journey had been hard and taken years. She'd stuck with them throughout, helping as she grew stronger. Though her new family wanted to know all about her, the only part she'd revealed was that she had some Romani blood.

She'd never repeated her past mistake about spending years in a single form. Her wolf had warned her it would be folly, but she hadn't listened to it. Nor did she assume her adoptive tribe would be tolerant if they knew what she truly was, so she dove headfirst into relearning Romani magic, remembering her affinity for it.

She'd been such an apt pupil she'd hidden just how potent her power was because she didn't want anyone to guess she was anything other than Romani mixed with human. As she'd developed her skills, she waited for the unknown to rise up and swallow her whole. Surely there was a reason the Rom avoided shifters. A reason why sexual congress was forbidden. Would her use of Romani magic leave her open to some hideous consequences?

Though she'd asked that question and others, taking care to be subtle about it, no answers were forthcoming. The lore books were written in Coptic, an old Egyptian language no one in her caravan seemed to have mastered at anything beyond a cursory level. Tairin spoke Coptic, but she'd never learned to read very well as a child, so translation was beyond her. Over the last century, she'd rectified being mostly illiterate, but her grasp of German and French didn't help decipher the lore books.

She stifled a frustrated sigh. Her current group of companions was the fourth one she'd joined since leaving Egypt. Given the rise of the Reich, it might well be the last.

The sounds of a horse galloping hard drew her back to the circle of wagons. Was Elliott returning? Or was an elder late to the party? She'd thought all were present and accounted for, but she might've been wrong. Tairin sent a slender thread of seeking magic outward. Elliott's energy resonated, making her heart flutter oddly.

The tall, broad-shouldered Rom with his long black hair and deep blue eyes moved with the grace of a large jungle cat. Seer power ran strong in him, and he dabbled in the darker side of Rom magic. Enchantments from Black Magick came easily to her, but she hid that particular ability from her fellows.

Sometimes she'd caught Elliott's gaze on her, sharply speculative. But if he saw through to what she was, he'd never said as much.

Elliott reined his horse to an abrupt halt, its thick hooves churning up clods of mud and stones. "Tairin." His voice rang with command and a surfeit of magic as he dismounted. "See to my horse." He tossed the reins her way and loped toward the wagon where the men held court. His leggy gait drew her gaze. He was so sensual, her body vibrated with wanting to throw herself into his arms. She'd never lain with a man, only with wolves, but she could imagine what it would be like.

Maybe it's time.

Maybe not. I got away with learning Rom magic. I might not be so lucky making love with one.

How would her half-breed blood react to joining with a Romani? She couldn't ask the question without giving away far too much about who she was.

She plucked the reins out of the dirt and sent soothing energy directly into the horse's mind. The stallion had been ridden hard. He needed a cool down, so she vaulted onto his back and walked him at a sedate pace until he stopped tossing his head and his breathing slowed. Some horses sensed her dual nature and resented the hell out of it, but the stallion seemed oblivious.

She'd tethered him near his fellows where he could graze and removed his saddle and bridle before curiosity drew her to the wagon where men's voices droned. Someone had shielded the conversation unfolding within, but she cut through the barrier with ease. Hunkering a few feet away, she eavesdropped shamelessly, wanting to know what would happen next.

Women fared better with the traveling folk than they did elsewhere, but Romani society was still run by men. When she sent her power spiraling outward to listen in on the men, the other women were all in their wagons, probably pretending all was well. The men—beyond the elders—milled about, busy with myriad tasks that needed doing each night. Younger children remained with their mothers. Older boys and girls helped the men do chores. Normally, they'd have set up their tents and wagons in Munich, soliciting local business, but the resident police force had made it abundantly clear they were no longer welcome.

Tension thickened the air. Even though everyone was acting as if tonight was just one more winter evening, they all knew better. Decisions unfolding one thin wall away from her would bind them to a course that might well spell their doom. A hissing snort bubbled up; Tairin smothered it fast before one of the elders heard and came out to investigate.

She swathed herself in invisibility and tilted her head, listening intently.

"You loosed a demon?" Michael thundered.

"How could you have been so irresponsible?" another voice she didn't recognize broke in.

"It's not as if that was my intent." Elliott's even baritone held a calming element. "I cast a scrying spell seeking visions, not one of Hell's minions." He paused for a few seconds, probably to strengthen the spell that lay beneath his words. "I did my damnedest to send the bastard packing. I wasn't strong enough, but we waste time speaking of him. We must decide how to proceed."

"Ye say the demon advised flight?" Stewart's Scottish brogue was unmistakable.

"Yes," Elliott replied.

"When we begin believing anything that emerges from a demon's mouth, we're finished," Michael said flatly.

"Och aye. Still, we canna remain here," Stewart said. "We canna work. We've been banned from the town."

"It won't be any different in Berlin or Heidelberg or Dresden," Elliott said. "The Reich have labeled our kind as undesirables. Our way of life is anathema to them."

"And ye know what happens next." Stewart's words sounded like a dirge. "We join the others. The ones imprisoned by those Nazi bastards."

"Let me say my piece," Elliott cut in. "Then you can decide what's best for your individual groups."

"I'm not certain I want to listen to someone who let a demon loose to feed off the poison spreading across Europe," another elder grumbled.

"Your choice." Elliott spoke clearly, but without inflection. "My path is clear."

"Really?" Michael's single word dripped displeasure. "Last time I checked, you were part of my group, which means you're bound by my decisions."

Elliott cleared his throat. "Nowhere is it written that you own me, nor that I signed on with you for life. Look, men, we have a problem. If we continue to ignore it, the Nazis may well add us to their genocide list—"

"They already have," Stewart broke in. "I, for one, would like to hear what the lad has to say. Listening doesna bind us to action."

"Fine," Michael muttered dourly. "Proceed, but make it quick."

After a period of silence when Tairin held her breath, Elliott began to speak again. "Very well. Escape from Germany is unlikely given our numbers. A few of us might get lucky, but most of us will end up trapped. Neighboring countries aren't a haven. Either they're already occupied, or they soon will be." He inhaled noisily and blew it out. "Our only option as I see it is to hide. If we remain in our groups, they're manageable enough we might be able to pull it off."

"What aren't you saying?" Michael demanded. "I damn near raised you, Elliott. I know when there's more than what's come out of your mouth."

"I'm impressed." Elliott laughed softly. "You do know me, probably far too well. I plan to leverage my magic and do what I can to sabotage the Reich. I'm not certain how it will play out, but if I strike fast and hard, I can catch them off balance. By combining my seer ability and maybe astral projection or invisibility spells, I should be able to determine where my efforts will create the most damage."

"So will ye be doing this on your own, lad?" Stewart asked.

"If need be, yes," Elliott replied. "I admit, it would be better if a small group of us signed on, but this will be extremely dangerous, and I won't ask anyone else to risk discovery—and maybe death—if things go wrong."

"You might have discussed this with me first." Michael's tone held censure.

"When would I have had a chance?" Elliott shot back. "This idea only took shape today, after the demon left me to stew in my own guilt for having offered it free passage from Hell."

"Mmph. The way I see it," Michael said, "we have three choices. Business as usual. Attempt to make our way to somewhere the Nazi scourge hasn't touched. Or conceal our presence."

"That was my assessment," Elliott murmured.

"Ye did well, lad," Stewart said. "Now leave us so we may determine if we all bet on the same nag, or if we separate our fortunes."

Tairin had crept so close, she leaned against one of the wagon's wheels. The sound of scuffling footsteps as Elliott exited the wagon happened fast. Too fast for her to scamper into the forest. Barely breathing, she wound another layer of spells around herself, hoping invisibility would hide her presence. Once Elliott retired to the wagon he shared with three other unattached men, she could make her way to her own bedroll in one of the women's wagons.

Elliott trotted by where she crouched. He moved fast enough, she let herself hope she'd avoided discovery. Listening in on the elders, particularly after they'd shielded their conversation against prying ears, would surely earn her a session with the bullwhip. If not far worse.

For long, tense moments, she thought she'd pulled it off. She was just starting to breathe again when Elliott's heavy tread first slowed and then stopped.

Shit! Crap!

"*Become me*," her wolf piped up. "*We can knock him down and be gone before he knows what hit him.*"

"*We can't shift that fast.*"

Magic, shockingly strong, probed her perimeter. The gig was up. Elliott might not know it was her, but he realized something was next to Michael's wagon. Something that had no business there.

More power pushed against her invisibility spell, growing in intensity until he punched through. His magic ceased abruptly.

"*Tairin!*" ricocheted through her mind. "*I know it's you. Don't bother denying it. Get over here. Now.*"

She rose to her feet, letting go of her spell as she moved to where he stood twenty yards away. She'd be damned if she'd cower, so she straightened her shoulders and stared him right in the eyes.

"Follow me," he ground out.

"Why should I?" she countered.

He spoke into her mind again. "*You have two choices. Either I call Michael, tell him what you were about, and let him decide what to do with you.*"

"Or?" She feigned bravado she was far from feeling.

"*We go someplace more private, and you tell me what the hell you were doing listening in on the elders' discussion.*" He narrowed his eyes to slits, but switched to speaking aloud. "I might still have to tell Michael. Just so we're clear about that. I owe him allegiance. As do you."

Tairin jerked her chin toward thick timber. "Lead out."

Elliott shook his head. "Nope. You first. I'll be right behind you. And I warn you, if you try anything, I'll flatten you with magic and ask questions later."

She made her way to the grove of pines and firs where she'd been earlier. It was starting to drizzle, so she pulled her hood over her head. Tairin took her time as she worked on organizing which blend of truth might fly better. He'd be able to sniff out falsehoods right away.

His energy pounded against her back as she retraced her steps from earlier. She picked out anger, disbelief, and oddly enough, disappointment. Where was that coming from?

Tairin ducked beneath a low hanging limb and turned to face Elliott. It was dark, but her shifter blood meant she saw quite well in low light conditions. Elliott's dark brows were drawn into a thick, disapproving line.

"Talk and talk fast, sister."

The sizzle of power surrounded her, and she recognized a truth casting. "Was that really necessary?"

"What do you think?" His voice was low, tight with something she couldn't interpret. "I find you swaddled in invisibility spells right outside Michael's wagon. You were obviously listening in. I want to know why."

"That's fair." She let go of her earlier intention of weaving a tale about idle curiosity mixed with boredom. Opening her eyes wide, she netted him with her gaze, trying her hardest not to pay attention to his high forehead, square jaw, and thick, curly hair that almost begged her to sink her hands into it.

"Come on, Tairin." He sounded exasperated. "Talk or you won't leave me any choices. What are you? A Nazi spy?"

Her mouth dropped open. "Awk. Jesus Christ! Oh, hell no." She bristled. "I have eyes and ears. I see what's going on about us. If you must have the truth, I was thinking about leaving, setting out on my own because I could hide myself better that way."

The edges of his magic probed her again. Along with it, his scent rose, tickling her nostrils with bay rum and piquant vanilla. She couldn't help herself, she breathed deep, inhaling the maleness of him.

His power jabbed her when he delved deeper. She rubbed her forehead. "Ouch. Surely that's more than enough. You must've picked up truth in my words."

"I did." Without warning, he closed the distance between them and clasped her head between his hands, pushing her hood back onto her shoulders. Rain pounded from the sky, soaking her.

The intense nearness of him made her knees weak, but she struggled, trying to get away. In all her years with the Rom, the only one who'd touched her had been that first fortuneteller, and the woman had a kind heart. She hadn't suspected a thing, and her touch was aimed at healing, not peeling back the layers of a secret Tairin had guarded for years.

"Stop!" She writhed in his grip.

His scent intensified, and the air around them turned silvery, glistening against the raindrops. Before he could dig deep enough to discover what she was, she wrapped her arms around his neck and pulled his mouth atop hers. The touch of his lips set fire to her blood, and she tightened her hold on him, kissing him as if the fate of the world rested on never letting go. Desire hot enough to set her heart racing sent sensation spilling through her.

After the briefest of hesitations, he buried his hands in her hair and sank his tongue inside her mouth. Something about the way he fell headlong into her embrace made her suspect he'd imagined kissing her just like this.

Whatever works. If this keeps him from unraveling my secrets, it's a small price to pay.

But she was deluding herself. She couldn't make love with him without telling him what she was. He'd never forgive her. More importantly, she'd never forgive herself.

His cock swelled against her belly, rigid with need. What would he look like? Taste like? She ached to wrap a hand around that hardness and drag him inside her body.

Reluctantly, she tore her mouth from his and let go of him. "Sorry," she managed through panting breaths. "I don't know what got into me." She stole a quick glance upward through lowered lids before adding, "I—I'm a maiden. Not a harlot."

"I know." His voice throbbed with yearning. "But you're right that this isn't a good idea. Not with all the problems we face."

She wasn't sure whether to agree, so she held onto a wary silence. Where would this go next?

He let go of her head. "Your magic is strong. As strong as any Rom I've ever come across. Yet you're not full blood."

She licked her swollen lips, anxious to change the subject to something other than her power. "I could help you."

"With what?"

She rotated one hand in a circle. "That plan you described. My magic is potent, and it would complement yours since I'm female."

"Hold on." He shook his head. "I was trolling for men. Women don't go to war."

"The hell they don't." She shook wet hair out of her eyes. Annoyance scoured her nerves, and she stuck out her chin. "Try me. If I don't pass muster, I'll either join the women and sew doilies, or more likely, I'll slip away and wage my own mutiny against the Reich."

His chiseled lips, lips she was having a hell of a hard time resisting, twitched into a smile. "You're on, woman. Feel like a ride?"

"Where are we going?"

"Somewhere we can plan our first offensive."

*E*lliott cut a path from the evergreen grove to where the horses were hobbled. Discovering Tairin outside Michael's wagon had been a shock. If Michael ever found out he'd taken matters into his own hands—without immediately reporting Tairin's presence—there'd be hell to pay.

Need to make certain he never discovers I made a decision he wouldn't have approved of...

Elliott pushed his desire for the woman walking next to him aside. She looked so fierce, and so vulnerable, he wanted to snatch her into another embrace and kiss her until both of them were breathless. He'd had his eye on Tairin for years, but she'd never seemed interested in men. She'd told the truth about being a virgin. He'd ascertained that little fact long ago.

Before tonight, he'd imagined she was either asexual or preferred women. The press of her mouth against his told him he'd been wrong on both counts. She wanted him as much as he wanted her. His cock throbbed hotly between his legs, hard as it ever got. He thought about the points of her breasts pushing into his chest, but it made his arousal that much worse. While not exactly virginal, his forays into sex had been brief and fumbling.

He'd always presumed he'd find a wife someday, but since most of his energy went into his magic, women found him too detached for their taste.

Elliott made his way to the horses with Tairin by his side. She was tall for a woman, only a few inches shorter than he was. Beneath her thick cloak, tawny curls cascaded down her back to waist level, and her deep brown eyes with their amber centers were pools of mystery. Slender like all of them after months of rationed food, her full breasts and flared hips were made for childbearing.

His cock twitched, loving the childbearing thoughts. Or what came before the bearing, most likely. The child making part. He tamped back a chuckle. His thoughts were wandering. No doubt because his cock wasn't in the mood for retreat.

"What's so funny?" Her voice was warm, like thick honey.

"Nothing." He bent to loosen the stallion's hobbles.

Tairin handed him a folded horse blanket. "Do you want the saddle and bridle?"

"Just the bridle. You good with riding bareback?" He tossed the blanket over the stallion.

"Sure." She fetched the bridle from where it hung from a tree branch.

Elliott settled it into place and laced his fingers into a platform to help her mount.

"I'm good. No reason to get mud all over your hands." Tairin vaulted into place, scootching forward.

Elliott jumped on behind and reached around her to hold the reins. The position, with her back jammed against his front and his arms pressed against the sides of her breasts, was sensual, tantalizing. He wanted to tighten his arms around her and press his rigid flesh into the curve of her buttocks. He breathed deep and held it. Her scent, an exotic blend of musk and wild things, did less than nothing to quell his arousal.

"Tell me where we're going," she asked again as he nudged the horse with his knees, and they trotted away from the Rom encampment.

He concentrated on the question to lessen his awareness of her nearness, her femaleness, and his intense desire for her. "To a special place that's just mine. It's difficult for me to cast spells in the midst of a Romani camp. Others seem to manage it, but the proximity of so much competing magic distracts me. It's not that I can't manipulate my power, but it's far easier if I'm by myself."

"I wondered why you always disappeared after we made camp." She hunched forward so her body wasn't plastered right against his.

It took a whole lot of self-control not to settle her firmly back against his chest, and the erection she had to feel jutting into her backside. "Where did you imagine I went?" he asked, curious about the answer, but mostly wanting to hear her melodious voice.

"Guess I figured you had a woman in every port, so to speak. We've made the same rounds for years, covering Germany north to south and east to west."

The thought of him as a Lothario was so preposterous he broke out laughing.

"Please don't laugh at me." She leaned farther forward and wrapped her arms around the horse's neck.

"I'm not. Your assumption amused me. I suppose I should feel flattered, but I've never had time for even one woman, let alone herds of them."

The stallion tossed his head. Tairin let go and straightened but didn't lean back against him. "Why not?"

"The seer magic twists me about and wrings me dry. I've never had much of anything left over to share with another."

She nodded. "I understand. It's much the same with me."

Elliott gave up struggling against his attraction and tugged her gently backward. She settled against him, but her posture felt tense, as if she might bolt from the horse at any moment.

He considered what she'd said about her power. It didn't add up, so he murmured, "Women's magic is rarely that demanding. Even our fortunetellers—"

"—are more smoke and mirrors than reality," she broke in. "That's why using magic doesn't drain them."

He leaned forward, placing his mouth near her ear. "Ssht. That's one of our dirty little secrets. I'd not be bandying it about. The women all have some level of magic. At least that part is true."

"Agreed." She turned her head and made eye contact. "But *some level* doesn't translate into many of their bold predictions. They're competent actresses. They want generous tips from the gadjo— their customers—so they play up minor magical hits. And pretend they've summoned someone's dead relative, even if said relative refused to leave the other side."

Elliott shrugged. "Sure. In truth, we're never around long enough for anyone to come after us. Our women aren't malicious."

"They do mean well. Once long ago, a Romani fortuneteller saved me—" Her words halted abruptly, almost as if she realized she'd become too comfortable, said more than she meant to.

"Saved you from what?" he prodded, curious about the woman in his arms. The motion of the cantering horse drove their bodies against one another rhythmically in much the same way sex would have. Still engorged, his penis pushed uncomfortably against the front of his leather trousers.

"Never mind. It was another family group."

"Yes, but how long ago could it possibly have been?" he persisted. "You can't be much over thirty-five. As I recall, you were maybe fifteen when you fell in with our caravan."

Tairin remained silent for long moments. When she spoke again, she asked, "How far is it to this quiet place where you spin spells?"

Interesting. She's not going to answer. Wonder why?

"Maybe ten minutes."

"What exactly will we be planning?"

His gaze slid over the darkened streets as the stallion's hooves clopped over cobblestones. It was late. Lights shone from a few windows, but most were dark. "We may be outside Munich's city limits, but it's past curfew. Safer if we don't talk much until we're beneath ground where the earth can shield us."

She didn't reply, but there wasn't much to say. He probed the edges of her magic, seeking the same information he'd sought earlier when he'd held her head between his hands.

She kissed me, sidetracked me, and I forgot about everything except her body next to me and her mouth on mine.

Had she done it on purpose? To divert him so he wouldn't discover something she was hiding? The more he thought about it, the more convinced he became that he'd stumbled on the right track.

Elliott moved delicately, teasing the edges of her mind so gently he hoped she wouldn't notice. To redirect her attention while he worked, he murmured, "My stallion likes you. He's not fond of very many people."

"Some horses like me. Others don't. What's his name?"

"Flame."

"But he's black," she protested.

"Not when he was a colt, he wasn't. He had a cinnamon coat that shone in the sun. It was only as he grew, his pelt came in the shade it is. If you look closely in midday light, you can still see traces of red mixed in with the black."

"Maybe he's a changeling horse." She laughed.

The musical cascade reminded him of wind chimes, and he wanted to cradle her, protect her, reshape the world so she'd be safe to laugh as often as she wanted.

"Wouldn't that be something? Have you ever met one?" He replied to her changeling horse idea.

"Can't say as I have…"

Continuing his slow, thorough transit of her magical barriers, he gradually moved deeper as he continued feeding her questions. When the answer he sought with his mage skill reared before him, it took all his finesse to hide his reaction.

A shapeshifter.

Tairin was a shapeshifter. Oh, she had Romani blood to be sure, but one of her parents had definitely been something other than Rom.

He wasn't certain what variety of shifter she was, but the power was unmistakable. His first instinct was to react, shout at her for misleading all of them all these years, but he buried it deep. Tairin had never caused one whit of trouble in their caravan. She was unfailingly polite and helpful. Her loyalty remained unquestioned.

Or it had until he'd caught her outside Michael's wagon earlier.

Obviously, she wasn't biding her time to make off with one of their children some moon-drenched night. What was she doing? Why had she joined her fortunes to theirs? He understood full well why she'd kept her dual nature hidden. The Rom were extraordinarily suspicious of magic beyond their own, and they hated shapeshifters. Strong prohibitions against any congress with them were part and parcel of the rules governing Romani groups.

That she was the product of forbidden love gave him a whole new understanding of a woman he thought he'd watched grow up —except she never looked any older. Now he knew why.

"You're quiet," she observed.

"I'm usually quiet," he countered. "We'll be there soon."

He should turn her in to Michael, but he didn't know if he could make himself do that. Better for her to strike out on her own as she'd suggested. A deeply buried part of him rebelled. It was too dangerous for a woman by herself. Even one who could mutate into another form. His next thought rocked him. Her animal essence could be invaluable. Whatever she was could slip unnoticed behind Nazi lines. Maybe even into the death camps…

He shielded his thoughts and slowed the horse to a walk, drawing him to a halt in a deserted walled courtyard. The remains of an enormous stone castle rose behind them, its upper floors long since gone.

"Here's where we get off," he said. "Flame will stay here. He'd have the devil's own time navigating the steps into where we're going."

Tairin waited until he dismounted before throwing her leg over the stallion's broad back and sliding to the ground.

He whispered spell words to bind the horse within the courtyard until his return and ducked around a corner to where an overgrown thicket guarded his entry point to the hidden walkway beneath the castle. Most old castles had such things. They'd served as escape hatches for royalty during periods of civil unrest. A small magical assist moved the bushes aside, and he gestured Tairin into the hole. "You'll need a light," he told her.

"Maybe not quite yet," she replied and worked her way down earthen stairs that had all but caved in.

Elliott followed her, the crackle of bushes snapping into place loud against his ears. He started to summon a mage light, but one bloomed next to her, shedding a golden glow. The feel of her magic lapped against him like a warm tide. He'd never been close to her before when she'd done much of anything magical. Many of the other Rom might not have felt the differences in her power, but he did.

Maybe I'm more open to it because of what I found out.

Rats and bats chittered angrily about being disturbed, but they fled readily enough. At least the tunnel system was dry at this end; he'd explored plenty of castle and manor house escape routes riddled with mud and damp.

They walked in silence until they came to the first side branch. "Which way?" she asked.

"Straight on. The remains of what was likely a hideout is in about fifty more paces. Those old kings and dukes sometimes needed a safe place to sequester themselves."

"Or to cuckold the neighboring king's mistress," she said and chuckled.

"Probably that too," he agreed and extended an arm to point. "Duck through the opening."

Tairin followed his directions and walked to the far side of the chamber where he practiced magic. "I don't get it," she said. "How is there a window here? We're underground."

"Whoever built this room constructed it in this spot for a reason. It's on the edge of the hill that the castle was built on. In daylight, you can actually see the courtyard wall."

"So whoever was hiding here could determine if it was safe to come out. I understand." Turning, she surveyed the ten-by-twelve-foot space. "Wonder if anyone died down here from thirst or starvation?"

"Not thirst. If you follow the tunnel a little farther, there's an underground stream. It might not flow year round, but it runs fairly well this time of year."

He walked in front of her and placed his hands on her shoulders. "You don't have to do this."

"By this, do you mean helping you?" At his nod, she went on. "I know that, but what's happening around us is so hideous, so unconscionable, I have to do something." She tilted her head and met his gaze. "Right now, it's us, immigrants, mental defectives, cripples, and the Jews. Soon others—everyone who doesn't meet the definition of Aryan—will join the list of undesirables. First they steal your citizenship. Then they lock you up for the crime of not being a legal resident."

Her voice turned low, almost into a savage growl that made him wonder again what kind of animal shared her body. "Hitler cannot win. He cannot. If I ran away, tried to save my own hide while millions perished under his tyranny, I'd never be able to live with myself."

He opened his mouth, but she waved him to silence. "I'm not done. Even before the elder council tonight, I'd been planning to leave. To take on the Reich myself if I had to. The real reason I was listening was because I wanted to know if the caravan was going to fight or run."

"When we spoke earlier—" he picked his words carefully "—you said you were planning to leave, but nothing about fighting back."

She shrugged, displacing his hands. "As you so succinctly put it, women aren't warriors—not in Rom society. Germany, Italy, the States, and all the rest of the players in this war haven't been shy about incorporating their women. Maybe not as front line soldiers, but in factories to support the war effort."

"Guess you read the papers."

"You sound surprised." She furled her brows.

"Where do you get them?"

Color rose from the neck of her cloak until her cheeks splotched rose. "Michael's trash."

Elliott laughed. "Don't worry, I'll never tell."

"Won't matter if you do—" she eyed him speculatively "—since I suspect neither of us will be returning to the caravan for much beyond our clothes."

A small thrill of delight raced from his toes upward, but he needed to make certain he'd understood what she meant. "Say more."

Tairin nodded. "It's easy enough. We'll plan something tonight and carry it out. If it goes well, we may choose to work as a team. If not, we'll go our separate ways. You'll deal with the Reich as you see fit, as will I. Nowhere in that scenario do I see myself returning to the caravan to live. You might feel differently, though. What was it that Michael said earlier? That he'd almost raised you? So for you, it's more like abandoning your family."

"We've provided shelter and a home for you for twenty years," he pointed out. "How can that be easy to walk away from?"

"It's not, but I've done it before." The color in her face deepened, and she clapped a hand over her mouth. "Not what I meant," she mumbled.

There it is. Her shifter side means she could be old.

Instead of pushing her to reveal her secret, he said, "Let's get our first project off the blocks. I'd thought we could do a little reconnaissance at Dachau. It's not far from here."

"No, it's not," she agreed. Relief spilled from her in waves, but she hid her emotions with skills she'd obviously honed for years. "Define reconnaissance."

"Maybe it's a little more than that," he admitted. "At least a hundred Rom were just interred there and are working at the munitions factory they built on the grounds. Beyond that, though, it's where they train new SS officers." He took a deep breath and grasped her hands. "Once I map this out, I will not allow you to leave my side until we've completed our mission."

She nodded solemnly. "I understand. Too much risk. You're not sure you can trust me. And in truth—" she cocked her head to one side, eyes narrowed to slits, "—the feeling is mutual."

He buried admiration for her. Even cornered and at his mercy, she was quite the little spitfire. Maybe she wasn't all that *cornered*, though. She could shift and annihilate him, unless she was an owl or a hawk or something he could overpower. Maybe he could hold her in her human form with his power, but he wasn't at all certain of that. He'd come across shifters before, but only in a peripheral fashion. They'd all been men, and he'd never fought any of them.

"This is what I plan to do." He let go of her long enough to kindle his power so that light crackled from his fingertips. Kneeling, he drew a glowing diagram on one of the more solid wooden flooring planks. "Here's the main gate, and the rear entrance. I'm expecting we can mask our presence with magic and sneak inside. Once we're there, we'll make our way to the rear quadrant of the camp where the SS have their training area and special kitchen."

Tairin leaned closer. "Can we poison the bastards?"

"That's exactly what I plan to do."

"What will we use?" Her question was low, feral.

"Magic. What else? We'll spell the food to turn into parasites once it's eaten. Parasites that will eat them from the inside out."

"I have a better idea." Before he could ask about it, she forged ahead. "We spell the food to thin their blood so they bleed to death, choking on their own fluids as their lungs become useless."

"I like it," Elliott said. "Might be faster."

"It is faster," she said. "Both from the casting end and the results end." She set her lips in a thin line. "How can we guarantee no one but the Nazis eats the tainted food?"

"We can't. Best we can do is show up right before a meal to deal out maximum damage."

"We can mesmerize the kitchen workers, make certain they leave the food alone."

Elliott's eyes widened. "You can do that?"

"You bet." Her dark eyes gleamed with determination.

"Good to know. Are you ready to leave right now?" he asked. "We can be in position in time for breakfast."

"Never readier. Where will we tether Flame?"

"We'll work that out when we get there."

"Sounds good to me." Tairin trotted back into the passageway. Elliott followed her. The more time he spent with the enigmatic half breed, the more he admired her. And wanted her, but he'd have to move beyond the desire that heated his blood. He wasn't certain of the rationale behind prohibiting congress between Romani and shifters, but it probably sprang from the soundest of reasons.

He inhaled her scent and encouraged power flowing from her to surround him too. Just his luck, he'd finally found a woman he could love, and she was off limits.

Could he work with her feeling as he did? Would it get in the way of becoming a lethal and efficient team?

Guess I'm about to find out.

One thing was certain. He wasn't going to confront her about her shifter side. No. That was something she'd have to tell him. Maybe after she did—assuming it ever happened—he could find out why shifters and Rom weren't supposed to have anything to do with each other. While she was at it, she needed to let him know why she'd chosen Romani caravans when discovery of her secret would mean certain expulsion. Maybe even death.

If she was going to pick a side, why hadn't she thrown her lot in with her shifter kin?

Tairin already had the thicket open, and Elliott ducked through, branches crackling in his wake. He had a lot of questions, but very few answers.

"Are you scared?" he asked and helped her onto Flame's back.

"Of course," she replied. "I'd be a fool not to be."

airin grasped handfuls of Flame's mane to stabilize herself as Elliott kneed the horse into a trot. It would take a couple of hours to reach Dachau, a medieval town about ten miles northwest of them. Two hours was a long time. She hoped he wouldn't ask any more uncomfortable questions. She'd slipped up in a major way when she'd disclosed his caravan wouldn't be the first she'd left.

Yet he hadn't jumped on her words. Why? He was smart enough to have intuited something wasn't quite right.

I'm reading too much into this. Maybe he was so focused on what we're about to attempt, he skittered right past my faux pas.

Tairin didn't exactly believe her rationalization, but shy of asking him outright, there wasn't much she could do. She'd also used her magic to kindle her mage light right next to him. She hadn't needed it. Her shifter vision was more than adequate to see in the underground passageway, but it would have looked odd if she hadn't summoned her light.

All in all, it had been the better of two bad choices. Despite her gamble, he hadn't commented on her magic feeling different. Magical ability ran the gamut among the Rom, from those as strong as Elliott to others with barely enough ability to light a candle. She'd always taken care to use her own power as little as possible, particularly once she'd rediscovered how strong the Rom side of her magic was.

Elliott didn't seem inclined to chat, and she was grateful for silence rather than subtle, probing questions boosted by his considerable power. The sound of a distant engine reached her ears, and her heart beat faster. It was late. Past curfew—both in the city proper and beyond.

"We have to get off the road," she said, keeping her voice low.

"Why?"

Too late, she understood he couldn't hear the approaching vehicle—yet—since he lacked her shifter senses. "I hear a car—or maybe a truck. It almost has to be military at this hour."

She felt the magical net he sent zinging ahead of them. "Good call," he muttered and guided Flame down a dirt side road that led into increasingly thick timber. Once they'd put about fifty feet between themselves and the roadway, he turned the horse around so they had a filtered view of the road.

"Lucky we're not traveling by car," she said. "We'd never have been able to find a place to conceal ourselves in time." The roar of a reciprocating engine grew louder. Headlamps created bizarre shadow patterns as two good-sized trucks, gray-green with canvas tarps slung over framing, rumbled past.

"Definitely military. Wonder if that's the end of them," Elliott muttered.

Tairin cocked her head to one side, listening intently, but the diminishing roar of the trucks moving toward Munich drowned out most everything else. "I don't know. Are there back roads we could use?"

"Yes, but If we do, we won't reach our objective in time for breakfast." He kneed Flame, and they started down the roadway again, this time at a gentle canter.

To forestall questions about how she could've heard the trucks so soon, she said, "Tell me about yourself. I'm guessing you grew up in this caravan, but if Michael raised you, what happened to your parents?"

"It's not a pretty story," he warned. "Maybe not the best tale for a dark night when we're keyed up anyway."

"Sometimes those are the best times for the not-so-pretty tales," she countered and felt his muscles tense where her body leaned against him. "I'll let you know if I hear more trucks."

"Might not be so lucky finding cover a second time. The forest thins out before much longer, and we'll be traveling through farm country."

What he didn't say was they'd still have to get back in full daylight, but she saw the thought clearly in his mind. She considered telling him it wouldn't be the end of the world if they had to go to ground until the next nightfall, but didn't want to admit to trespassing on his thoughts.

"You were going to tell me about yourself," she urged. Part of her insistence was to direct his attention away from her, but she also wanted to know more about the man who sat ramrod straight behind her.

"I suppose I was." Breath whistled through Elliott's teeth. "I was born in Bucharest, Romania, not quite forty years ago. My parents were old, and they'd given up on ever producing a child, so I was more than welcome. After I was born, we left our home caravan and struck out on our own, remaining independent of any caravan until..." Elliott's voice faltered. "Well, until they died, and Michael's group took me under their wing."

"Did they become ill?" Tairin asked. "Smallpox or perhaps diphtheria?"

"I wish it had been that simple." Elliott's voice turned even more somber. "Father's ability was linking with animal intelligence, so his talent for training horses was legendary. He could also coax hens to lay, goats to produce milk, and rats to turn on one another rather than us."

"Sounds like an amazing man," Tairin murmured and tried not to think about the shifter father who hadn't wanted her.

"He was. Mother's skill was weaving magic into garments. She could create dresses that made you beautiful—or gowns that would eat you from the inside out. I was too young to understand the power she wielded, but I remember a hideous argument. A couple came to our wagon one night when we were camped on the outskirts of Hamburg. They wanted to commission a dress for one of their enemies, with the intention of destroying them. Mother refused. She took me outside and told me to remain with the horses, probably to shield me from further harsh words, but they were impossible not to hear.

"About that time, Father returned from wherever he'd been that day. The argument grew more heated. The male half of the couple threatened Mother with a curse if she refused to comply. Father said if the man had that kind of power, he wouldn't have been soliciting a death gown."

Tairin moved a hand to Elliott's thigh, seeking to comfort him. "Sounds terrible. What happened then?"

"Nothing I could ever put my finger on. The man cursed my parents in Romanian, and then in a language I've never heard before or since. I'm not even certain it was a curse, but given what happened next, it almost had to be. I didn't understand what I felt, but I sensed darkness, evil, as it surrounded our wagon. Mother came to get me and held me tight while I cried.

"I asked if we were going to die, because death's presence thickened the air around us. I felt it soaking into my skin and attacking me from the inside every time I breathed. Mother soothed me, but didn't exactly answer my question."

"How long did it take?" Tairin asked around a dry throat and eyes that pricked with tears.

"Not long. Mother died first, maybe a week later. Father was stronger, but he was gone a few days after that." Elliott's arms turned rigid with pain and outrage where they lay against her sides. "Whatever it was wanted me too, but I fought it. And kept right on fighting. Michael found us—my dead parents and me—when I was close to the end of my reserves. He knew right away what had happened, and he cast spells to counteract the one that wanted to kill me. Just him by himself wasn't enough. It took six more men, all working together, to cast out the evil and save my life."

Tairin's heart twisted in her chest. To have loving parents ripped away might be even worse than what she'd lived through. "If that couple—or the man, anyway—had that kind of power, why did they solicit a death garment from your mother?"

"I've asked myself that same question." His voice was low, vibrating with pain and outrage. "Only thing I could figure was they wanted to distance themselves from whomever they planned to kill. All magic is unique to the one who casts it, and they didn't want anyone to know what they'd done. I made a vow over my parents' funeral pyres that I'd become strong enough to never, never get trapped the way they were."

"They knew the spell would kill them?" Tairin asked.

"Yes, and were powerless to stop it."

She tightened her hand around his thigh where it cradled her body. "I'm so sorry."

"Told you it wasn't the best of tales." His voice had a catch in it, and he cleared his throat.

"Life isn't a fairy story. There's a whole lot of evil in the world. It's why we have to make certain Rom magic doesn't die out."

"A worthy goal, but easier said than done. We're almost to Dachau. You don't have to come inside with me, Tairin. You can stay with Flame."

"Nice try, fellow. I'm coming. Wasn't the whole purpose of tonight to determine if we have what it takes to be a team?"

Instead of answering, Elliott guided the horse down a side street and then another, until the prison camp's walls came into view in the distance. Light from multiple guard towers turned the night into one harsh glare. He drew Flame into an alleyway that appeared mostly unused and dismounted.

She got off too and began the incantation to render her invisible.

Hands dropped onto her shoulders from behind; Elliott turned her until she faced him. Tairin let go of her fledging spell. Before she could ask what was going on, he gripped her head between his hands. Eyes that had darkened to midnight bored into her.

"Talking about my parents reminded me how hard it is to lose someone I care about. I've kept an eye on you for years. When you first joined our caravan, you were kind of like a little sister, and I watched out for you but made sure you didn't know it. I don't want to have to live with your death on my conscience."

She creased her forehead and worked to make sense of what he'd just said. "Your parents' deaths weren't your fault."

"I wasn't able to save them."

"You were five. No child has that kind of magic." She gripped his forearms. "Hell, you're lucky you're still alive."

"Alive and planning to remain so," he said through gritted teeth. "If you come with me, you have to do exactly as I say. Understand?"

"I'll do my best," she hedged. If things turned to shit, she'd shift to protect both of them. Hopefully, it wouldn't come to that.

"What I told you riding here," he went on. "It's not a tale I've bandied about. Michael and the men who labored to save me are the only ones who know. I was ashamed, felt I'd failed Mother and Father, so I asked Michael and the others who came to my aid not to tell anyone what condition they'd found me in. They agreed."

"Why'd you tell me?"

His eyes, deep pools of inky blue, snared her. A woman could get lost in those eyes and never resurface.

"I don't have an answer for you," he said, "and we need to get moving."

He let go abruptly and stepped away. She felt the zing of magic as he shrouded himself in spells. She did the same and followed his broad back as he ran lightly to the walled enclosure a quarter mile distant.

Tairin had to remind herself no one could see her. Brilliant lights mounted on every tower made her feel vulnerable, exposed. The wall was solid brick and concrete. Eight feet tall, rounds of barbed wire scrolled across its top. Clearly, the gated entrances were the only way inside.

Elliott loped toward the front gate. Relief rattled through her when she saw it was open. A phalanx of uniformed prisoners was filing out. Hopelessness radiated from their slumped shoulders, dead eyes, and thin bodies. When she looked hard at them, her heart hurt. It was clearly a work detail heading out for the day that had yet to begin.

"Careful." Elliott breathed the word into her mind. *"Some of those are Rom."*

Which meant they might sense her and Elliott. Tairin thought it unlikely. The men and women walking double file were beaten. They'd long since given up focusing on anything beyond their own misery.

I hope.

Tairin buried her shifter magic deep just in case. Rom might not react to sensing their own brand of magic, but they'd pitch a fit if they glommed onto shifter emanations. Tairin reined in her apprehension. Even if someone recognized the scent of power, what the hell would they do about it?

One of the women raised her shaved head and looked right at Tairin with cloudy, dark eyes. Her nostrils twitched as she tested the air, and a knowing smile tugged the edges of her lips.

Breath clotted in Tairin's throat. The Rom woman "saw" her. Should she try mind speech? Indecision rocked her as she ran past the slow-moving line, twisting sideways to avoid touching anyone.

Words formed at the bare edges of her consciousness. *"Help us. Please."*

She wanted to reach out and reassure the woman that help was indeed imminent, but caution—and fear—stayed her tongue. What if some of the guards had Rom blood? Or some other kind of magic? No. Her best bet was remaining as well hidden as she could.

She and Elliott passed the end of the line, and he sprinted for the northwest corner of the prison complex and the smells of food cooking. Tairin followed, trusting he knew where he was going. Drab cellblock buildings were arranged around a central courtyard. The stench of human waste and misery rose from everywhere. Not just shit and urine, but vomit, blood, and putre-fied wounds.

Death too. Decay from dead bodies, and those at the brink, twisted her stomach into a hard, painful knot.

"This is a very bad place." Her wolf spoke into her mind.

"Worse than bad," she told it.

Elliott stood aside as a man dressed in food-splattered white clothing tugged a five-gallon bucket of grease out a doorway. The grease was rancid, and her already nauseated stomach lurched. She swallowed back sickness. She could hide herself, but not vomit spewing from her.

She skittered around the man with his revolting ancient fat bucket and entered the kitchen. Any doubt she had that she was in the right place evaporated when a swinging door at the far end slammed against its stops and a blond man, who could've been a poster child for Aryan perfection, screamed at the kitchen staff.

"You are late. Again." He punctuated his words with a closed fist jabbing the air. "We ordered breakfast for half an hour ago. Get it served. Now." Without waiting for a reply, he slammed back into what was presumably a dining room.

One of the cooks looked up from a large pot he was stirring to make an obscene gesture and spit into the pot. It was all Tairin could do not to laugh.

Guess we're not the only ones who hate those bastards.

Elliott made hand gestures that let her know she was responsible for creating spells to poison the pots to her right. He'd take the others. She didn't lose any time and focused lethal magic into the pots' contents. Once she was done, she switched up her power and sent subtle suggestions into the kitchen workers' minds. There were five of them, including grease-man, who'd just come back into the kitchen.

"Do not eat this food."

She kept her incantation simple. No reasons. Just the one sentence. It would do the trick. She also rode herd on her spell to make certain none of it leaked out into the assemblage of SS officers and trainees she sensed on the far side of the swinging door.

Because she was occupied, she managed to keep fear from immobilizing her. When Elliott quirked a brow her way, clearly wondering if she was done, she nodded. He faded out the back door, and she shambled after him. Her knees were weak, and her stomach still threatened to rebel.

They'd done what they came for, but they still had to get out of the complex before they ran their magical wells dry. The specter of being discovered made her teeth chatter from fear, and she clamped her jaws tight so the noise wouldn't give her away.

The slow-moving work brigade was still shuffling through the front gate, but their nice, neat double file line had disintegrated. Apparently, there'd been some kind of altercation. Prisoners lay on the ground, moaning, while guards in SS uniforms clubbed them. The crack of a bone breaking punctuated by a howl of pain shot through her, and she wanted to kill the guard who'd just broken a man's leg.

Fucking bastard. He was laughing and swinging his baton with abandon, clubbing whomever he could reach.

Fury boiled from Elliott, turning the air around him shades of red that only she could see. He raised an arm. Power arced from his fingertips, and the guard pitched facedown onto the ground.

Competing emotions racked her. She was proud of Elliott. Proud he'd killed the son of a bitch. And scared to her bones they'd never escape. Not now. People would run to aid the fallen SS officer. They already were. The crowd at the gate would become even thicker, more impenetrable...

Elliott ran to her and gripped her hand. It would interrupt the magic shielding both of them to some extent, but no one was looking their way. He pulled her along with him and raced for a small opening in the crowd of bodies jammed up against the gate. Tairin wrenched her hand away. Fear left a sharp, bitter taste in the back of her throat.

Elliott disappeared through the gap, and it closed right behind him. She couldn't see if he'd gotten through, and she hurried forward, frantic to find a way past the opening before the guards wised up and shut the gate. Where was Elliott? Had he crossed the perimeter? Was he safe outside?

Almost as if her thoughts about closing the gate had been an invitation, it creaked, beginning the trajectory that would seal her —and maybe Elliott—inside.

Can't let that happen. Can't.

Fear narrowed her airway until her head spun, and her grip on her magic almost slipped its bonds. The prisoners were so tightly packed together, no one would notice if she jostled them. They'd think it was the man or woman standing next to them.

Tairin pushed, prodded, dropped to her knees and crawled. But she made it. The gate brushed against her as she slithered through sideways just before it clanged shut. She wanted to screech her victory, but a dozen SS milled around the courtyard, guns raised and trained on the gate, ready to kill anyone trying to escape.

Tairin rose from her crouch, sidling away from the guards with their weapons.

Where was Elliott? She didn't see him. Did that mean he was well on his way back to Flame? She offered a prayer to the goddess that he was safe and pushed more power into her invisibility casting. *Goddammit!* She was shocked by how close she'd come to running herself down to bedrock. Once that happened, she'd no longer be invisible.

And the gig would be up. The SS would rape her before they killed her...

"Not on my watch," her wolf piped up. *"Head for the end of the street. If Elliott isn't there, we—"*

"Tairin. Dead ahead. Take the first right."

Relief and joy vied for ascendency at the sound of Elliott's voice, and she understood how worried she'd been he hadn't made it out.

"We did good tonight," she told her wolf.

A low, growly purr filled her mind. *"Proud of us,"* the wolf said.

Tairin was proud of them too, but before she could tell her wolf, it added, *"When are you going to tell him about me?"*

Tairin didn't have to ask who *him* referred to. She knew well enough. *"The Rom don't like us very well,"* she reminded the wolf.

"Yes, but he likes you."

She bit back a bevy of questions, including how the wolf could possibly know that, and wheeled right. She hadn't gotten half a block when Elliott looped an arm around her and dragged her between two buildings.

He clasped her so tightly against him, his heart hammered against her ear. Breath rasped from his throat. "Thank all the gods you're safe. When you weren't right behind me, I tried to go back for you, but I couldn't get through."

"It was tight—even for me, and I'm smaller than you." Her voice was muffled against his chest, and she wrapped her arms around him, splaying her hands across his back.

She tried not to think about how good he felt crushed against her. Tried to focus on the distance that remained between them and Flame.

Elliott let go of her. "We have to hurry. Once we get to Flame, we'll figure out what to do next."

"Hey!" She closed her fingers around his arm before he could leave. "We did it."

A crooked smile lit his even features. "We sure did."

"*Me,*" the wolf crowed. "*Tell him about me.*"

Elliott whipped his head around. "What was that? I could've sworn I heard a voice."

"I didn't." She clapped him on the back. "Let's get moving."

"*Coward,*" her wolf observed, but it sounded disappointed.

"*Soon,*" she said. "*I promise.*"

"*Like you promised me time to run?*"

Her bondmate's sarcasm pricked deep, but Tairin didn't react. She deserved the rebuke and vowed to do better. On all fronts.

CHAPTER 4

*E*lliott set a quick pace for where they'd left his horse. The easy part had been casting the spell to turn the food deadly. Getting out of the prison camp had proven far more intricate than he'd anticipated. They almost hadn't made it. From now on, he'd make certain Tairin was ahead of him. Once he realized she wasn't with him—and he'd sensed her still within the walled compound—he'd gone insane with worry. He'd tried to shove his way back inside, and almost got clubbed in the process. One of the prisoners had taken a beating in his stead, and he felt rotten about it.

He rebuked himself for tonight. He'd been flying by the seat of his pants, and the whole mission hadn't been well thought out. He and Tairin needed to practice working together. A deadly undertaking wasn't the best of proving grounds.

Yeah. My arrogance almost got her killed.

He winced at truth in his words—and at a savage protectiveness that flared within him. He'd do damn near anything to keep the woman next to him safe. But how could he do that if he dragged her into dicey situations?

"Maybe tonight wasn't such a good idea—" he began, not quite sure what to say next.

Tairin saved him from his dilemma. She skidded to a halt before he could get any more words out and grabbed his arm, forcing him to stop too. "I know where you're going with this," she hissed, "and I don't like it. I did my job—and I did it well. You didn't have the magic to make sure the kitchen staff didn't die right along with the SS. I did."

"Ssht." He pried her hand off his arm. "Come on. We'll talk once we're well on our way out of Dachau."

She clacked her teeth together, clearly far from done with whatever was percolating in her brain.

Flame nickered softly once Elliott broke the spell keeping the stallion shrouded in shadows. Without waiting for assistance, Tairin vaulted onto the horse. Elliott took his place behind her, considering what to say next. He'd expected her to be disappointed. What he hadn't anticipated was her righteous anger.

Guess I don't know her as well as I thought.

He muffled a rueful snort. Since she'd totally hidden what she was from him—and everybody else—he clearly didn't know Tairin Jabari at all.

Light from a gray day surrounded them. Daytime was a mixed bag. The evening curfew that forbade them from being out and about wasn't active, but their options for hiding themselves lessened too.

Should they chance the ten miles between them and Munich? Or would they do better covering half that distance until they reached the relative cover of forested hills? He could borrow from the trees' energy to conceal himself, and Tairin could take whatever her animal form was. It would be a far better disguise than he could cook up.

He kneed the stallion into an easy lope, and they passed the vestiges of Dachau's medieval walled enclosure. The town dated back to the ninth century, and its castle, situated on a hill high above town, stared down at them almost as if the old building knew what they'd done.

"If you're planning to come up with some lame excuse to jettison me from more operations like tonight, spit it out and get it over with." Tairin's words jolted him out of the place his thoughts had sidetracked. She'd been sitting stick straight astride Flame, careful not to let her back touch his front.

Elliott sucked in a tight breath. "What we did tonight turned dangerous far more quickly than I anticipated. I'm a seer, not a soldier. I assumed being invisible would make slipping in and out of the camp easy—"

"It made it possible," she broke in. "I never figured it would be easy, and I was plenty scared. That didn't mean I couldn't do my part." She stared dead ahead, not turning to look back at him. "I did as well as any man would have. Better than many. Why'd you say tonight was a bad idea?"

Because I don't want you getting killed on my watch.

He took a chance and wrapped one arm around her. "I care about you, Tairin. I don't want anything to happen to you. And if that *anything* happened because of a scheme I'd cooked up, it would be damned hard to live with."

"Look." She did turn around then and shot him a look full of hurt and reproach. "You're not my husband. Or even my boyfriend. I make my own choices. No man chooses for me. We're Rom from the same caravan. What that means is we look out for each other and work together for the common good. What we did tonight was important. More important than whether you or I lived through it."

Her words stung, and he choked on a mouthful of excuses justifying his feelings. He was acting like a heavy-handed husband. She'd nailed him on behavior he had no right to display. "Even if I were your husband," he ground out, "it wouldn't give me a right to tell you what you could and couldn't do."

"Not all men feel that way." She spoke carefully, her words devoid of inflection.

"True enough, but that doesn't make it right."

"I'd rather talk about how we follow up on tonight's victory than trade philosophy—" She quieted abruptly and swung her head from side to side as she raked the newly risen day with her gaze.

"What do you hear?" Elliott switched to mind speech. His magic needed to recharge, but he had enough left for that.

"Trucks. Lots of them. We need to get off the roadway fast."

Elliott glanced about. Farms to support Dachau with food were tucked into nooks and crannies in the foothills of the Bavarian Alps. Most of the trees in this area had been cut down for fuel or building materials long since, and miles remained to reach the area he'd hoped would conceal them. He spied an overgrown track off to their right and guided the horse along it. Flame didn't care for the choice and tossed his head repeatedly.

"Doesn't feel right to me, either," Tairin said, keeping her voice low.

The farther they went, the worse it felt to him, but even he could hear the rumble of trucks now. He rounded a bend and walked the stallion in a tight circle until they faced back the way they'd come. "We'll wait out the trucks here," Elliott said. "We're far enough from the road, it's unlikely anyone would be looking this way."

"I want to get off."

Elliott considered arguing she was safer on the stallion. Instead, he asked, "Why?"

"So I can figure out what feels so rotten. Maybe it's something we can fix."

He jumped down lightly. "You're not going alone. Neither one of us has much magic left."

Tairin tossed a leg over the horse and slid to the ground. When she turned to face him, her features were drawn into a mask of such grim determination he almost didn't recognize her. "Don't ask me to explain, because I won't, but my senses are sharper than yours. I smell death, but there's a wrongness to it. Like whatever it is isn't dead the way you and I understand it."

She lowered her voice and spoke right next to his ear. "Men armed to the teeth are here too. Not so far from us. They may have something to do with the not-dead stench. If that's true, I want to know what's going on."

Elliott scattered his depleted power as widely as he could—and didn't care much for what he found because he couldn't interpret it. Familiar, yet not. Dark magic soured his stomach and made his fingertips burn unpleasantly. What the hell were they walking into?

The day that couple had sought out his mother reared up and slapped him. Whatever those people had been held the same feel as what was unfolding a few hundred feet from them. He gripped Tairin's arm to keep her from leaving without him and catalogued what he sensed to make certain he wasn't mistaken.

"What?" She narrowed her eyes.

"I don't fully understand how it could be, but the power we're sensing has the same signature as whatever murdered my parents."

"Do you think it will recognize your blood?" She spoke into his mind, and to her credit she didn't sound rattled.

Elliott hadn't even considered that possibility. *"I have no idea. It's been years."* He thought fast, trying out theories and discarding them when they didn't fit. *"My first guess is whatever fell force killed my parents wasn't the only manifestation of it. For all I know, it's some sort of Black Magick cult with a following we can only guess at."*

"Could be," she murmured, retreating to whispered speech. "If it offers power, it would appeal to the Nazis."

"Certainly would. No matter what the cost," Elliott growled. "Let me go first. I'm going to work an invisibility spell, but I have no idea if I have enough power left to pull it off."

A jolt of something electric started in his toes, moving upward. He stared at Tairin. "You're offering me magic?"

"What else?" She grinned roguishly. "I have more than you—and we're a team. At least until you lose your mind and dump me."

He wanted to say a lot of things, including that he'd been a fool. Instead, he nodded sharply. "Thanks. I'm going to approach whatever's there nice and slow, and I'll circle round so they can't catch our scent—or our magic—on the wind."

"Smart." She gestured with one arm. "Lead out."

Elliott borrowed lavishly from the power she'd given him and swathed himself in spells, muting his presence as much as he could. That done, he set an oblique path for the slimy wrongness that set his teeth on edge and raised fine hairs on the back of his neck.

He sensed Tairin behind him. Sensed her determination, and her solid presence. The caravan hadn't fully appreciated her. They'd seen her as one more woman with marginal magic.

Because she didn't want any of us to discover what she is... And she was strong enough and canny enough to shield herself.

The wrongness escalated with each step. It jabbed against his warding, seeking a way inside. Elliott curled his hands into fists and tried not to breathe too deeply. Rot, charnel pit decay, burned his nostrils and dragged his stomach into a sour knot. What the hell was wrong with the nearby farmers? It didn't take magic to smell the evil tainting their bucolic environment.

Maybe he was wrong, and it did.

He cast a net, hunting for animals that might tell them something, and didn't find so much as an insect within range. *"No animals or birds nearby."* He glanced back at Tairin.

"I already figured that out. We left Flame at the perimeter of the dead zone."

Elliott worked his way cautiously through squelching mud. He would have given anything for trees to shield them, but maybe they couldn't have withstood the evil, either. He topped a small rise and halted abruptly.

A scene that defied credibility spread before them. Tairin dropped to a crouch by his side, and he mirrored her posture. When he gripped her hand, her fingers were cold. The reeking miasma that tipped him off in the first place grew to a choking cloud. Breathing shallowly didn't cut the stench, so he cupped his free hand over his nose and mouth.

A series of shallow trenches held open caskets. Radiating unearthly beauty, a dozen vampires—mostly male, but two were female—had paired up with SS officers and were drinking from them, but sharing blood in return. Elliott focused on one of the bizarre couples with shielded magic and felt power transfer from vampire to human.

Had the humans who killed his parents traded blood for unnatural power? Given the feel of the SS officers, it was likely but he'd never know for certain. He hadn't run into any vampires before, so his only knowledge came from the lore books. He focused more intently on the vampire half of the couple he'd targeted with his magic. The creature, a male, had long, shimmering, red-gold hair that hung to its waist. Black robes sashed with deep blue covered its body. Midnight eyes with swirling golden centers were focused on the SS officer in its arms. Unable to look away, Elliott watched as the vampire lifted its mouth from the officer's neck. Blood dripped from extended fangs, and the abomination spread its lips in a satisfied smile and arched against the human in its arms.

It looked as if it was in the throes of coital bliss. Though robes covered its body, the front was tented like it would be if the thing had an erection. Elliott swallowed back disgust. Christ! Could vampires have sex? What would the impact of that be on their victims? Or did they only fuck other vampires?

Elliott shoved discomfort and horror to a distant part of his mind. He felt well beyond his depth. The lore books said very little about vampires, and their sexual appetites hadn't been part of any book he'd studied.

Now that Elliott had focused on it, the creature's hunger—for sex and blood—was palpable even from where he crouched. He sensed how difficult it was for the vampire to not simply drain the human, toss his corpse aside, and move on. Elliott told himself to get moving. He'd seen enough. No way could he and Tairin take on an entire vampire nest.

Despite strict exhortations to leave this hideous place, he remained frozen, mesmerized by the scene unfolding before him. Even though the vampire had no idea he was watching, it exerted such a strong pull, Elliott couldn't force himself away from the tableau. Man and vampire looked like an unholy pair of lovers, and Elliott wanted to know what would happen next. Would the creature tug the sash holding its robes open and do something perverse to the human?

More perverse than drinking his blood?

Ach Christ! I have to get Tairin out of here.

But Elliott couldn't move. He couldn't even turn his head to look at Tairin. The vampire's power drew him like a lodestone, and that more than anything scared the crap out of him.

The vampire tore its wrist open and held it to the man's mouth. After a few moments when the inert SS officer didn't react, he fastened his mouth to the vampire's streaming wrist and slurped, making little grunting noises as he fed. His face that had grown ashen, turned a warm shade of rose.

The vampire pulled his wrist away. "It is enough."

A wicked smile started in the SS officer's eyes, not quite making it to his mouth. "Of blood, perhaps." He reached down, snatching the front of the vampire's robes and reaching beneath them. Groaning, the vampire angled his head and crushed his bloodstained mouth over the man's lips. The pair crumpled to the ground grappling with one another, hips pumping as they ground their cocks together.

Fascination vied with disgust. Maybe it was the combination, but Elliott finally found the strength to look away. Was this why so many Nazis seemed invincible? Drinking from vampires would make humans fast, deadly, and much harder to kill. Who the hell knew what traits fucking them would confer? He glanced around at the other couples. All of them were locked in heated clinches. Breath hissed from between Elliott's teeth before he cut off the sound, so it didn't give them away.

Tairin squeezed his hand hard enough to hurt. When he looked at her, she tilted her chin back the way they'd come and extricated her fingers. The crippling inertia from before had lifted. Elliott said a quick prayer of thanks to whichever god or goddess killed the chokehold the vampires had on him. Straightening, he followed Tairin. She was already astride the horse, arms wrapped around his thick neck when Elliott jumped on behind her and guided Flame toward the roadway.

The trucks were long gone, and he snugged an arm around Tairin. His mind had been busy while they made their way back to the horse. "I'm sorry you had to see that," he murmured. Opting for honesty, he added, "I kept thinking we should leave, but those bastards had me hypnotized."

"You deployed so much magic hiding your presence, you didn't have enough left over to shield yourself from their poison."

"You don't have to make excuses for me," he said, feeling miserable. "I failed you. No woman should have to bear witness to what we just saw—"

"Stop it!" Her tone was pointed. "Sex between vampires and humans is scarcely new. It's one of the many ways they bind humans to their will. Semen and blood are one hell of a one-two punch."

"I see what humans get out of the deal, but what's in it for vampires?" Elliott asked.

"Who knows what the Reich promised them," she countered. "Maybe free rein in their camps. As much blood as they can drink.

Sex with all the humans they want." She shrugged. "The possibilities are endless. One thing is certain—whatever the Nazis offered was enough to entice the vampires into cooperating."

"Do you suppose that's the only nest?" Elliott said.

"I haven't seen a vampire since I left Egypt." Her voice trembled a little. "I'd heard they made this part of Bavaria home long ago, but I figured they'd moved on."

"Egypt? You'll have to tell me more about that but not right now. What we stumbled on back there explains a lot." Elliott spoke slowly.

"No kidding." She leaned into him, her body vibrating from strong emotion.

"Are you afraid?"

"Who wouldn't be?" she countered. "I'm angry too, though. Nazi fuckers. As if things weren't bad enough already, and now they're borrowing power from pure evil. What horrifies us today is bound to grow worse. Lots worse."

"We have to do something about it." The words slipped out before he could ride herd on them. What they'd done today at Dachau paled to a child's game compared with taking on a nest of vampires.

"We?" Her voice was soft, low, and a cross between entreaty and a threat. She stiffened in his arms, waiting for him to answer.

"Not the two of us by ourselves," he amended hastily. "We'd be worse than rubes not to secure all the help we can." He quieted, considering the Romani in his caravan and some of the others. Perhaps Michael and Stewart might help. He couldn't see the others volunteering to face down a nest of vampires—unless said vampires threatened their caravans directly.

"I might be able to find…others to help us. Don't ask me to say more because I won't. And it might not work because—" Her voice faltered, but she tried again. "Because it might not."

Questions rioted through him. Was she referring to her shifter kin? If so, why would they ignore her pleas for assistance?

Maybe the same reason most of the Rom would rather walk over hot coals than face down a vampire.

He scanned the countryside and empty roadway. "We're halfway back. Do you want to chance making it the rest of the way to the caravan?"

Tairin nodded and turned to look at him, her expression somber. "Yes. We need to figure out who our allies will be—or if we end up walking this road alone."

He'd always thought well of her, but his admiration for her spirit and courage soared. "You're one amazing woman."

"Not at all." Her gaze never left his. "Just one who wants to come through this alive—after every single one of those Nazi bastards dies a slow, horrible death."

"Couldn't have said it better myself." He snugged his arms closer about her.

Elliott smothered an impulse to nudge Flame into a nearby copse of trees so he could tumble Tairin off the horse and taste her mouth again. Wanting her filled him with sweet yearning. His cock had reacted to the vampires' sexual heat, and his arousal made him feel dirty. Not the kind of energy he wanted tainting anything to do with the woman tucked between his thighs.

He cared about her. Intended to protect her from everything vile and wicked in the world. That would have to be enough for now. Exploring the delights her body offered could wait for a better time. One where they weren't beset with evil from all sides. Beyond that, they had a lot of ground to cover before they moved from friends to lovers. He wouldn't take her casually. He thought too much of her to act on the attraction burning a path through him. If he couldn't offer more than his body, better not to travel that road.

He had to figure out if the secret that stood between them would kill any possibility of a mutual future. Why had the Rom steered clear of shifters? Was there some hidden reason?

Elliott vowed to find out.

Tairin paid out magic as they rode toward Munich to make certain the road was as deserted as it appeared. She was tired but forced herself to remain alert, so she didn't miss any clues. Maybe it was the early hour, or maybe everyone who could was keeping the lowest profile possible. If the Nazis couldn't see you, they wouldn't drag you in for the interminable questioning that had become commonplace once their chokehold on Germany expanded.

She was grateful for Elliott's solid presence behind her and equally grateful for his silence. For once, her wolf wasn't saying anything, either. Coming upon the group of vampires had been a shock—one she could've gone the rest of her days without facing.

They'd been a scourge in Egypt, where there'd been thousands of them. Her strategy in those days had been avoidance. It worked because that part of the world played host to myriad magic wielders two hundred years ago. Temples to various Egyptian deities dotted the landscape like grains of sand, and legions of priests and priestesses kept the vampire population under some semblance of control.

What a difference a couple of centuries made. Magic had all but died out of the world. What was left traveled dark alleyways, remaining out of sight. Kind of like the Rom, who plied their various trades apologetically, not owning their magical birthright.

Better to be labeled as quacks and charlatans than deluded crackpots.

She swallowed hard. Her path was clear. She had to try to marshal shifters to address the vampire problem. Even if the strongest Romani banded together, they didn't have enough magic to take on a nest of vampires. All they'd end up doing would be getting themselves killed.

"When are you going to tell him about me?"

Tairin snapped her head up, surprised her wolf wouldn't bring up the vampires.

"This is about the vampires," the wolf inserted smoothly, proving it had helped itself to her thoughts.

"How so?"

"He has to understand why the Romani need to find a way to work with shifters." A pause. *"Not so different than convincing our people to pitch in."*

"Do you have any ideas for how to make that happen?" she asked.

"Of course not. I never understood why they banished us in the first place."

A sad, lonely note in the wolf's comment tugged at her heart. Bitterness filled her at what the shifters' refusal to acknowledge them had cost her wolf. She'd dealt with the specter of social isolation by joining with the Rom and shrouding what she truly was—so at least she'd fit in somewhere. The wolf hadn't been as fortunate. Since wolves were pack animals, the enforced segregation from its kind must have cost it dearly, yet it had never complained. And it had stuck by her. At least it could visit other bond animals in the place they roamed when they weren't actively engaged with their bondmates.

"I'm grateful you never abandoned me," she began haltingly and stopped, not sure what to say next.

"How could I? We're pack. You dreamed me when you were still a child, and I heeded your call. Those bonds can be severed, but only at the risk of great pain and ill fortune. We talked of this not long after your first shift."

Guilt kicked her in the guts. She'd taken time to learn about the Romani half of her heritage, but not the shifter one. Never mind opportunities for the latter weren't as apparent. She hadn't viewed the wolf as a source of information—and she should have.

"I—I'm sorry, I should have realized—"

"No time for your misplaced sense of obligation to our bond. Or your guilt. Not now. We have bigger problems. You have to tell him about me. About us. And about how Rom magic isn't a match for vampires."

Behind her, Elliott shifted position atop the stallion. Given what they'd faced in Dachau, he'd comported himself well—until he started making over-protective noises about including her being a mistake. He seemed to have gotten over that part.

She hoped.

Tairin inhaled briskly, blew it out, and did it again. They were passing the outskirts of Munich. If she was going to blow her cover, better to do it before they got back to the circle of wagons and many sets of prying ears.

"Are you all right?" he asked.

"Find a place to stop," she replied, not answering his question directly. "Before we get back to the caravan."

"Why?" a note of alarm ran beneath the one word. "Are you leaving?"

"Sooner or later, I'll have to. I wanted a private spot so we could talk."

Elliott guided the stallion back to the same crumbling castle where they'd begun the previous evening. "Is this all right?" he asked. "It's the most comfortable location safe from being overheard that I can provide on short notice."

"It will be fine. I should have thought of it." Tairin winced. This was the second item in as many minutes when she wasn't thinking clearly. First about her wolf, and now about Elliott's grotto. She was tired, but she had to pull herself together. Convincing Elliott was critical. If she failed, he'd gather Michael, Stewart, and maybe a few other men and ride into that vampire nest like an Old West posse out for blood.

She'd seen how easy it was for the creatures to hypnotize Elliott today, to leech away his free will. And they hadn't turned anywhere near the full brunt of their power his way because they'd had no idea they were being watched. If the vampires' attention hadn't been on feeding and fucking—activities that were almost synonymous for them—neither she nor Elliott would be alive right now.

He brought Flame to a stop in the same place he'd left him before and slid to the ground. Tairin joined him and worked her way down the falling-to-ruin stairs leading to the tunnel. This time, she didn't waste power on her mage light. No reason to. Elliott would either accept what she had to tell him—or be furious and reveal what she was to the caravan.

Even if he wasn't outraged, Rom law still forbade him from holding her identity secret.

Good thing I was mostly ready to leave anyway.

Light flared from behind her as he kindled his mage light. "Hold up," he called.

"I'm good," she replied without looking back. "I don't need light to see." She ducked into the side chamber where they'd decided Dachau was a worthy goal.

Elliott joined her. "Only place to sit is on the floor or my clothing chest, I'm afraid."

"I won't be doing much sitting." She turned and faced him head-on. Here it was. Either she told him and got on with things, or his death—courtesy of a nest of annoyed vampires—would sit squarely on her shoulders. Not that the vampires might not be the death of them anyway, but at least he'd be going into things with his eyes open.

An unpleasant thought pricked—and made things that much worse. She was stalling, but she said, "That demon you raised earlier?" At his nod, she continued. "The odds of it finding the vampires are good. Evil attracts evil."

He drew his brows together. "Yeah. I'd already come to the same conclusion while we were riding back. Not much we can do about that but address it once it happens. If it happens. That can't be why you wanted to stop here, though." He watched her speculatively, waiting.

"Go on," the wolf urged. *"Do it now. It's not going to get any easier."*

The corners of her mouth twitched. *"I love you."*

"We're pack," the wolf replied, and its simple words warmed her heart.

She clasped her hands behind her. "I'm only half Romani," she said. "My father was a wolf shifter."

He skewered her with his blue eyes. "I know. Not what type of shifter," he amended, "but I knew you had shifter blood."

Out of all the reactions she'd anticipated, this one hadn't been anywhere on her list. "B-but how?" she sputtered.

He turned his hands palms upward. "How else? I looked with magic, but I was subtle about it. Subtle enough I hoped you wouldn't notice, and you didn't."

"See?" The wolf smirked. *"Wasn't hard at all."*

"That's him, isn't it?" Elliott asked. "That voice I can't quite make out."

"Might be a her." Tairin grinned, relief spilling through her.

"Don't you know?"

She shook her head. "The bond animals are genderless, but that's not important. How come you're not outraged? What my parents did is a cardinal sin. After my first shift, the Rom in Egypt made it clear I wasn't welcome, and shifters are an even stodgier lot. They only accept those with pure blood."

"I was upset at first," he admitted. "But I got over it fast. No one likes to find out they've been hoodwinked for years."

"No. I suppose not."

Elliott moved next to her and placed his hands on her shoulders. "Why'd you tell me? It must be important since you broke your silence. You could've just quietly left the caravan with no one being the wiser."

"You would've been," she pointed out.

"Yes, but I'd have kept your secret."

She shook her head hard to force herself to focus. "You asked why I fessed up. It's because I know more about vampires than you do." She thinned her lips into a hard line. "Remember earlier, when you couldn't look away?"

An uncomfortable look washed over his face. No man liked being reminded of a time when he was helpless.

Tairin kept talking. "They had you in thrall, and they didn't even know we were there. Do you have any idea how much worse it gets when they train their attention on you?"

"No. First time I've laid eyes on those bastards."

"What it boils down to is this." She wrapped her hands around his forearms. "You're not strong enough to take them on." Before he could protest, she added. "Not you personally. Rom magic, even the stronger varieties like what you wield, are no match for vampire seduction."

"But I wouldn't go alone."

"Wouldn't matter. Even if you brought a dozen Rom all as capable as you, the vampires are still stronger. If they perceive you as a threat—and they will—they'll drain you or worse."

"Do you mean turn me into a lackey like those SS officers who traded blood for power?"

"Exactly. Not only power. Speed, stealth, and a total lack of conscience—in case there's a Nazi alive who still has one."

"How do you know so much about vampires?" He quirked a curious brow.

"There were lots of them in Egypt. And dedicated groups of high priests and priestesses to ride herd on them."

"High priests, huh? How long ago was that?" His question wasn't unexpected.

She held his gaze. "Two hundred years."

"That would explain why you've left caravans and started over multiple times."

"It would."

"Ask if he wants to meet me." Her wolf was back, but she didn't exactly think it had gone anywhere.

"I will, but I want to finish the conversation first."

"What did your wolf want?" Elliott asked.

"To come out. It wants to meet you properly."

"What did you tell him?"

"That we needed to finish talking. Curious that you keep referring to my wolf as him. Anyway, if I can get cooperation from other shifters, we might have a fighting chance against the vampire nest—assuming it's the only one in this area and they haven't already teamed up with your demon."

Elliott dug strong fingers into her tight shoulder muscles, rubbing them. "It's not exactly *my demon*. How likely are your shifter kin to help the Romani?"

She rolled her eyes. "The question you should be asking is how I'm going to go about even locating them. If they won't show themselves to me, I'll never get an opportunity to ask for help."

"They're here." Elliott sounded certain.

"How do you know?"

"I may not have come across vampires before, but I've run into dozens of shifters—of all persuasions—over the years. Wolf, bear, bird, mountain lion."

"They revealed themselves to you?" she asked, incredulous.

"Not exactly. Some of my trance states run deep. When I'm coming out of them, I'm quite sensitive to anything magical nearby. Most of the shifters I sensed probably never realized I detected their presence." He hesitated for a beat. "I'd have known about you sooner, except I made a practice of moving far from the caravan to cast my serious spells."

"Fascinating." She closed her teeth over her lower lip. "If you weren't planning to turn me in to Michael right away, I'm hoping you'll wait until I determine if any shifters in this area are willing to talk with me—"

"I wasn't planning to turn you in to Michael at all," Elliott broke in. "And I can help you locate your kin. At least I think I can. What happens if they say no?"

She bit on her lip until she tasted blood. "I have no idea."

"They can't say no," her wolf piped up. *"Not if another of us requests aid."*

"Not sure that rule applies to those like us," she replied.

"It should." The wolf sounded so fierce and resolute, she could've hugged it.

Tairin considered Elliott's statement about not revealing what she was to Michael. "Don't get me wrong," she said. "I'm touched by your offer to guard my secret. But not telling Michael about me violates the Romani creed—and leaves you subject to banishment. I won't put you in that position."

Elliott wrapped his arms around her and drew her close. She tucked her head into the hollow between his neck and collarbone, listening to the strong, steady beat of his heart. He cradled the back of her head in one hand and threaded his fingers beneath her hair.

"I know those things." His voice rumbled against her ear. "Have you ever revealed yourself to any caravan?"

She shook her head. "No. Not since the one I was born into kicked me out." She reared back enough to look up at him. "You wanted to know more about me. Now's as good a time as any. Thirteen was...different two hundred years ago. I was considered an adult—and fair game for any man who wanted to have his way with me. After the Romani banished me for having mixed blood, I went to my father's people. They shunned me as well. After a couple of near misses where I was almost abducted and raped, I spent the next hundred years as a wolf, traveling with local wolf packs."

She took a measured breath. "When I finally wanted my human form again, it was nearly impossible to shift back. I got stuck half in one form, half in the other for days. I'd just solidified my hold on my human body when a kind, old Romani fortuneteller came upon me. She nursed me back to health, even helped me learn to talk again. I'd forgotten how."

"Lucky she found you when she did. If she'd happened on you while you were half wolf, her caravan would have burned you."

"Yes. I know that."

"What happened to your parents?" Elliott didn't loosen his hold on her.

"What do you think?" Bitterness scored her from the inside out. The passage of time hadn't moved her any closer to accepting her mother's death or her father's disappearance. "You know Romani rules. They burned Mother for having had sex with someone they determined was unclean, forbidden. I have no idea what happened to Father."

"His shifter clan took him back on the condition he never transgressed again and agreed to give up any claim to you—his daughter." The wolf spoke up.

Shock must have registered on her face because Elliott angled his gaze to capture hers. "What?"

Tairin repeated the wolf's words, her voice dull with pain and shock, and then added, "My wolf never told me before now." She smothered the sob that wanted out. "All these years, and my bondmate never told me."

"Because he loves you and knew the truth would hurt." Elliott's voice was soft.

"That's exactly correct," the wolf said. *"I planned to tell you someday, but the opportunity was never quite right—until now."*

Tairin kicked herself. Her father's abandonment had hurt—so much she'd never dug through the wolf's memories for information. What an idiot she was for not having explored her shifter side as thoroughly as she knew her Rom heritage.

"If it's any comfort," the wolf went on, *"your father suffered for his choice. And he still does. He never took another to wife. You're his only child."*

"I'm not trying to pry," Elliott massaged the back of her head, still cradled in his hand, "but I can't make out what your wolf is saying, and I'd like to be part of the conversation."

"I can fix that." Tairin extricated herself from his embrace. "Basically, the wolf said Father never came to terms with his choice, never mated again."

She moved to a dim corner of the underground room. Light from the new day filtered through the cracked window. "Turn around," she told Elliott.

"Why?"

"You'll see." Tairin could have shielded her nakedness with magic, but this was easier. She waited until he turned away and quickly stripped out of her clothing before opening herself to shifter magic. *"Ready?"* she asked the wolf.

"Never readier."

Tairin felt the change take her. Magic prickled from her head to her toes as her torso shortened and fur sprouted. Maybe because of how hard her journey back from a hundred years as a wolf had been, she'd never minded the minor discomforts shifting produced.

"You can turn around now." She used mind speech because it was the only option available to her.

She watched Elliott's face as he twisted so he faced her. Expecting horror and revulsion, she readied herself to gather her wolf legs beneath her and bolt down the passageway. She could blend in with the local wolf packs. She'd done it before. Leaving twenty years' worth of belongings with the caravan would rankle, but it wasn't the end of the world.

Rather than disgust, Elliott's features glowed with fascination and wonder. He hunkered into a crouch and held out both hands in clear invitation. She shook off the last of the change magic and padded to him, letting him take her head between his hands and stroke her fur.

"You're beautiful," he murmured. "Gray with black and tawny markings. And your eyes are the same. A beautiful, deep brown with amber irises." He ran his hands from her head down her flanks, rubbing gently. "I love how your fur is soft underneath."

"Thank you." She aimed her mind voice for him. *"Now that we've talked this way, you should be able to hear my wolf when I'm in human form."*

"Can we run?" The wolf asked.

Their dual nature didn't change. Regardless which form she took, the wolf had its own ideas, thoughts, and personality.

"I don't see why not," she replied and butted Elliott's hands with her snout.

"Do you want me to wait here for you?" Elliott asked, which meant he'd heard the wolf's bid to run and her reply.

"No. Return to the caravan. I'll be there soon."

"Can I ask your wolf something?" Elliott gazed at her as if she were one of the world's seven wonders, and she glowed under his affirmation of her twofold nature.

"Of course," the wolf spoke up.

"Do you know where Tairin's father is?" Elliott switched to mind speech.

"Yes."

Shock roiled through her. *"Have you known all along?"*

"Yes. You never asked."

"That might be a good place to begin convincing your shifter kin to help," Elliott said.

She nuzzled his outstretched hands, licking them and whining softly. So many things had never occurred to her.

Yeah, I was too busy being lost in feeling sorry for myself—if I thought of Father at all, which I tried not to.

"Will you tell us where he is?" Elliott pressed.

Images flashed through Tairin's mind. It was how the wolf communicated about places. Her previous caravan before Michael's, and locations it had stopped, formed a collage. She opened her magic so Elliott could see too.

He scrunched his forehead into a thoughtful expression. "Austria. Somewhere in the forests and mountains between Innsbruck and Salzburg. Accessing that region won't be easy, given the Reich's reach."

It certainly wouldn't. Tairin didn't have anything to add to his assessment, so she remained silent.

"Let's run," the wolf urged.

Tairin shook herself from snout to tail tip. After a final nuzzle, this time to Elliott's neck, she ceded their shared body to her wolf, and they slithered into the passageway. The disintegrating stairs were easy with her claws extended for purchase. The magic shrouding Flame apparently masked their presence because the stallion didn't so much as whinny when they flashed past, heading for thick woods above the town.

"If you know where Father is," Tairin began, "does that mean you know where other shifters are as well?"

"Yes. Our kind are all around us, but Elliott's suggestion about tapping into our blood kin first is solid. Your father is less likely to turn his back on you, and he can convince others to come to our aid."

"I thought you said shifters weren't supposed to refuse life-and-death requests from other shifters." Now that she knew what a staunch resource the wolf was, she was determined to mine for information.

"Supposed to and doing are two different things. I want to enjoy my freedom, not worry it to death with talk."

Tairin would've grinned if she'd been human. As it was, she let the wolf's jaws loll into a lupine version of a smile. Not wanting to dilute her bondmate's joy in the wind against their fur and the adrenaline rush as their muscles pumped, she cleared her mind. Later, when she was human again, would be time enough to worry and plan.

$\mathcal{E}$lliott straightened from his crouch. Wonder at Tairin's transformation from woman to a timber wolf with long, straight legs, lush fur, and a clean, animal scent filled him. The musky, outdoor world odor that clung to her as a woman was mirrored in her wolf, and he inhaled hungrily wanting to fill his lungs before the enticing smell dissipated.

He'd had no idea how seeing her shift would affect him. Hell, he hadn't known what she was about to do until she asked him to turn aside. After the rustle of her clothing hitting the floor, he'd felt unfamiliar magic pour from her, knowing it had to be from her shifter heritage. Longing filled him. He wanted Tairin by his side forever. Romani and their rules be damned. Tairin's mother and father had fallen in love and produced a child. Apparently, the father was very much alive, and her mother might well have lived out a normal lifespan—if her own people hadn't murdered her.

He'd spend the time Tairin and her wolf were running free to find out what he could from the lore books. Dusty tomes, they were stacked in boxes in the back of Michael's wagon. Elliott hadn't looked at them in a long while and hoped his mastery of Coptic wasn't as rusty as he feared. The Romani had originated in

India long ago, but it wasn't until they'd migrated to Egypt that they'd exchanged oral tradition for memorializing their rules, customs, and information in written form.

Elliott rolled his eyes. Everything came full circle, and Rom magic had reverted to oral tradition rather than an organized course of study with the dawn of the twentieth century. Except it wasn't working very well since their native abilities were fading with each passing decade.

If the Rom ever saw the far side of the current mess with Germany, they'd need to address that problem. If not, nothing would matter because they'd fade into nothing beyond memories.

After a last look around the cozy underground room, Elliott ducked through the doorway and chugged down the passageway toward where he'd secured his horse with magic. Daylight meant he couldn't sneak into the caravan unnoticed. Michael would want to know where he'd been—and if the demon had been contained.

Elliott choked back a snort. Chances of the demon even responding to one of his spells were less than zero, but maybe there might be a way to mute its power and lessen the odds of it stumbling across the vampire nest. He released the warding around Flame, and the stallion nickered a greeting as Elliott vaulted atop his back and started for the caravan.

There was no love lost between horses and wolves. Could Flame sense Tairin's bondmate? If he could, why didn't it bother him? Some Rom had an affinity for communicating with animals, but Elliott had never been one of them. As he rode, he thought about the varying manifestations of power among his people. Their magic had definitely dwindled since they'd dispersed from their Middle Eastern origins. Hell, it had faded during his lifetime by dint of underuse. How could it be otherwise? It was difficult to immerse themselves in magic in a world that no longer believed in supernatural beings or events.

As he understood things, the Rom had once been a deeply

magical people, fascinated by their power, which they saw as a gift from Isis, mother goddess of the Earth. But magic and modern religions didn't coexist well. Many Romani had been persecuted for practicing their craft, and it had been enough of a wakeup call to warn the rest of them to keep their magical rituals well hidden.

He ground his teeth together. Whenever something couldn't be practiced in the light of day, it was bound to weaken—and eventually fail. Sorrow for his people filled him. Had they come this far to end up nothing more than penny-ante, marginalized performers, telling fortunes and sharpening knives for a pittance while the mainstream passed them by?

He rode Flame to the area behind the wagons where the other horses were hobbled and got him a bucket of feed and another of water. The horse whinnied his gratitude and set about chomping hay mixed with dried grass the women had cut with scythes.

Many of the horses were missing. Had the elders come to a decision and returned to their home caravans?

The boy assigned to caring for the horses waved cheerily and went back to cleaning hooves and mucking horseshit. Elliott waved back and said, "If Flame finishes his feed, you can give him a little more."

"Got it."

"Did the elder council complete their business?"

The boy, who wasn't much past ten, shoved greasy strands of long red hair out of his eyes as he straightened to glance at Elliott. "Who knows? They left, right enough, but were close-mouthed about where they were headed or what they were doing."

"Thanks." Elliott clapped the boy on his shoulder and walked toward Michael's wagon.

The caravan was long past awake, and men and women traded greetings with him as he threaded his way through the circle of wagons. They'd have to relocate soon—before local authorities showed up again. He mounted the steps to Michael's brightly painted wooden door and knocked, waiting for the man's rough voice to invite him inside. When it didn't come, he pushed the door open relieved he could root through Michael's boxes of books without the older man looking over his shoulder.

Elliott thought back to the group of horses. The set of bay geldings Michael used to both ride and pull his wagon had both been there. Did that mean Michael had doubled up with another elder, or that he was still somewhere in camp? Something was afoot. Elliott felt leftover energy hovering in the familiar wagon and considered getting back on Flame and using magic to track the men who'd left—assuming they'd all gone the same place, which was far from certain.

No reason I can't do that if no one is back before I finish with the books.

Decided on a path, he invoked the spell to unlock the chest where Michael stored the caravan's supply of lore books and settled on the dusty floor next to it. The books weren't indexed, and his Coptic was worse than rusty from disuse. By the time he located which volume held information about shifters, an hour had slid by.

Elliott sifted through two sections that looked promising. It was slow going, and he ended up skipping over words he couldn't puzzle out from context. The missing words didn't matter, though. As the meaning from the passages scribed on stained parchment sank in, his chest tightened in amazement. Mixing magical lines produced stronger magic than either strain possessed. Long ago, a half-breed created from Romani and witch blood had joined with another half-breed, who had shifter abilities. The result had been a child so powerful—and so inherently wicked—he'd wiped out hundreds of Romani before they'd set a successful trap and killed him, taking care to burn his remains so nothing could resurrect itself to haunt them.

Rocking back on his buttocks, Elliott reached for a wineskin hanging from a nearby hook and drank deeply. At least that explained why Tairin was so powerful. Maybe it took the addition of witchy genes to create evil progeny, but more likely the child described in the lore had been overcome by the mix of magics in his blood. With no mentors to train him, perhaps he'd gone mad.

Elliott set the book aside, and rooted through the others, searching for the one addressing vampires. He'd skimmed that section years ago and had surely missed critical information because he'd lacked application for the knowledge. This time, the volume he sought revealed itself quickly. Magical tomes were sometimes cooperative like that, particularly when they were concerned about their own survival.

His grasp of Coptic gradually returning, he read carefully. There were still words he didn't recognize, but fewer than there'd been in the previous volume. Where the information about Tairin had been heartening, the section addressing vampires made him feel worse, the more he read.

Creatures born of night, they resulted from a blood pact between the devil and Sekhmet, Egyptian goddess of death and slaughter. Though they could have sex—and did with great frequency—new vampires were created by draining humans to the point of death, then letting them feed from the vampire who'd taken their blood. That vampire became their sire, and they owed allegiance to him forever. It was how master vampires formed nests that sometimes numbered in the hundreds.

Lesser variants of the draining-feeding continuum produced humans with unnatural, dark power who weren't exactly vampires in that they didn't feed on blood, but nor were they human anymore, either. This was likely what he and Tairin had witnessed. While vampire power was enhanced by darkness, they were perfectly capable of functioning in broad daylight too, a fact that surprised him. He flipped pages, skimming for more valuable tidbits.

Vampire perversions and societal structure didn't interest him, so he paged forward, crinkling the parchment is his haste to discover how to kill them. The answer he sought was simple enough. Beheading would do it. So would a silver stake through their hearts. Whoever had penned this segment cautioned that vampires held supernatural strength and speed, so getting close enough to employ either method required stealth. According to him, the creatures were wily, but vain, and flattery could sometimes get a person within range. Of course, it also put you within striking distance of their deadly fangs.

That section brought him to the end of the book, so he closed its cracked leather binding. Rising to his knees, he piled it and the others back inside Michael's trunk and secured the lid. Hours had passed while he dug through the books. Where was Tairin? Had she returned? His magic had recovered somewhat, and he sent a thread zinging outward in search of her energy. While he was at it, he looked for Michael.

Neither was anywhere close. Alarm drove him to his feet. Michael was probably with the other elders. They could take care of themselves, but Tairin was by herself…

She's a wolf. And she has stronger magic than any Romani. She'll be fine.

His words made sense, but they didn't mitigate his fears for her. Elliott headed outside, intent on saddling Flame and hunting for Tairin. She might not need him, but he needed her. The insight rocked him to his bones. Once he'd kicked the door to his feelings open, longing for Tairin spilled through him. He'd always cared about her, but he was a master at shunting his own emotions aside.

No more. He'd find her and tell her how important she was to him. That he was falling in love with her and wanted to join his life to hers.

He tossed a blanket over Flame's back, following it with his saddle.

The boy tending the horses rose from a hay bale and trotted to Elliott as he mounted up. "They're none of 'em back yet." The boy sounded uncertain. "You thinking there's trouble? Should I round up the women and wagons and get us moving down the road?"

Elliott stared hard at the young man, impressed by his courage. He was clearly frightened, but he'd already assimilated the lesson that men took care of women. "Alert everyone that we might be pulling out before the end of today, but don't leave yet," Elliott said tersely. "We need a plan of where we're going, and right now, we don't have one."

"I'll make sure everyone is ready." The lad took off running for the far end of the circle of wagons.

TAIRIN GAVE the wolf its head. They ran through shadowed hills looming above the busy, convoluted tangle of Munich's streets. She didn't have to warn her bondmate to skirt small farms and other places they might run into a disgruntled farmer with a shotgun.

After its "I told you so" about Elliott's unexpected reaction to their transformation and its disclosures about her father, the wolf had been uncharacteristically silent. Tairin was grateful because it offered her an opportunity to think about the tall Romani. Many of the men were players, moving from one willing woman to the next, but not Elliott. If he'd had dalliances, he'd kept them brief and private. In truth, she'd viewed him as married to his magic. A concept she understood.

The sun moved higher in the sky, and she was about to suggest they head back to the rundown castle where she'd left her clothes when a hint of Rom magic reached her hypersensitive lupine nose. What were Romani doing all the way out here? She lifted her snout, sorting scents. When she identified Michael and Stewart, she was certain it was the group of elders.

Had they taken to the hills to weave some arcane brand of magic?

"We should see what they're about," her wolf said.

"Spying on them feels wrong," she retorted.

"How is it any different from what you were doing outside Michael's wagon last night?"

If she'd been human, it would've taken effort not to laugh. Her wonderfully pragmatic wolf had thrown her hypocrisy in her face. "It's not," she replied. *"Just don't get us caught."*

"Elliott caught you last night. I'd say that turned out pretty well," the wolf observed archly.

She thought about saying she had no idea how last night would turn out, but held her tongue. She wanted Elliott, probably more than was good for her, but a Rom and a shifter had no future together. Her parents were living proof of that, and she didn't plan to repeat their mistakes. The expression of awe on Elliott's face once she'd shifted filled her mind, and her resolve weakened.

Tairin shoved the dilemma aside, grateful she didn't have to solve it right now. She'd end up doing the right thing, whatever it might be—even if she left pieces of her heart along the way.

The wolf picked a path parallel to the group of Romani men, following them to a deserted cottage at the edge of a meadow. Sharp escarpments rose on two sides behind the stone structure, and a rushing creek burbled not far from it. The wolf shinnied beneath a bramble thicket on its belly, selecting a vantage point that gave them a clear view of the cottage. She watched the group of elders shuffle over the lintel and into what had likely been a sheepherder's cottage. From the smell of things, the place had been deserted for many years.

Romani magic swirled around the little house—obfuscation spells designed to keep words spoken within from anyone else's ears. Tairin carved a small, unobtrusive opening. What was the point of putting herself at risk if she couldn't hear what the men had to say?

"We need consensus," Michael thundered. "I wasn't about to

have our shouting match continue where my people could hear and worry themselves sick. We're leaders for our people. That means we provide clear direction as free from dissension as possible."

"You just didn't care for our assessment," a man whose voice she didn't recognize cut in.

"Indeed. Half of us wish to take our chances traveling back toward Egypt. Our reasons for leaving the Middle East evaporated a hundred years ago," another voice said.

"Ye'll never make it." Stewart's brogue was unmistakable, his tone flat. "Too many countries and too many borders to cross. Once the Rom were welcome everywhere, not anymore. Winter will make travel difficult too."

"We can't wait until spring," the first man said in a more reasonable tone. "I've thought this through. Clearly, we all wouldn't leave together. Maybe we could stagger the caravans by a week or two. And some of us could take a more northerly route through Poland."

"Another bad idea," Michael said. "Anywhere there are Germans, we'll run into the same hatred that's driving us out of Germany's cities."

"I refuse to believe our kind will die out at the hands of the Reich," another voice said. "As leader for my caravan, I've made my decision. I'm leaving. Wish me luck."

"We're leaving with him," the first man who'd spoken said. "No point remaining all the way out here a moment longer. There's serious work to be done before my caravan is ready to depart."

Amid a spate of muttered apologies, the cottage door that was hanging half off its hinges opened, and seven of the twelve men filed out. After a hurried exchange of wishes for good fortune, open fires, and wind at their backs, the group got on their horses and took off at a lope for town.

Sadness rose, making Tairin's heart hurt.

"Romani killed your mother," the wolf reminded her.

"Yes, but they're also the closest thing I have to family."

If she'd been in her human body, she'd have blinked back tears as frustration vied with anger and shame. She should hate the Rom for what they'd done to her mother, but she couldn't find it in herself to hang onto her outrage.

"They've only become your family because they have no idea what you are," the wolf retorted.

No one would ever come out on top in this conversation, so she didn't pursue it. The wolf had an uncanny way of cutting to the heart of things. While its observations were often uncomfortable, it didn't make them any less true.

Tairin cleared her mind, preparing to continue listening in on Michael, Stewart, and the other three men. She thought about who had left and decided Keenan and Alex were inside. She didn't know the last man's name. A tall, rangy blond, his long hair was turning gray, and he spoke German with a strong, Romanian accent.

"What'll it be?" Michael sounded defeated. Tairin could almost imagine his shoulders slumping. See his dark eyes pinched with worry. Like many Rom, he was dark and swarthy with a thickly built body and legs bowed from long years on horseback.

"We canna verra well move all five of our caravans together," Stewart said. "As 'tis, we attract notice."

"Should we sell the horses and buy automobiles?" Keenan asked in his gravelly voice. Michael's twin, he was leader to his own caravan.

"I wish I knew," Michael replied. "Before we left, I tasked our strongest women with looking into the future."

"If Elliott failed, surely they will as well," Stewart muttered. He'd kept to his native kilts, and his red hair always hung to his knees in a series of tight braids.

"There are checkpoints at every border," Keenan said. "Whether they stop us and tear our wagons apart or our cars, I'm not sure it makes much difference."

"We have waited too long as it is." The man she couldn't name spoke up. "If you recall, my counsel was that we should leave many months ago."

"Aye, Valentin. I do remember that," Stewart said. "'Tis sorry I am I dinna heed that advice and move my caravan back to Scotland."

At least now I know his name, she thought.

"We can't live in the past." Weariness rode beneath Michael's words. "What will each of you do with your caravans? Will you go to ground here or flee?"

Tairin's attention shifted to the pounding of hooves closing fast, but still at least a quarter mile distant. Before she could direct her magic in that direction to see who was coming, her wolf said, *"It's Elliott and his mellow stallion that likes us."*

"Did he track the men—or us?"

"Does it matter?" the wolf replied.

"Yes. If he came looking for us, we need to meet him far enough from the cottage the others don't see him cozying up with a wolf."

Lupine whuffling that passed for laughter rolled through her mind, and the wolf backed out from under the bramble thicket and loped downhill, toward Elliott and his galloping horse.

*E*lliott urged Flame to move faster. He'd come across the seven Rom elders on their way back to the wagons, and they'd told him where to find Michael. No one had said anything about seeing a wolf, and Elliott hadn't asked. He'd been tracking both Tairin and Michael when he ran into the tight knot of men with faces serious enough to curdle new milk.

It couldn't be accidental she'd traveled so close to the men's track. A grin played about Elliott's mouth. Apparently eavesdropping came naturally to her. The men crossed her path had probably been happenstance, but once they did, it piqued her curiosity and she ran with it.

Flame whinnied and reared, tossing his head. Elliott sent soothing magic into the stallion's mind while he raked the countryside with his gaze, trying to figure out what had spooked his mount. A short, gruff bark sent him catapulting off his horse. He stopped long enough to hobble a nervous Flame with magic and took off running toward the sound. It had to be Tairin. Her energy was thick here, and Flame had no doubt sensed the wolf.

Elliott threw his magic wide open. Tairin's unique feel pulled him like a magnet. He ducked into a copse of trees, delighted when he saw the wolf, tongue lolling, tail pluming, breath steaming in the chill air. He halted abruptly. If she'd been in her human body, he'd have wrapped her in his arms.

No reason not to now.

He sank into a crouch and held out his arms. Like she'd done earlier in the underground grotto, she came to him and leaned into his touch while he buried his hands in her fur, inhaling her clean, wild scent.

"I was worried about you when you didn't return. Checked the grotto and found your clothes, but you hadn't been there." He kept his voice low. He didn't sense any other people about, but it paid to be safe.

I would have been back long since. Actually, I was on my way to retrieve my clothes when the elders trooped by us.

"And you got curious, huh?" He riffled her fur.

I figured we—" she stressed the last word "*—needed all the information we could lay our hands on. So yes, I stayed to listen.*

"I got a rundown from the men heading back to their respective caravans," Elliott said. "Did Michael and Stewart and the ones left here come to any decisions?"

They hadn't when my wolf sensed you. We thought it best to intercept you before you got close enough one of them might have seen you talking with us.

Elliott furrowed his brow in thought. "Too bad your clothes are so far away. We could both show up at the cottage and join in the discussion."

No point wishing for the impossible. You need to go right now and talk with them. Once they know about the vampires, it will change everything.

"Maybe." Elliott wasn't so sure about that. The Rom had enough to worry about without fighting a war they might not see as theirs.

But it is their war. Sorry. I was inside your head just now.

"No need to apologize. How is it their war?"

"Vampires are strengthening the SS. By that token, they're allied with the Reich. The Nazis hate us. We're part of whom they've targeted for destruction—"

Elliott stroked the soft fur on her muzzle. "You can stop. I understand. The friend of my enemy is also my enemy."

She nudged him with her nose. *"Right, even if it is a perversion of the original quote. Now hurry. It didn't seem to me that Michael and the other elders would be there much longer."*

"Where will you be?"

"I'll wait for you in your grotto. I'm tired, so I'll try to sleep once I'm dressed."

Elliott didn't think about it before he bent and kissed the tip of the wolf's nose. The wolf licked him effusively before jerking its head away. *"Get moving."*

"I will. No time now, but we need to talk about what I found in the lore books about shifters and Rom."

"What?" Her mind voice took on a closed off aspect, and Elliott kicked himself for opening an important topic when he didn't have time to finish it.

He reached for her head again, but she jerked away. "Tairin, sweetheart. It isn't anything bad at all. More like an urban myth that grew with the telling. Long ago two half-breed Rom produced a devil child. To be on the safe side, the elders forbade Rom from mating outside the blood. That's all." He hesitated. "Don't you see? There's no reason we can't care about each other. None at all."

The wolf whined softly. *"There's more."*

"Of course there is, but I just hit the important points. I'll tell you everything, plus I read up on vampires too. As soon as I get to the grotto, you'll know exactly what I do."

"Promise?"

"On all the gods' blood." Elliott invoked an old Romani saying.

"We like blood," the wolf chimed in. *"Now get moving."*

When he bent and hugged the wolf this time, it didn't wriggle away from his embrace. Elliott took it as a good sign. "See you soon," he said. "Both of you."

He dismantled the enchantment around Flame as he ran to the stallion and vaulted onto his back. Elliott didn't realize how close he'd been to the cottage until he felt Rom magic pulsate. If he hadn't been sensitive to its particular feel and scent—cloves mixed with cut grass—he'd have ridden right by the solid, stone cottage that looked as if it had been built at least a hundred years ago.

A staunch leap moved him to the ground, and he directed Flame to wait with the small group of mounts milling behind the cottage, partially obscured by the same spell that locked the house away from prying eyes.

He pushed through a door that had long since lacked hardware to lock it and walked into a single room running the length and breadth of the structure. It was cold inside, but no one had bothered to light the blackened hearth. Probably because smoke would have been impossible to mask.

"I had a feeling ye'd turn up." Stewart trained his shrewd, dark eyes on Elliott.

"Och aye." Elliott aped the other man's brogue. "I'm a sucker for lost causes, though I have reason to believe ours is not yet completely beyond salvage." He joined the men's rough circle and crouched to be on a level with the others. "We have another problem."

"Yes?" Michael raised one eyebrow. "Something that supersedes escaping the eye of the Reich?"

"They're entwined. Last night, Tairin and I snuck into Dachau and poisoned food for at least fifty SS officers and trainees. They'll be dead by nightfall or shortly thereafter."

"You took a woman with you?" A shocked look blossomed on Valentin's high cheekboned face. He looked like the Mongols who'd been his ancestors with sharp features, straight blond hair going gray, and eyes so dark the pupil wasn't visible.

"Hear me out." Elliott continued without waiting for permission. "On our way back, we got off the road to avoid a truck convoy. Fell magic battered us, so we followed its taint to see what we faced."

"Mayhap Tairin's a woman," Stewart cut in, "but she's a damned brave one."

Elliott felt pleased by the compliment aimed at the woman he was falling hard for. "Indeed she is. We came across a nest of vampires. They're trading power for Nazi blood. Probably why the Reich rose so quickly, and no one has been able to make much in the way of inroads into their powerbase."

A sharp intake of breath rattled through Michael's teeth. He hooked one hand into the sign against evil. "How many?"

"Twelve vampires. Ten males and two females. Each of them had paired with an SS officer."

"Fucking and feeding, eh?" Keenan tried to sound casual, but his tone revealed how troubled he was.

"Fucking and feeding," Elliott agreed, "but not in that order. The blood sharing came first, then sex." He turned his attention toward Michael. "I returned to your wagon and spent time with the lore books. We can kill them, but it won't be easy."

"Is that a battle we even want to take on?" Michael looked briefly at each man in turn. "It may be all we can manage to either flee or hide."

Stewart sifted his hands through his braids. They made little clicking noises from the beads woven in with the hair. "I doona see where we have much choice." His words came slowly, as if each one cost him.

"If we ignore this, it might truly turn into a thousand year Reich, just like their propaganda fliers and rallies predict," he went on.

"We don't owe the gadjos anything," Alex protested. "They haven't lifted a finger to help us." His green eyes were cold, and he crossed his arms over a broad chest. Farrier as well as leader for his group, he spent his days when they weren't traveling working the forge and making sure all the horses had shoes. He kept his dark hair shorn close to his head so nothing could escape into the heat of his fire.

"It's not about who owes whom," Michael said. His eyes held a pinched, resigned expression. "It's about doing what we must so there are some pieces to pick up once this is over."

"I fear if we do nothing," Elliott said, "there may not be anything left to salvage. If the Nazis grow much stronger, the world will become theirs because no one will be able to face them down and win." He paused, weighing his next words before giving voice to them.

"What?" Michael asked, clearly intuiting something remained unsaid.

Elliott inhaled raggedly. "If that world comes to pass, there will be no place in it for the Romani. We will be forced into the shadows forever. Without the light of day to sustain us, we'll die out. If we go, the natural world won't be far behind."

Stewart nodded. "Aye, 'twas what I meant about not having any choice." He pushed heavily to his feet. "We must hurry and catch the others afore they scatter to the four winds. When a Rom chooses to disappear, they can be verra hard to locate."

"I'll take care of that." Michael reared his head back, and a high, piercing whistle set Elliott's nerves on edge and made his teeth ache. He clapped his hands over his ears, but the sound intensified, so he realized he had to be hearing with his third ear.

Magic. Michael is calling the others back. It's what he meant when he said he'd take care of it.

The noise ceased as quickly as it had begun. Elliott shook himself to quell unfamiliar feelings cascading through him. A sensation he had to ride into battle or be swept away was so pervasive, it took all his self-discipline not to race to Flame and urge him into the enemy camp.

"What exactly did you do?" he asked Michael.

"You must have missed that part in the lore." Michael lumbered to his feet and clasped his hands behind him.

"What part was that?" Elliott gazed at the man who'd raised him.

"'Tis our ancient call to arms," Stewart answered. "So far as I know, no one has uttered it in my lifetime. It should bring the others back."

"Or sent them fleeing as fast as they can run the other way," Alex muttered dourly.

Elliott had a feeling any Rom would have a hell of a time running from that command, but he held his tongue. He thought about where he'd encountered the seven men—and how long ago. Even if they set their mounts to a full gallop—which was unlikely because of how much attention it would attract—it would take them a good three quarters of an hour to return to the cottage. Once they were assembled, the ensuing discussion would likely last long into the night.

Elliott got to his feet.

"Where do you think you're going?" Michael shot him a sour look.

"To get Tairin and bring her back here—"

"No women." Valentin bolted upright and faced off against Elliott.

"We never include women in elder council discussions." Michael hesitated. "By rights, we shouldn't include you, except you're who saw the vampires."

Elliott stood straight and spread his hands in front of him, palms upward. He'd be damned if he'd cower in front of men he'd known all his life. "Tairin's magic complements ours. If it weren't for her, I'd still be there, and the creatures would've discovered me eventually."

Stewart made come along gestures with one hand. "Ye needs must say a wee bit more than that, lad."

"Just being in proximity to their magic hypnotized me. I

couldn't look away. Leaving was out of the question. Tairin touched my arm and broke their enchantment. Once she did that, we both snuck away." He inhaled tightly. Should he reveal what she was?

No. If I do, they'll never accept her in our midst, and any chance we have of success will go up in smoke.

Elliott shrouded his thoughts. The group would find out about Tairin's dual nature soon enough. By then, they'd be in the thick of things, realize how much they needed her, and their antipathy would vanish. Or at least lessen.

Hopefully.

Stewart narrowed his eyes to slits. "There is something about her magic," he muttered. "I've caught glimpses of her power from time to time, but she's always careful to cloak it. Almost as if she doesn't want us to look too deep."

"Pah!" Valentin spat on the dirt floor. "Women. Secretive bitches. None of them want any man close enough to see their dark natures. How can you trust something that bleeds every month?"

Elliott looked away. Valentin liked men. He kept it under wraps for the most part because Romani culture viewed same sex pairings as akin to devil worship. He'd approached Elliott years before, otherwise he might not have guessed about the other man's proclivities.

"What'll it be?" Elliott looked from one man to the next. "Regardless, I'm going to meet up with Tairin. If I don't bring her back here, I'm returning to the caravan, and you can solve the vampire problem without me." Reacting to annoyance streaming from Michael, he held up a hand. "Don't remind me how much I owe you. This is one place I'm taking a stand. You get both of us or none of us, but I'll give you directions to the vampire nest. It's easy enough to find."

"Do you suppose there are others in this area?" Keenan spoke up.

"I have no idea," Elliott said. "They have a particular stink about them, though. If I'd run across it before, I'd have remembered. So either they're newly arrived, they've kept a very low profile—which is unlikely since they require blood—or this is the only nest. At least for now."

"My guess would be all three," Michael said, sounding more rational. "They just got here. They've kept a low profile, and they're the only group in this area—at the moment, but that could change." He rubbed his eyes with the backs of his hands. When he looked up, he jerked his chin in Elliott's direction. "Bring her here. These are unusual times. Perhaps it means we must suspend how we normally conduct our business."

"Nothing in Romani law forbids women from taking part in council decisions," Keenan said.

Elliott didn't wait to hear any more. The rise and fall of the men's voices followed him outside as he clucked to Flame and jumped astride. While he rode, he considered what would happen if Tairin refused to return with him. She was on the verge of leaving the caravan. She'd all but said so, plus she'd have to leave at some point. Either that or reveal what she was. Shifters might appear perennially young, but no one else did.

By the time he arrived at the ruined castle, he'd decided to present the facts and let her decide. Whichever way she wanted to go would be fine by him. He wanted to remain by her side, whether they stayed with the caravan or struck out on their own. Given the mess the Reich had made of Germany and much of Europe, they'd surely be safer as a couple than as part of a larger group.

He would help the men with the vampires, though. If Tairin chose to leave, he'd come up with a place and time to meet her... If she was willing.

Leaving Flame in his usual place, Elliott hurried down the tunnel, drawn by Tairin's lush scent and unique energy. Now that he knew what she was, she'd stopped wasting magic to mask her essence. He ducked into the room. Tairin lay curled on her side in one of the corners, looking young and vulnerable and heartbreakingly lovely. Eyes closed, she was deeply asleep, head resting on joined hands.

Elliott crossed to her and pulled her into his arms, cradling her body against him. Strong emotion coursed through him, and he vowed to all the gods and goddesses in the universe that he'd devote his life to being worthy of her.

If she'd have him.

"Tairin, darling."

She curved her body against his and threaded her arms around him, murmuring in an old Germanic dialect. He kissed her forehead. Her lips drew him, encouraged kisses, but they didn't have time, and he was afraid if he started kissing her, he wouldn't be able to stop.

"Michael called the men back." He stroked hair away from her forehead. "We need to return so that—"

"We?" she broke in. "They'll allow a woman…" She reared back and looked at him. He felt her magic slip inside his mind and welcomed it. "Did you tell them about me?"

"No, my love. That's for you to reveal. Or not. Just as helping with whatever we end up doing to try to annihilate the vampires is up to you."

She pushed away and sat up, scrubbing the heels of both hands down her face. "But you need me. None of you are strong enough to do this without me—and a whole lot of other shifters."

Elliott smiled crookedly. Her courage warmed him. Even after the raw deal the Rom had dealt her family, she was still willing to help. Thoughts rolled from one side of his mind to the other. When words came, they were halting and uncertain. "You're amazing. Your spirit shines like the sun. Your—"

She put a hand over his mouth and rose to her feet. "I'm inside your head. I see all those extravagant compliments. Better watch it. They'll go to my head."

He scrambled upright and caught her in an embrace. "I'm falling in love with you, Tairin."

She hugged him back, quick and hard. "I'm starting to care about you too. Way more than I should. Maybe. Tell you what. On that ride back, you can fill me in on what you discovered about why our two bloodlines are forbidden to mingle."

"Of course. I'd be glad to. By the time I'm done, maybe you'll throw caution to the winds and join your star to a poor sod like me."

"There are lots of words I'd use to describe you." Musical laughter warmed him. "*Poor sod* isn't anywhere in the lineup. We need to get moving, right?"

"That we do. Thank the goddess Flame likes your human form. Given a little time, he'll wrap that equine head of his around your wolf."

"Good you didn't forget about me." The wolf chimed in.

"How could I?" Elliott countered. "You're part of Tairin. Loving her means loving you too."

Deep in his mind, a pleased howl rose, followed by a bevy of several more.

Elliott took off at a quick trot along the passageway with Tairin by his side. Soon, they'd sit in on a Romani war council. He'd always assumed they'd take on the Reich, but he'd figured they'd employ stealth—like he'd done in Dachau. Vampires hadn't entered the equation.

Until today.

He had a hunch stealth wouldn't make a dent in those twelve vampires. They'd require direct confrontation. Some of his friends would likely die.

Not Tairin. Not while there's life in my body to protect her.

She shot him a pointed look. "What if I feel the same way about you?"

"We'll protect each other."

"I like the sound of that. Do you want me in the saddle or in front of it?"

"In it." Elliott settled behind her, enjoying the feel of her body pressed against him. Times might be dire, and their need desperate, but he'd found his life's mate. She'd been there all along, but he hadn't been paying attention. Or maybe she'd been too busy masking what she was to allow him—or anyone else—to see the parts that enticed him. Made him certain she was the woman for him.

"Tell me what was in the lore books," she urged.

Elliott began to talk, filling in details as they rode back to the cottage and the Romani elders.

*L*ight was fading from the day when they reached the clearing. Tairin had listened intently to Elliott's recitation of the lore, and she could see how both shifters and Rom might well have adopted Draconian measures against a perceived threat. The event had happened long ago when folk were far more superstitious than now, and the blanket prohibition against shifters cozying up with other magical beings made sense. The devil child who'd started it was certainly an anomaly, but folk from an earlier era wouldn't have interpreted it that way.

She leaned against Elliott, enjoying the feel of his arms around her and remembering the press of his mouth on hers. Not a good idea to get lost dreaming about the man behind her, though. What he'd said about vampires was enough to offset any joy she felt in discovering there wouldn't be dire, cosmic consequences if she and Elliott made love.

Or fell in love and made a life together.

Elliott guided the horse to the back of the cottage. Dismounting, he waited for her to climb down. The number of mounts milling about meant all the elders were within.

Tairin turned to him and focused her mind voice. *"I'm going to tell them what I am. We need help from my shifter kin—if they'll give it. Nothing you said about your research into vampires convinced me that twelve—or even twenty—Romani would do more than amuse a vampire nest."*

Elliott winced, and then nodded slowly. "About the same conclusion I'd come to," he replied out loud. "Shall we?"

"Michael will kick me out of his caravan."

"You were leaving anyway." Elliott switched to telepathy and sent a meaningful look skittering her way. *"If it comes to that, and I'm not certain it will, I want to go with you—if you'll have me."* He held her gaze, resolute, determined, all things she knew about him. Elliott was capable of amazing single-mindedness, and now it was focused on her.

Unfamiliar feelings spilled through her. Caring. Gratitude. Desire to build a life with the man by her side. She pushed them away. What would unfold over the next hour was far more important than her personal needs. Reaching up, she cupped the side of his face. "Hold onto that thought. First, we have to find a way to survive."

He placed a hand over hers, trapping it against his cheek. "You didn't say no." Something hot and feral and hopeful blazed from the depths of his eyes.

"I didn't say no," she agreed and tilted her chin toward the cottage. "They know we're out here. Let's get this next part behind us."

He swung her hand to her side without letting go, and they walked to the cottage, ducking through the damaged door. Twelve pairs of eyes focused intently on them and their joined hands.

"Nice of you to come inside," Michael said.

"Aye, we sensed the two of you arrive this quarter hour past—more or less," Stewart cut in.

Elliott made a grunting sound. "It wasn't that long. Since you're all here, did you come up with any ideas for dealing with the vampires?"

"Lots of ideas," Keenan muttered. "Just not anything practical."

"Nor anything that willna get the lot of us killed," Stewart said dourly.

Michael narrowed his eyes to slits, skewering Elliott. "Did the lore mention silver bullets? Or iron? Or perhaps a mixture of the two?"

Elliott shook his head. "No. I was expecting something like that, but never found it. Maybe if I read more thoroughly—"

Stewart made a chopping motion with one hand. "Wouldna matter. None of us—" he made an expansive gesture with his other hand "—recalled aught beyond beheading or a silver stake driven through the heart, likely same as what ye read. Means ye'd have to get damned close."

"We might do away with one or two," Alex said, "but the others would pick us off sure enough before we did much more damage."

"Given all that," Michael spoke slowly, "perhaps we'd be better served to ignore the problem. No reason to sacrifice all of us for nothing."

"Our survival is far from certain," Valentin muttered from where he sat in a corner. "All this would do is ensure we'd die sooner."

Elliott opened his mouth, but before he could voice arguments, Tairin extricated her fingers from his and stepped forward. She kept her gaze downcast as befitted a Romani woman. "Permission to speak before your august group."

"No!" Valentin bellowed. "We have enough problems without whatever you might bring into the mix."

Elliott walked to Michael, but didn't kneel next to him. "What was the point in your consent to include Tairin if she can't be a part of this conversation?"

Michael lumbered upright and looked Elliott in the eye. "The discussion appears to be over. We won't engage in a battle we're sure to lose. Our people depend on us. Without the elders to guide them, everyone is likely to end up in a work camp."

"*Work camp* is a euphemism. What our people will be is dead." Valentin shouted the last word. "Dead. If we take on the vampires, it's the same as sentencing our people to die."

Tairin smothered an instinct to roll her eyes. When had the man turned into such a drama-ridden coward? She squared her shoulders and raised her gaze, looking at each man in turn. Some averted their eyes, but most didn't. Tension thrummed through her, and she balled her hands into tight fists.

"I asked for permission, and you argued, so I will say what's in my mind. Once I'm done, I'll leave if that's your decision."

"Leave now," Valentin snarled.

"Let the lass speak her piece." Stewart trained guileless eyes on her, but she wasn't fooled. The Scot saw more than most of them, perhaps on account of his Celtic roots.

She inhaled deeply and blew it out. The words wouldn't grow any easier with waiting. "You think you know me," she began, "but you don't. Michael's caravan is the fourth I've joined. I left the earlier ones—and I'm well prepared to leave this one—so no one would realize I didn't age."

Hissing grew, and the men made forked signs against evil.

"None of that," Elliott thundered. He strode to her side and stood shoulder to shoulder with her.

"What?" Valentin leered. "You're fucking her. That's why—"

Elliott covered the distance to the other man so fast, she could've sworn he had shifter blood. The sharp crack of a slap filled the room, and a reddened spot bloomed on the side of Valentin's face. Elliott doubled up a fist and drew it back, prepared to break the man's nose.

"Apologize. Now." Elliott closed a hand around Valentin's shoulder, holding him in place.

"When hell freezes over. This is what comes of allowing women into our midst."

"Let go of him," Stewart said, compulsion strong in his voice.

"Once ye do that, Valentin will leave and remain outside for the remainder of this discussion."

"You can't magic this away," Elliott said through clenched teeth.

"Och, but I can." Power thickened the air, and the salt smell of the ocean mingled with bayberry wafted around Stewart.

Elliott released Valentin; the man rose to his feet and walked out the door as if he were in a trance. The scent of Stewart's magic departed as quickly as it had risen, following Valentin.

Tairin started talking before any of the other men decided she was a bad omen and needed to be silenced. "My mother was Romani. My father a wolf shifter. As you might guess, neither side wanted me once I began to bleed and the ability to shift came with my moon blood."

She hurried on before she lost her courage. After centuries of silence, talking about her beginnings felt unnatural. "Mother was burned by her people for transgressing. Father returned to his people on the condition he'd not have any contact with me. I spent my first hundred years as a wolf. After that, I've traveled with Romani caravans. No one died because of me. No one went mad. No one did anything unusual..." Tairin was babbling, and she reined herself in.

"The only reason I broke my silence now is you need shifters to defeat the vampires. My wolf believes local shifters will help because they know how dangerous the Reich is to all magical creatures." Tairin stretched the truth about her certainty shifters would do anything but tell her to get lost and said a small prayer she was right.

"What makes you think we'd ever want to do battle side by side with shifters?" Michael asked, sounding as if the words choked him.

Tairin shrugged. "Desperate times require desperate solutions. Even if you refuse to help, I'm betting shifters will take on the vampires." She cloaked her mind now that she was lying outright.

"It appears we have a few unknowns here." Stewart's brogue was welcome. "How long will it take to raise your kinfolk?"

"Not long," she replied. "A day or two. I'll travel in wolf form, not human."

More hisses and hooked fingers.

"I'll go with you," Elliott said.

"But I require your help with the caravan," Michael said, still sounding as if something were stuck in his throat.

"Really? I never help with the caravan. Mostly, I'm off on my own spinning magic." Elliott drew his brows into a tight line. "What Tairin is makes you uncomfortable, and you're trying to protect me. Don't."

He hooked a hand under her elbow. "We're done here. Let's hunt down your shifter kin."

Tairin unkinked her fists and held out a hand. "Not quite done. We'll return to the caravan—or Elliott will if you want me to leave —by nightfall two days hence."

"We'll wait for you afore we make any decisions," Stewart said. "I'll see to it."

"You're welcome to return," Michael said stiffly. "If only to recover your things."

"If you banish her, you'll lose me too." Elliott pushed her toward the door before Michael could reply.

The buzz of voices followed them into the yard. Words like besotted and ensorcelled made her sad and angry that no one believed Elliott could care about her for herself. Valentin lounged against a tree, smoking, oblivious to everything but the spell that still held him in thrall.

"Let's get Flame. We can talk once we're away from here," Elliott said.

"Fine, but we're not going far. I was serious about hunting in wolf form. I can cover more ground that way, and perhaps the other shifters will take me more seriously if I'm in my animal body."

"Wise of you," the wolf observed.

"I was wondering what happened to you," she said.

"Watching to see which way the wind blows."

Elliott angled the stirrup, and she sprang lightly onto the stallion's back. He got on behind her as he'd done earlier, but let her manage the reins. "I apologize for Valentin back there."

"Not necessary." She kneed the horse to make him trot. "You're scarcely responsible for other Romani. What are you going to do while I'm gone?"

"I've been thinking about that. Seems like a good opportunity to delve into the lore books. I was in a hurry earlier. There are better than twenty volumes in Michael's chest, and my Coptic came back to me as I spent time with them. I'll be far more efficient now than I was then."

"Still hoping for a magic bullet?" Turning, she stole a glance at him over one shoulder.

"More like a miracle. Besides, if we leave the caravan, this may be my last opportunity to study a collection of Romani lore books."

Tairin guided the stallion back to the same copse of trees where Elliott had found her earlier and waited for him to slip off the horse's rump before jumping down.

Elliott closed his arms around her from behind and nuzzled her neck. She should shift and leave. Instead, she twisted in his arms and turned her mouth up for a kiss. Who knew if she and the wolf would find her kin? Even if she did, would they do anything but chase her away? Worst case, they might try to harm her. If they held the same narrow worldview as the Romani, it was a distinct possibility. She might prevail against two or three shifters, but not an entire wolf pack intent on her destruction.

His magic rose around them, bay rum and vanilla, and she felt the touch of him in her mind. "You don't have to go," he said. "Not if you don't want to."

"But I do. Have to go, that is. Now that we know about the

vampires, we can't just walk away and pretend we never saw them. It could mean the difference between the Reich succeeding or failing."

She twined her arms around him, hands spread across his back. "We cannot let that happen. The Nazis can't win. If they do, everything good in the world will die out."

He tipped her chin upward. A savage light burning in his eyes turned them midnight blue. "You're braver than that whole roomful of Romani elders."

Pleasure at the compliment filled her. "Maybe because I've survived worse than any of them. I've sure as hell lived longer. All I know is we have to try. And that means me coming out of hiding. I dropped my mask in front of half the Rom caravans in Germany tonight. Letting the other part of my blood know I'm still alive won't be any harder."

"Except I won't be there."

"Ah, but I will," the wolf said. *"I can reason with my kin. They're not cowards like the Romani."*

"I feel shame for my blood kin," Elliott told the wolf. *"Please don't hold their weakness against me."*

Tairin's heart hurt for Elliott, but she was proud of him for not making excuses for the other Romani. She tugged him hard against her. Standing on tiptoe, she brought her mouth down on his. Moaning low in his throat, he crushed her against him and kissed her with a fervor that stole her breath. He nibbled, licked, and sucked her lips. Explored her mouth with his tongue and welcomed hers. The kiss developed a life of its own, and time slowed while he teased her with tongue and lips. Sensation coursed through her, lighting her blood with desire.

Their breathing quickened as they ground their bodies against one another. Her nipples turned into stiff peaks, and the dark, secret place between her legs ached to be full. He moved a hand from her back, sliding it beneath her cloak to cup one of her breasts and rub her nipple. Sparks raced to her belly, and she straddled one of his legs, rotating her hips to increase contact with her nub. His cock swelled, pressing against her belly, and she sandwiched a hand between their bodies to cup his erection.

Before she was totally swept away by sensation swirling through her, she tore her mouth from his. "We can't. I have to leave."

"Please, Tairin. Making love properly will have to wait, but I have to touch you. This is one genie we can't stuff back inside a bottle. Not now."

Elliott jammed a hand between her legs, pressing upward. She thrust her hips against him and worked his cock through his trousers, too aroused to manage the laces holding everything together. He kissed her again—hard, firm, demanding—and angled his hand to rub the distended nub beating like a second heart between her legs. Layers of clothing didn't mute his ability to find the right spot.

She knew how to make herself come. Had done so many a night when the sounds of lovemaking from other wagons aroused her. But the touch of his fingers in what had been a private place was intensely erotic. He pressed his cock up and down in her hand, closing his other around it to show her the pressure he needed.

His penis grew harder still cupped in her hand, and an orgasm spooled deep in her belly. When it roared through her, wave after wave of white heat, his cock exploded, pulsing with a climax of its own.

Gasping and panting, they clung to one another. "I love you, Tairin," he managed, his voice harsh with passion. "I suppose I've loved you for a long time, but I never let myself see what was plainly in front of me."

She stroked his hair and his face, overcome with tenderness. "That's the sex talking."

"No. It's not. I've been searching for a way to tell you I want to marry you. Make an honest life for us. Not one where we hide in shadows and pretend things are legal, like so many of the Romani."

Hope lodged in her breast. Rather than kicking it out, she found a home for it. "I hope you mean it. I want to believe you."

He kissed her forehead, her lips, her chin, and pried her fingers off his still-hard cock. "It'll be a mess inside my trousers. I need to clean myself up, but I'll do that after you're well on your way."

She removed her cloak, folding it and leaving it in the crotch of an evergreen tree. Next, she removed her boots and stockings. Elliott's gaze never left her. "No privacy?" She quirked a brow in an attempt at humor.

"You'll be my wife. Sooner or later, that means I'll see you naked."

"You opted for sooner, eh?"

He smiled, and her heart cracked wide open. Before she lost her nerve and threw herself into his arms, she undid her skirt, folding it atop the cloak and followed it with her long tunic. Goosebumps raised along the length of her arms, and she shivered. She drew her shift over her head, leaving it on the very top of the pile. If she survived her meeting with her kinfolk, she'd need her clothing, particularly if Michael rescinded his offer to allow her to collect her things from her wagon.

"Gods but you're beautiful." Elliott whistled long and low.

"Thanks. Too bad there's not time for you to display your wares as well. I'll meet you in the grotto," she said through teeth that were beginning to chatter.

"Not here?"

"How would that work? You'd have to keep coming back to check for me. At least if we choose the grotto, you can bring Michael's lore books there and work. You can bring my clothes back with you too."

"Wise as well as beautiful. Be safe. Hear that, wolf? Keep both of you safe!"

"You can bet on it," the wolf said. *"I'm not planning to let some other shifter be the death of me. Besides, we might find her father. Bastard is so eaten up with guilt, he'll help all he can."*

"I thought he was in Austria," Tairin said.

"I put out a call when we first talked about finding him." The wolf sounded smug. *"Who knows? By now he could be much closer."*

She summoned magic to shift, and the scent of her spell filled her nostrils. Musk and the wooded glens where her wolf loved to run. The change took her, torso shortening, fur sprouting. Fur would cut the winter night's chill, and she welcomed it.

Elliott waited until her transformation was complete, and then gathered her against him and kissed the tip of her snout.

She licked him and wriggled free. *"I need to leave. I've stayed too long as it is."*

"Come back to me."

"We will." The wolf spoke for both of them before it ran between shadows, taking them away from everything familiar and into the unknown.

Tairin gave the wolf its head. For a time neither of them spoke, caught up in the simple joy of running free. Earlier clouds had dissipated, and the inky sky was shot with stars and a newly risen moon.

"You didn't ask, but I approve," the wolf said.

"Of what?" She felt confused. *"Hunting for our shifter kin was your idea."*

"Not that. Elliott. He will be a good mate for us." The wolf hesitated, maybe gathering its thoughts. *"Because you weren't raised among shifters, you wouldn't know this, but I have to approve of your choice of a mate. If it's another shifter—which is far more common—the bond animals must agree to the mating."*

A thought slapped her hard. *"If I link my life with Elliott's, does that mean you're destined to never have a mate of your own? Help me understand how this works."*

"It does mean that, but bond animals don't engage in physical relationships. We walk in a spiritual realm."

"But I had sex with other wolves." Tairin worked to make sense of the wolf's statement.

"It may have been my body when you lay with wolves, but it was

your soul. You needed that connectedness or you'd have slipped beyond where I could call you back."

"I almost did."

"I haven't forgotten. Elliott will be a good partner for us both. When you dreamed me when you were just a girl, and I agreed to the bond, I knew about your mixed blood. And I also understood it meant we'd likely never mate with anyone. Neither shifters nor humans would want to be part of such a pairing."

"Funny, but I'd come to the same conclusion. It seems miraculous Elliott can look beyond our dual nature."

"Indeed. We will both welcome him, but now is a time to turn our thoughts outward. Let us hunt for our kin."

They ran through much of the night in a generally westward direction. Tairin let the wolf pick which dark glens they skirted, invisible as a passing shadow. They stopped to drink from rushing brooks and even caught the odd field mouse that crossed their path. Hours drizzled by. So many, the eastern sky was turning pearlescent with the coming of dawn.

"We need to go to ground," she said as daylight grew around them.

"We would except we're almost there," the wolf replied, not bothering to elaborate what it meant by *there*.

Tairin waited. She could be patient. It was one of the traits that had stood her in good stead through her two hundred years. They'd left anything resembling a main road hours back. The land grew rougher, marked by abrupt escarpments and rocky cliffs, and they slithered through increasingly thick timber. The wolf halted in front of a solid granite cliff face. It howled, and power built within their shared body before boiling over in a torrent that lapped against the granite walls.

The feel of her bondmate's magic shocked her. Beyond the ceremony formalizing their bond that it had walked her through after her first shift, she'd rarely known the wolf to wield its own ability—even during the century they'd spent in lupine form.

Then they'd been motivated to blend in with a normal wolf pack, though. Any unusual displays would've gotten them booted out.

The stone before them took on a shimmery appearance, and the scent of magic tickled her sensitive nose. The wolf's power smelled a lot like her own, but heavier on the wild animal side. Clean, bracing, fresh, it reminded her why she loved being a shifter. Tairin trained her gaze on the stone, ready for damn near anything.

Footsteps—human, not wolf or any other animal—approached from somewhere beyond the wall that was fading to nothingness. A man with copper-colored hair braided tight against his head came into view. Tight-fitting leather garments made from tanned deer hide hugged his tall form. Leather boots laced to his knees. He stopped in the doorway and looked at her from eyes eerily like her own.

Tairin swallowed hard. Her father hadn't changed at all in two hundred years. Being in her wolf's form muted her emotions, but joy vied with fury anyway. *At least you opened the door for me this time, Father,* she gritted without preamble.

"Come inside." His low voice was gruff. "This isn't a conversation to have where any might overhear."

Tairin growled; hackles raised the length of her back. *I'm not going inside a place controlled by your magic until I know more.*

A look of grudging admiration etched into his high cheekbones and square, stubble-covered chin. Austere features, yet the man before her was handsome in an ascetic way.

He knew we were coming, the wolf informed her, following it with, *We ran most of the night to get here. Don't let your temper stand between us and securing help against the vampires.*

Her father angled his head to one side. "Are you going to follow me or not? The magic won't allow me to hold the gateway forever."

The wolf stepped forward. Tairin considered fighting her bondmate, but she'd trusted its instincts most of her life. If it thought traveling through stone that wasn't stone would be safe, she'd go along with it.

"I have strong reservations, but we will follow you." She kept her tone formal. Her long-lost father had abandoned her in favor of his own self-interest, and she'd be worse than a fool to forget or even lay it aside.

He spun on his heel, walking fast. She moved through the gateway, feeling the zing of unfamiliar power turn the air electric. Small jolts of power buffeted her until she was well clear of the illusion that maintained the rock wall. It grew darker, and she assumed the cliff was back in place.

Her wolf's vision provided enough illumination to see a rounded tunnel, clearly constructed by human hands, and not all that long ago from the looks of the materials. *"What is this place?"* she asked.

Without answering, he led them through a door into a small, cozy room, closing the door once they were inside. The walls were lined with lumber and bricks, much like the tunnel had been. Fire crackled in a hearth carved out of one end of the chamber. A table and chairs sat next to one wall, and a small sofa graced the other. Illumination came from the fire and her father's mage light.

He walked across the room and pulled an armoire open. Gathering a robe, he laid it over the sofa. "Shift, daughter. It will make it easier to talk."

Daughter. He called me daughter.

At least he acknowledged me.

Tairin froze in place. Part of her wanted to launch her wolf form at the tall man with the chilly eyes and drive him to the carpeted floor. She could rip out his carotid. Get even for him abandoning her all those years back—

"Get hold of yourself," her wolf snapped. *"Now. If I'd realized how much bitterness you harbored, I never would have brought you here."*

"Your wolf is wise," her father said. "I'll turn around while you shift and cover yourself."

Tairin swallowed saliva dripping from her mouth. *Before I settle in for tea and crumpets—*" She winced. Even her mind voice sounded sarcastic. *"My wolf went behind my back to summon you, which means you must know about the vampires too. Will you help the Romani kill them?"*

Her father, Jamal Jabari, twisted his mouth in what might have been a grim smile. "Not much love lost between us and the Rom, but nothing says shifters can't take on vampires on our own. We scarcely require Romani magic to augment ours."

"You're just as stubborn as your daughter," her wolf sputtered. *"The magic is complementary, additive. You're stronger working together than either of you separately."*

Jamal gestured toward the robe. "Please. I'd rather argue with you in human form."

"My wolf will still be here. Still have opinions."

He snorted. "You think I don't know that? My wolf has given me hell for the last two hundred years. Ever since I walked away from part of my pack to honor the other part." Shaking his head, he added, "No matter which path I'd chosen, it would have been wrong."

Words rioted through Tairin's brain. So many words. All the internal conversations she'd held with her father—and her mother—in the years since she'd been on her own. The epithets she'd hurled their way for being careless enough to produce a child burned the back of her throat, and she loped to the robe, not caring if Jamal turned around or not.

Shift magic augured into her, but she welcomed the pain as her human body formed. Snatching up the robe, she wrapped it around herself before the air stopped glimmering around her.

Tairin spun to face her father. "The Rom murdered Mother. I've been on my own since I was thirteen. Did you know that? I spent my first century as a wolf to keep from being raped."

Guilt and resignation streamed from Jamal. His forehead creased in pain, and his eyes developed a pinched look. "I didn't know the last part. How were you able to recapture your humanness after so long?"

"An old Romani woman found me. Luckily, it was after I'd managed to complete shifting. It took a week. A week of pain so bad I longed for death, but didn't have hands to kill myself. I tried to throw us off a cliff, but my wolf refused. It never stopped believing in me. In us."

"That's what fathers are for," he said in a voice laced with regret. "No number of apologies can make up for what I did to you, so I won't even try. What I did instead is gather a cadre of shifters willing to go after the vampire nest you uncovered."

Tairin's mouth gaped open. She shut it with a snap. Just like that. Jamal wasn't going to let her wallow in feeling sorry for herself. Or get lost in anger she had every right to indulge in. She crawled out of the pit she'd been digging herself and set her jaw in a hard line.

"What about the Romani?"

"What about them?" Jamal countered. "I'm having a hard time believing they want to join us on any battlefield. They don't trust us. And we don't trust them." He blew out a tight breath. "Make no mistake, daughter—"

"You will not call me that." She straightened her spine, facing off against him. "When you chose your other obligations over me, and agreed never to see me again, you lost the right to call me daughter."

"Fine. Make no mistake, *Tairin*, killing even one vampire would be hard, and there are twelve to dispatch. We cannot afford any distractions."

"Romani will strengthen you." Her wolf joined the conversation.

"Maybe," Jamal conceded. "If we weren't too busy watching our backs to take advantage of whatever shared magic might buy us."

"How many shifters agreed to help?" Tairin asked.

"Twenty-five. Some wolves, some ravens, one vulture, some mountain lions. I was grateful for the birds because vampires can't fly." He crossed his arms over his chest. "Tell me where the nest is, and I'll leave."

Reality reared up, socking her in the gut. "Wait a minute. I'm part of this."

"No, you're not. We never include women in battles. We're no different from the Romani in that regard."

Tairin curved her fingers until her nails cut into her palms. None of this was going as she'd planned it. A vicious laugh bubbled up. Since when had any of her life gone as planned?

"Did you know about this part?" she asked the wolf.

"Not exactly, but I figured including the Rom—and us—would be an uphill struggle."

"Hurry," Jamal urged. "The others are waiting for me. It's best to take care of things like this when energy is running hot. One of the few things we hold in common with the Romani is knowledge that the Reich abhors magic. I'm certain they have a secret 'final solution' to rid themselves of the vampires as soon as they no longer need their power. If they secure their chokehold on Europe, we're done for."

Tairin longed for Elliott. As another man, maybe he'd hold the key to talking sense into her father. He wasn't here, though, so she'd have to do what she'd done all her life. Find a way through. Not capitulate—even when things looked impossible.

Jamal opened his mouth, but she made a chopping motion with one hand. "Take me with you. You want the vampires dead, need to cut off the power they're funneling into the Reich. I know where they are." Tairin leveled her gaze at her father.

"I can pluck the information out of your mind," he said.

"Ha! Try it. You'll find I'm not the puny thirteen-year-old you deserted."

He grimaced as if she'd slapped him. *Good.* Bastard needed a wakeup call. "Your choice." She crossed her arms beneath her breasts. "Take me with you, or my wolf and I are leaving. We'll do the best we can with Romani magic."

"Have you forgotten? Other shifters don't accept you."

She shrugged. "Neither do the Rom after last night when I told them what I am. I can live with that. Besides, that whole thing where Romani and shifters are forbidden congress is based on a legend. Apparently, a Rom-witch mix and a shifter produced a devil child long before anyone understood genetics. I'm sure the kid was an anomaly, an aberration, but the ancients were superstitious and decided the safest route would be to make certain it never happened again."

She watched understanding play across his face. "You're saying my people forced me to choose based on a legend, a myth?"

"Yup. Are you going to take me to whoever signed on to fight vampires, or not?"

"What about including the Romani," her wolf persisted.

"One battle at a time," she replied.

The muscles in Jamal's jaw worked. "I'll bring you with me, but I can't guarantee your safety."

"We'll take our chances," the wolf spoke up.

A tightly wound place deep inside her relaxed just a little. "Human or wolf?" she inquired.

"Human. We're not going far." He strode past her and out of the room.

"How far is *not far*?" she called after him. "I don't have shoes."

"You asked for this," he told her, without so much as looking back. "Don't complain."

Tairin watched where she walked, mage light suspended over one shoulder. The passageway was cold, but the ground outside held a layer of frost. The false cliff was open when she got there, and she strode through. Once she was outdoors, she doused her light. The soles of her feet burned before they turned numb as she followed her father's retreating back. Anger kindled at his callousness, but she relegated it to a minor role. It took far more than blood to call someone family. Jamal had made his choice when he walked away, and if she'd nurtured a secret hope he'd gush over her with apologies, she needed to get over it fast.

I don't need him. Once I did, but that time is long past.

"Steady," the wolf said. *"This will grow harder before it gets easier."*

Jamal stopped in front of another cliff, twin to the one that had sheltered his spot from discovery. Magic rose around him, turning the air iridescent. "What are all these places?" Tairin asked.

"If you'd grown up with shifters, you'd know we have shelters scattered everywhere. They're all concealed with similar magic, and each has a subtle...draw to it. When one of us runs into trouble, if we project our magic on a particular frequency, it will lead us to the closest place we can hide."

She bit her tongue to avoid telling him he'd made certain she lost out on her shifter birthright. Two-hundred-year-old ire had no place here, but it was damned hard to let go of. "How can I get out if I need to leave in a hurry?"

Jamal sent an appraising glance her way. "Good question. You may not hold any fondness for me, but you inherited my practical side. Your wolf possesses the answer to your query." Her father turned to her. Power flared from his hands and the stone illusion began breaking into motes of nothingness. "Once you're inside, the only way you'll leave is if the others let you. Just so you're clear about that."

"They'd kill their own?" She shuffled from foot to foot, trying to move blood into toes that felt like blocks of ice.

"No. But they don't include you in that group. You could still escape a confrontation with the ones within." Compulsion wove into his words, subtle but noticeable. She felt herself weakening and longed for her wolf's warm fur and weatherproof paws.

"Tell me where the vampires are, daughter. It's all I require."

His last words broke through her vacillation. She stood tall, shoulders squared. Even though she was a few inches shorter than her father, she skewered him with fury. "I required a lot of things from you, and you didn't deliver a one of them. Why the fuck should I accommodate you? Finish the spell. Open the door. We're doing this my way, or not at all."

"As you will. Don't say I didn't warn you if things go badly once you're inside."

She curled her lips back from her teeth, mimicking the wolf's snarl. "I get it. You abandoned me once. Easier a second time. I know exactly where your allegiance lies, *Father*, and it's not with me."

"Was that truly necessary?"

"Yes. Take care of the goddamned door."

"*I can do that,*" the wolf said. "*Open your mind to me.*"

"Not necessary." Jamal chanted a few words in Gaelic, and the remains of the illusory cliff fell away.

Good thing to know that their spell language was different from what the Romani used. Even better, her Gaelic was passable since she'd spent long hours with Stewart, letting him teach her the lyrical tongue.

"*Let's go,*" the wolf urged. "*If the tide turns against us, follow my lead.*"

If the tide turned against them, they'd be dead. At least according to her poor excuse for a father. She considered asking the wolf what it had in mind, but it might be better if she didn't know. What wasn't front and center in her mind couldn't be stripped from it.

Her stomach twisted from tension, and the sour taste of adrenaline flooded her mouth. She pushed it all aside. Shifters could smell her fear, and she'd be damned if she'd go into a room full of the bastards in a one down position.

CHAPTER 10

*E*lliott was tucking several books into his saddlebags when Michael, Stewart, Valentin, Alex, and several others rode into the circle of wagons. It was closing on nine in the evening. At first, he ignored them, planning to ride for the grotto, but that was his pride talking. His resentment at how rude they'd been to Tairin. He reminded himself they were all in this together, and people in tight spots often said and did things that were self-defeating.

It would be wise of him not to join that particular herd. The one that reacted rather than thinking things through. Smarter to shove his feelings to a place where they didn't color his actions. Latching the saddlebags, he made his way to Michael and Stewart. "We need two plans," he said, not bothering with a greeting. "One that includes shifters and one that doesn't."

"Agreed." Michael nodded tiredly. "And we must be ready to deploy one or the other as soon as we know if Tairin's shifters will lend their magic."

"'Twon't be easy fighting side by side with shifters. Most Rom consider them enemies, same as they view Nazis," Stewart muttered.

199

"Yeah, well, I'm sure shifters feel the same way about us," Elliott said. "In truth, they don't need us as much as we need them."

"They may be stronger than we are magically, but even a group of shifters might not have enough power to take on a nest of vampires." Valentin joined them, seemingly recovered from his earlier snit.

"I was going to return to my grotto to read—" Elliott glanced around the group "—but maybe I'll remain here for a while. When I was deciding which of the lore books to take, I came across an interesting section."

"What was in it?" Michael sounded intrigued.

"Not sure. I didn't give it much time beyond chapter headings, but it seemed to address commingled power and how it's stronger than any of its individual components." He paused, thinking. "Tairin is living proof of that. Her magic is potent. I have no way to compare it to shifter power, but she's far stronger than any Romani."

"Go get the book," Stewart said. "I'll put a kettle on. We'll brew tea with whiskey and puzzle through it."

Elliott dug through his saddlebags until he found the volume he wanted. Its cracked, leather binding revealed its age. They were one of the only caravans that still kept lore books, mostly because the ability to read Coptic had declined among their folk. By the time he walked up the steps and into Michael's wagon, the men had started on Stewart's tea and whiskey concoction.

Elliott settled in a corner and opened the book on his lap, thumbing through its dog-eared pages. Someone thrust a glass into his hand, and he sipped as he read. Fortunately, the arcane form of Coptic took all his attention, otherwise his thoughts would've strayed to Tairin. Where she was. How she was doing. Most importantly, if she were safe.

Her wolf would do its best, but if a pack of shifters turned on them… Elliott dragged his full attention back to the lore book. He was too far away to help. What he should have done was insist on coming with her.

Why hadn't he?

When the answer came, embarrassment filled him. He wasn't fond of shifters, and his presence might've tipped the tables against the other magical creatures aiding them. He could shield his thoughts, but maybe not well enough to fool a roomful of shifters, who'd all have been focused on him.

Tairin was a shifter. Loving her meant he needed an attitude adjustment. And damned fast.

"Ye're daydreaming." Stewart's voice broke into Elliott's thoughts.

He glanced at the canny old Scott. "Indeed I was."

"What did you find?" Michael moved next to Elliott, scanning the open pages.

"Unfortunately, nothing concrete. The lore includes vague allusions to combined power being stronger, but it also mentions the age-old antipathy between Romani and every other magic wielder out there." Elliott frowned. "When did we become so insular and stop trusting everyone?"

Michael shrugged. "Probably when vampires, shifters, faeries, and mages drove us out of Egypt."

"The antagonism between us and the rest of our magical kin predates that by a long time," Valentin said. "They hated us long before Egypt, and the feeling was mutual."

"History is fascinating, but not particularly relevant," Michael cut in.

"Agreed." Elliott glanced at the men packed into the small space. "Did you change your minds about tackling the vampires by ourselves?"

Color rose from the neck of Michael's shirt. "Yes. Walking away was never the right path. Listening to Tairin—a woman— say 'desperate times require desperate solutions. Even if you refuse to help, I'm betting shifters will take on the vampires,' was quite a wakeup call for the rest of us."

"'Twill take a lot of us," Stewart cut in. "Sixty to be precise. Five for each vampire. We will attack simultaneously. One Rom will leverage magic while three hold the vampire down with more magic. The last man drives a silver stake through its heart."

Elliott's eyes widened. It was a bold plan. One requiring split-second timing and absolute dedication. If even one Romani got cold feet, he'd put the entire group in mortal danger.

"So we can do this without the shifters," he said, not quite believing the others' assessment.

"Maybe," Michael replied. "If we tap five men from each caravan, at least our losses will be spread evenly—if things go against us."

"How can we protect ourselves from becoming immobilized—like I was? And they didn't even know Tairin and I were there."

Stewart reached over and plucked the book out of Elliott's lap. "There should be amulets we can craft to stymie their power." He glanced at the book's spine and said, "Aye, this one's as good a choice as any other."

Stewart turned a few pages and nodded. "'Tis right here. If we mix garlic paste and holy water and tie them into a leather pouch that also contains rosary beads, a crucifix, and consecrated earth, we should be safe enough. At least for a short time. And this willna be a battle that lasts overlong."

"But we're hardly Christian," Elliott protested. "Where will we get holy water and rosary beads and consecrated earth? Let alone sixty crucifixes."

"We could steal them from a church," Keenan spoke up. "Probably several churches."

"Wouldn't stealing negate their 'holy' quality?" Elliott asked, and then added, "Don't bother to answer that. It goes against the grain, but we need to find a priest, tell him why we need religious items, and hope to hell he decides to provide them. At least that way, we'll have a man of the cloth to bless the consecrated earth and holy water."

"Mayhap more than one priest," Stewart said. "Since we need enough to outfit sixty men."

Michael clapped his hands together, and the buzz of side conversations quieted. "Elliott will approach the Catholic Church near the center of town. The big one. I'll go to the Anglican Church nearby. Their priests live there, and hopefully haven't retired for the night quite yet. Regardless of what the shifters decide, we'll need those amulets. While we're about securing materials, the rest of you return to your caravans and select four other men to join us. Return here by midmorning tomorrow. If the goddess is good to us, we'll have what we need to craft an amulet for each man. Shouldn't take too long. We'll bind everything with magic."

Elliott rose. "Once I'm done with those tasks, I'm going to the place Tairin agreed to meet me. And I'll remain there until she shows up."

"What if she doesn't?" Michael's gaze augured into him.

"Then I'll hunt for her." Before his caravan leader could protest, Elliott added, "You'd best have someone besides me selected among your four—in case I'm not back in time. If Tairin doesn't return, it means the other side of her bloodlines turned on her. She risked herself for us, and I won't rest until I find her."

He crawled over the others and let himself outside. Michael hadn't argued, but maybe that was because he recognized Elliott wasn't about to capitulate. The roar of planes flying low spooked the horses, and he sent calming magic into their minds. It also decided how he'd get to the huge, old Catholic Church in downtown Munich. After making certain Flame had feed and water, he dragged an old bicycle out from beneath a storage wagon and pedaled into town. It wasn't far, but he couldn't fire his mage light. Not where humans might notice.

Without the books to divert his attention, he worried about

Tairin and sent prayers to whatever deities might be listening, asking them to keep her safe. Did shifters have their own gods? He had no idea, but from now on, he vowed to accept them as brothers. The war with them would stop with him. They had a common enemy in the Reich and their vampire sidekicks. Every single being with magic would do well to remember it.

~

TAIRIN'S FEET stung as blood returned to them. The passageway was warmer—and much longer—than the one in the other shelter. Jamal had remained silent after his warning, and she'd considered it a blessing since her ability to be civil to him was in serious decline.

Shadows flared on the tunnel's walls, and she scented a fire burning. Rather than a room off the tunnel, this one opened into a large, circular chamber with a fire pit in its center. Men crouched around the fire, dressed similarly to her father in formfitting leather garments. Some had long, full beards.

A vulture winged its way from the chamber's dim recesses, cawing. Tairin recognized shifter magic and gazed at the bird. She hadn't seen any other shifters since fleeing Egypt. None she'd recognized as such, anyway.

"Meara!" One of the men shot to his feet and shook a fist at the vulture. "You were to remain hidden." Tall and lanky, the man's coppery hair was chopped unevenly to shoulder length. His hazel eyes radiated censure.

The bird snapped its beak in his direction and continued straight for Tairin. Midflight, shifter magic simmered with the scents of new mown hay and wild rosemary, and the bird sparkled into a woman with long, gray hair. She executed a graceful somersault and landed on her feet right in front of Tairin. Her hair cloaked her nakedness, trailing on the room's wooden planked floor. Shrewd amber eyes examined Tairin from head to toe, digging into her soul.

"I was expecting you," Meara said in a low, melodious voice. Power spilled from her in bright, multihued waves, and something ancient surrounded her aura.

"Glad someone anticipated my arrival—besides my father," Tairin muttered. "Are you a seer?"

The man who'd shaken his fist at Meara stalked toward them. "I told you not to interfere with what Jamal brought back to us. We planned for information, though, not his half breed daughter in the flesh." Derision added an unpleasant twang to his words, and he looked pointedly at Tairin and sneered.

She girded herself for a battle that would likely mean her death, but her wolf said, *"Hold. Don't be hasty. The vulture was one of the first shifters. Her presence is significant."*

Interesting information, but Tairin remained vigilant. Just because the bird shifter was old didn't mean she'd be any more kindly disposed to a Romani than any of the rest of her kind.

With an oddly avian gesture, Meara angled her neck to regard the man who was closing on them. "You lack power or authority to order me about. I am your prophet. As such, I decide what I will—or will not—do." She raised a hand, and the man stopped in his tracks, his face working with disbelief and fury.

"You offer us a call to arms." Meara addressed her words to Tairin.

"Yes. More than that, though. My offer entails fighting a common enemy with the Romani."

"Aye." Meara cackled softly. "Vampires. I saw them in my glass too."

"Did you see if we won?" Tairin asked.

A low hissing rattled from between Meara's teeth. "Such is not for anyone but me to know. I forgive your question this once because you do not know our customs."

"So I can't ask you anything?" Frustration soured Tairin's stomach further. Perhaps Meara wasn't quite the ally she'd appeared at first. Tairin rocked from foot to foot. Feeling had returned to them, and the rough planked floor was studded with splinters.

"Trust that I will provide what information you need. Hold still, child." Meara shuffled closer and placed a hand on either side of Tairin's head.

She steeled herself. Was the ancient seer about to send a killing blast of magic through her skull?

Meara cackled again. "If I wanted to murder you, I'd scarcely require proximity. I wish to sort through the years of your life."

Heat flashed through Tairin, prickly and uncomfortable, but not to the point of pain. Her wolf preened under the attention, whuffling inside her. The sensation ceased abruptly, and Tairin resisted an impulse to shake her head. The shifter had taken her measure. No more. No less. She stared into Meara's amber eyes, noticing they had bottomless pupils. "Did I pass inspection?" she asked.

The corners of Meara's mouth twitched, but stopped before curving into a smile. "Now that's the sort of question I will answer. Yes. You have courage and have grown into a woman we shall include in our ranks. No more Romani caravans for you."

"Wait a minute. I get a choice in this, right?"

"Why would you desire one? We are superior to them magically—and in every other way as well."

Tairin bit hard on her lower lip. She wanted to argue, but it would be a waste of time. Besides, it was hard to defend a culture that had lashed her mother to a bier and set fire to it. She squared her shoulders. "Will you help the Romani defeat the vampires? It's the reason I came. To secure help." She hurried on. "Vampires are strengthening the Reich. We cannot let them win. If they do, magic will die out of the world."

"While I agree with your conclusion, the nest you stumbled on are hardly the only vampires in all of Germany."

Meara's words were quiet, but Tairin felt naïve, young. She'd underestimated their opponent, but that wasn't a reason not to press forward. "Probably not. But if we come up with a way to deal with the ones we know about, when the next nest shows up, we'll have a method in place." An idea blossomed, and she ran with it. "The more of us who know how to dispatch vampires, the better the odds we can defeat them. Make certain they can't help the Nazis anymore."

Meara did smile then, but it held bitter edges. "You're determined for us to join forces with the Romani. Why?"

Tairin dug deep. "Maybe because I hold both bloodlines, and so long as you're at war with one another, there will always be a part of me that feels offensive, unclean."

"That was a good answer. Wait there." Light flashed around Meara, and she materialized in front of Jamal. "Why did you bring your daughter into our midst today?"

Her father, who'd sank to a crouch next to the fire pit, scrambled to stand in Meara's presence. "Because she wouldn't reveal where the nest was any other way."

"Why did you abandon her as a child? Nay, back up a few years. Why did you mate with someone forbidden in the first place?"

Color stained his cheeks, visible even in the room's dim light. "I tried to stay away from Aneksi, but I loved her. Would have taken her away from both our people, but she refused to leave her caravan. Her parents were old, ill. She was their caretaker." Jamal spread his hands before him. "If I had it to do over, I'd have taken them all into the hills. I'd found an oasis where we—"

"Enough. What would you do to correct a very old wrong?"

Jamal continued to stare at his feet. "I'm not certain what you mean."

"It's a simple enough question."

"Maybe so, but with you, nothing is ever simple. You're testing me."

Meara nodded. "Aye. Have you learned anything these past two hundred years?"

Jamal looked past her to where Tairin stood, watching. "I'm not certain quite what I've learned, but I want to find a way to honor my daughter's request to aid the Romani who took her in when I forsook her. It's the only thing she's ever asked of me since I closed my door on her long ago."

Something hitched painfully in Tairin's chest, and her throat thickened with emotion. She'd misjudged Jamal. He'd been icy and abrupt to dissuade her from entering a circle of his kin where he wouldn't be able to protect her if things went sideways.

"We will never fight alongside Romani." The man who'd rebuked Meara jutted his chin defiantly.

"Never is a long time," Meara observed, her tone devoid of inflection. "And *we* is a big word. You can speak for yourself, but not for others."

"But I lead this pack," he sputtered. "The wolves who are part of this gathering answer to me."

"Pah. I outrank all of you. Once all magic wielders—except vampires—viewed themselves as allies. We have moved into an era where that must happen again. All things come full circle, and this is no exception. The Reich is our common enemy. Not the Romani. Or witches. Or Druids. Or any odd mages practicing their craft independently." She swung in a circle, eying the collection of men scattered about the room. "Do any of you disagree with me? If so, you may leave now. I will sever your connections with your pack, and you will become a pariah to our people. Rather like Tairin has been all these years."

"Y—You don't have to do that," Tairin stammered.

"I never act unless it is in the interests of all my people," Meara informed her.

None of the men moved. Even the pack leader shuffled to a corner and hunkered next to a wall. Resentment streamed from him, but living with it was apparently preferable to becoming a lone wolf.

Jamal moved to Tairin's side. "How many of us were you hoping would assist your Romani family?"

"I hadn't exactly gotten that far. Maybe two dozen. Two shifters plus several Romani could target each vampire."

Meara glided to them. "Are you confident the Romani will welcome us?"

"No." Tairin swallowed hard. "One will. Maybe two for certain. The rest I don't know."

Meara's thin lips stretched into a genuine smile. "I've always appreciated honesty. Shall we find out just how many Romani will embrace our aid?"

"I'd like that. Thank you." Tairin extended a hand.

After a hesitation, Meara grasped it. "Not one of our customs, but I recognize it as important to you. Where is this caravan of yours?"

"There's a well-hidden spot where I'm to meet one of the Romani who believes in me. I can travel in my animal form more easily if I wait until nightfall. You could all shift and run with me —or fly."

"The rest of us will want our clothes—and our human bodies —if we're to sit and parlay with a group of Romani," Jamal said. "Describe where we're to meet. Each of us will get there in our own way."

She didn't have to say very much before most of the shifters recognized the ruined castle and left the room in small groups. The wolves' pack leader slunk past her, keeping as much distance between them as he could.

"Would you like to rest for a few hours?" Meara asked her. "I know where the castle is, and you must've run most of the night to get here."

Tairin was tired—and hungry. "Is there anything to eat? Or maybe I could shift and hunt."

"I have food. Return with me, and I'll watch over you until nightfall makes it safe for you to return," Jamal said.

"Shift and run with her," Meara said, her words an order. "Perhaps one of the Rom will take pity on you and loan you a shirt and trousers after you arrive."

"If they don't, it's scarcely the end of the world. I'll make certain no harm befalls Tairin on her way back to the Romani." Jamal started toward the false cliff.

Before Tairin followed her father, she turned toward Meara. "Will you meet with the Romani too?"

"You asked me that for a reason. What is it?"

"I have a…friend. He's seer to the Romani. You two might have a lot of common ground."

Meara's eyes crinkled knowingly. "Somehow I sense he's more than a friend. Yes, I will be there. I've hated vampires for millennia. Wouldn't miss this opportunity for the world. Now hurry along and get some rest."

"Does that mean you'll fight too?" Tairin asked.

"Indeed, it does. Why would you even ask?"

"Fath— I mean Jamal said shifter females don't take part in battles."

"Generally, that would be true, but I'm one of the first shifters. I do what I please. No man directs my actions." Power streamed from Meara, cloaking her in a swirl of color.

Tairin inclined her head. "I came prepared not to like any shifter, but I respect you."

"The feeling is mutual, child. Now go."

Deep within, her wolf howled its happiness. Tairin felt like dropping to her knees and howling right along with it. Today had come out so much better than she'd hoped, she still couldn't believe something awful wasn't waiting in the wings to nab her.

Vampires are waiting, she reminded herself. *They're about as wicked as things get.*

Jamal stood outside the false cliff face. "Would you like me to carry you? The ground is frozen."

"It's kind of you to offer, but I can walk. You were right about it not being far. It didn't take all that long for my toes to thaw out. After a while, the wooden floor was almost worse than cold dirt because of all the splinters."

He shot her a solemn look. "You have strength. I'm not responsible for any of it, but I admire what you've become."

The words rang sweetly within her. She walked by her father's side, curious to know more about him. About how he'd spent the years they'd been apart.

No rush. We'll have time.

She shut her eyes for a moment, willing her thoughts to be true.

"No matter how much time we have," Jamal's deep voice rumbled, "I'm grateful for a chance to repair the chasm I created between us. Sorry for gleaning your thoughts, but I want to know everything about you, so I'm cheating. I'll stay out of your mind if my presence there offends you." He glanced away.

"It's all right. I want to know more about you too. Mother never would tell me much except that business called you away a lot. She finally admitted what you were not long before they dragged her off to burn her."

"You'd shifted by then, so you must have figured that out on your own."

"Yes. Me shifting was how the Rom found out. And why they burned Mother. It was a hell of a price. I felt responsible for her death. Then when I went to your people—" Her voice broke and she willed herself not to cry. Not over centuries-old pain.

"Yes. I know what happened then. I've had a long time to replay that day, even though I didn't find out about it until months later." They reached the cliff and Jamal said, "You open it this time. Repeat after me. That way shifter shelters will show themselves to you when you have need of them."

Tairin was grateful for something else to focus on. Magic flowed through her, and the gateway formed. She walked through with Jamal behind her. "Do me a favor," she said without glancing back.

"Anything, as long as it's within my power."

"For the rest of today, teach me shifter lore. I can't focus on the past. It's too distracting."

"I understand. Let me get you something to eat. Bread and cheese and wine. I'll tell you about the first shifters. Your wolf knows, but you would have had to ask it. Just like you're asking me."

She curled onto the sofa, tucking her cold feet beneath her, half-dozing in the warm room. Jamal placed a plate of food next to her and moved one of the chairs close.

"Shifters date to the making of the world," he began. "Meara was one of the first. She flew out of heat and light when this world spun out of the sun…"

*E*lliott glanced at his watch again. It was almost midnight. An assortment of shifters had begun arriving several hours before, and they were still showing up in groups of twos and threes. He'd asked the first ones about Tairin, and they'd reassured him she'd be along. She had to shift, whereas they'd traveled as humans. Unlike the Romani, they'd made a full transition to motorized vehicles. Some rode motorcycles, but most came in an assortment of cars and trucks. The courtyard where he kept Flame was quite crowded. Enough so, he hoped all the vehicles didn't draw unwanted attention from the Reich.

Driving after curfew was an offense punishable by internment in a prison camp, but none of the shifters appeared concerned. Perhaps they had ways of shielding their vehicles with magic. He would have asked, but the presence of so many of those he'd heretofore considered enemies was unsettling.

He'd accepted their explanations about Tairin, but enough time had elapsed he was growing concerned. Had the shifters done something to her? He thought it through, and it didn't make sense. If they'd killed her, then why bother to show up in his grotto? He considered, and then discarded, summoning a vision to track her. His last attempt at scrying had gone horribly awry, and he didn't want to give the shifters reason to see him as incompetent. Besides, the level of concentration he'd need wasn't possible with so many shifters milling about, moving in and out of his room as they wandered from the passageway to the courtyard and back inside.

In truth, that many Rom would have interrupted his ability to concentrate too.

All of them had said the same thing, even a grumpy, dour wolf shifter. Tairin was with her father and someone named Meara, and all three would arrive as soon as they could.

A different brand of shifter energy buffeted his raw nerve endings. The swoosh of wings announced an enormous black and gray vulture. It flew through the doorway and landed on his shoulder, its talons cutting deep.

"You must be the one," the newcomer said in mind speech. Lidless, amber eyes regarded him intently.

"I'm afraid you need to say a bit more than that," Elliott replied in kind.

The bird nipped his ear with its beak. *"You're supposed to be a seer. What kind of seer requires information about future events?"*

"The kind who hasn't had sufficient privacy to cast any sort of spell for the last several hours." He hurried on before the shifter could chide him further. *"Do you know where Tairin is?"*

"Who am I?" The bird didn't answer his question, instead asking one of its own.

Elliott pushed outward with magic, seeking information about the bird still perched on his shoulder. Talons flexed hard enough blood trickled down his chest. Images filled his mind, and he sorted through them.

"You're old," he ventured. *"Maybe as old as the earth. Your human form is female. You're the prophet for your people."* He rammed his power forward, but ran into an impenetrable wall. *"That's all you'll let me see."*

The vulture clacked its beak together. Light so bright Elliott had to shut his eyes surrounded them, and magic rose, pungent with the scent of clay baked under a sun far hotter than it ever shone in Germany. Herbs mingled with the clay smell, rosemary and fresh cut hay. When the light faded, a woman as tall as himself stood before him. Gray hair shrouded her from the crown of her head to her feet, and she was thin to the point of emaciation. Her eyes were the same warm amber as the vulture's, with ringed, avian pupils.

The other shifters left the room. Had she ordered them out? Or did her people find her as intimidating as he did?

"You must be who the others call Meara," Elliott said. "No other women here."

"I am. What you couldn't puzzle through with magic, you solved by deductive logic. I would have your name in return."

Heat rose to his face. "Sorry. I'm Elliott Brend, and I am seer for the Romani caravans in Germany." He bowed formally.

Meara bowed back. When she straightened, she said, "Are the Romani prepared to join us in battle?"

"At the point I left the group, the answer to that was yes. But we've gone back and forth, nor are all of us of one mind—except regarding the necessity of dealing with the vampires, so they can't add any more of their insidious strength to the Reich."

"Good that you're honest with me." Her nostrils flared. She reached a long-nailed index finger forward and plucked his amulet out from beneath his shirt. It hung from a length of leather, ripe with the smells of garlic and freshly turned earth. "This is newly made."

It wasn't a question, so he nodded. "We crafted three for each of our groups. It won't stop a vampire, but we're hoping for some small level of protection from their mind control power. Originally, we'd planned on an amulet for each of us, but it takes time to create some of the ingredients, so we went with what we had."

Meara narrowed her eyes to slits and let the amulet drop back against his chest. "Holy water, consecrated earth, rosary beads, and bits of a crucifix all mixed with garlic. Where the hell did you get such items? You're not any more Christian than we are."

"Where else? From a church. The clergy aren't kindly disposed toward vampires or anything wicked. Only difference between holy men and most humans is they believe in evil, so it didn't take much talking to convince a couple of priests we needed their help."

"But you're Romani." The word rolling off her tongue sounded like a curse. "I'd have expected you to steal what you needed."

The Rom did have a long, colorful history as thieves, and her statement was too close to true for him to be offended. "We considered it, but the thing about holy water and consecrated earth is they require a priest's blessing. We had no idea if you'd help us, so we concocted a plan on our own. It entailed sixty of us, five for each vampire. The amulets were an important part of buying us enough time to stake the vampires."

"Can you make more of those things?"

Her question took him by surprise. "The amulets? Shifters would wear something crafted with Romani magic?"

"If it keeps us safer, of course." Meara drew herself straight. "In the old days, all of us worked together—except vampires. We must close ranks again—lay our differences aside—or all of us will perish. I've seen it in my glass."

Elliott tried to stop himself, but words blurted out. "Last time I looked toward the future, I raised a demon. Tried to send him back to Hell, but he was too strong. I haven't scryed since then, but I've spent time with our lore books, and they all say much the same as you just did. They also suggested that our combined power is stronger than either of us working alone. Is that true?"

"Yes and no. If the combination 'takes' we become stronger. Tairin is an example of that. But some combinations don't work nearly that well—or at all. It seems related more to an individual's magical vibrations, not what type of magic wielder they are."

Elliott thought about it. "When we pair up to fight the vampires, we'll have to be careful we don't pair any of the Romani with shifters whose energies aren't compatible."

"Aye. You've got a quick mind. You asked about Tairin. She and Jamal will be here soon. I feel them closing on us. If you were to look, I imagine you'd sense the same thing."

Hope raged through him like an out of control wildfire, and he sent magic skimming outward. Tairin was indeed near, and he wanted to run past Meara to meet her.

"The woman you love will be here soon enough. You and I aren't yet done, and you will remain until we are." Meara had clearly intuited his thoughts about intercepting Tairin. Probably not much of a feat, given the power cloaking her in multicolored light.

"What else do we need to cover?"

"Do you have materials for two dozen more amulets? I actually agree with your first plan, the one that included one for each person fighting the vampires."

Elliott thought about it. "Probably not, but I was the one who approached the Catholic priest—actually he was a Bishop. He said if I needed more, to let him know."

"Excellent. It saves time if we don't have to figure out how to get our hands on such things. We will remain here. A sorcerer once lived in this castle, and bits of his energy remain. Enough to keep us safe from prying eyes. Vampires are strongest at night. We will attack day after tomorrow midday."

Elliott wasn't at all certain they'd be ready by then, but he wasn't about to contradict her. "This blending of energies. Can you tell which of us will pair well with a particular shifter?"

"Of course. Once the amulets are ready, all the Romani who will be part of this mission will congregate here. We will divide into our twelve groups, move into position, and finish off that nest. Once we're done, we'll have to burn the remains. There may not be much, depending on how old these vampires are. I have yet to figure how to finesse that part because no magic known to me will mask that amount of smoke."

"What did you mean about not being much left? I know very little about vampires, and our lore books said nothing about burning them, although that makes good sense."

Meara pursed her lips into a straight line. "When a vampire dies, its body reverts to its actual age. If we kill one that's several centuries old, its corporeal form will shatter into a heap of decomposing bones."

"Fascinating. Not much to burn there."

She angled her head to one side. "No. But the odds of all twelve vampires being that old are very thin. Usually there are one or two old ones and an assortment of others that they've turned to create their pod or nest."

"Assuming we prevail during this current battle, I'd like to know more."

"I'm not going anywhere. All you have to do is ask me."

"Thank you. Returning to practical matters, do you agree with one group of us targeting each vampire?" At her nod, he asked another question. "How many Romani in each group? Absent your help, we'd settled on five."

"Three will do it, and two of us. So thirty-six of your people and twenty-four of mine. Plus me."

He almost asked what she'd be doing, but it felt disrespectful, so he held his tongue. "Should a few extra Rom show up? In case the energies don't blend well?"

Meara drew her gray eyebrows together in concentration. "Wouldn't hurt. Although I should have been clearer. It's rare for there to be such a mismatch of magics, people can't work together for short periods of time."

Tairin's wolf loped into the room accompanied by another, larger black and gray timber wolf that was probably her father.

Elliott dropped to his knees holding out his arms. It wasn't dignified, but he didn't care. Joy and relief washed through him in waves. Tairin ran into his arms, and he buried his hands in her rough pelt, breathing in her clean, animal scent.

"I'm so grateful you're here," he murmured. "I was getting worried."

"Happy to see you too." She leaned into him and licked his nose.

"I want to hear everything, but it can wait. Is that your father with you? Your differences, did you…" Elliott wasn't sure how to phrase things.

Tairin saved him the trouble. *"I'm not angry anymore. The goddess granted us a second chance to be family, and we're taking advantage of it."*

Meara had joined the other wolf. Power shimmered about them, so they must be conversing.

Tairin wriggled out of his arms and bounded to where he'd folded her clothing in a corner of the room. The air around her turned first bright then dark, shielding her from his vision. When it cleared, she was kneeling to lace her boots.

He hid a smile. She'd had the ability to cloak herself all along, yet she'd shown him her body in the grove of trees. Her trust warmed him to his toes. Another flash of power drew his attention to the other wolf. It had transformed into a tall, naked man with Tairin's chestnut-brown hair and dark eyes.

Elliott strode to him and held out a hand. The other man grasped it. "I am Jamal Jabari."

"Elliott Brend. Nice to meet you, sir."

Jamal snorted. "You can drop the sir part. I scarcely deserve it, and we're equals. Sir is reserved for those you consider above your station. Any chance of something I can cover myself with?"

"As a matter of fact, yes. I always keep clothing here. We're close enough to the same size, my things should fit." He pointed to a carved, wooden chest sitting against the wall. "There are magic accoutrements in there, but dig beneath them and take what you need. The only thing I don't have extra of is shoes, but I can correct that when I return to the caravan."

Tairin made her way to Meara. "Would you like me to find you a cloak or a robe and something for your feet?"

"Thank you, child, but no. I haven't worn clothing in a very long time." She turned her attention to Elliott. "Return to the Rom. Tell them we await them. Construct the amulets and return here by this time tomorrow night with those willing to work side-by-side with us to defeat the vampires. I will use the time between now and then to coach my people—and capture the demon you set free. We cannot let it remain on this side of Hell. Its wickedness could lay waste to our efforts."

So that's why I told her about it. He recalled the words he'd tried to hold inside that had streamed out anyway.

"By rights dealing with the demon should be my job," Elliott protested, guilt vying with determination. "I created the problem. I should be the one to take care of it."

"Admirable sentiments, but your time is better spent gathering your people and creating more of the protective talismans. Besides, if your power were enough to defeat that brand of evil, it would already be back in Hell."

"What demon?" Jamal had donned dark trousers and a black sweater. He raised an inquisitive brow, sounding interested.

"From the feel of things in this room—" Meara focused her unnerving gaze on Elliott "—my guess would be Ba'al or Grigori. The thing got away from you here, correct?"

"Yes."

"Jamal and I will create a drawing spell. It will be easy enough to lure it back to its entry point." She dusted her hands together.

"There's enough time for me to help," Elliott insisted. "At the least, I can add power to your working."

"This isn't up for debate." Meara shot a sidelong glance his way and folded her arms across her chest.

"I'm going with Elliott when he returns to the caravan," Tairin said sounding fierce and protective.

"Of course you are." Meara laughed. "I can do many things

with my power, but I know better than to stand in the way of love. Final plans to address the vampire problem will have to wait until all of us are together."

Tairin looped an arm beneath Elliott's and tugged. "Best go before she changes her mind."

"Be safe. Tell the others to remain outside until we call them. We don't need any distractions until we've dispatched the demon." Jamal turned back toward Meara, and the two of them lapsed into Gaelic.

Elliott walked out of the room and through the tunnel with Tairin by his side. They shooed the few shifters in the passageway into the courtyard, and he dismantled the magic holding Flame in place.

"Why don't you use a car?" one of the shifters asked, sounding more curious than hostile.

Elliott shrugged. "We've stuck with our old customs, most of them anyway. Horses and wagons are how the Romani have always traveled."

The shifter inclined his head. "That's a good horse. Most of them hate us."

"He wasn't any too fond of me the first time he met me as a wolf," Tairin said, "but he's fine with me as a human."

She clambered into the saddle, and Elliott vaulted up behind her. He reached around, ostensibly to take the reins, but mostly he wanted to feel her pressed against him.

Tairin relaxed into his embrace, and they set off for the caravan at a trot, keeping to shadowed byways. Curfew was curfew. It might be easier to hide a horse than a car, but the consequences of being caught were the same.

"What happened with the Rom while I was gone?" she asked.

"They changed their minds about taking on the vampires." Elliott chuckled. "You shamed them, made them see their duty."

Breath rattled from her in a hissing sigh. "We have so many problems. That thing we did in Dachau, we should be planning more stealth attacks just like it. Not only in that prison camp, but all of them. Instead, we got sidetracked by vampires. Not that they aren't important, but everything else is too."

"I believe some of the Rom will continue to fight with us, once we finish off the nest."

Tairin angled her head back to look at him. "*If* we finish off the nest. The outcome is scarcely certain, although Meara knows what will happen."

"Are you going to tell me?"

"I would if I knew. That knowledge is hers and hers alone, but she's planning on being part of the attack, so maybe that bodes well for us. Gods but I hope things go well. Romani aren't warriors. You said the Rom might take part in guerrilla warfare against the Reich, but I have my doubts."

"Your Rom blood doesn't get in the way of you being a capable fighter." Elliott tightened his arms around her.

"Yes, but I've had a long time to get used to blending my two disparate sides. And I've had help. Those first hundred years when we lived as wolves, if it hadn't been for my wolf, I'd have lost my mind. I was so lonely I couldn't stop howling. It used to croon to me at night, lull me to sleep. And it watched over us while I rested."

Elliott's heart ached for what she'd lived through. His life hadn't been easy after his parents were murdered, but he'd been surrounded by loving, caring folk in the caravan. After a while, they stood in for the family he'd lost.

"You'll never be alone again." Fierce protectiveness raged through him.

"Neither will you." She threaded her arms around his and hung on tight. "Once we get to the caravan, we're picking who'll be part of this undertaking, right?"

"Not exactly. They'll already have been selected by their caravan leaders. The thing that will take time is making amulets for the shifters." The sound of an approaching truck drove him down a deserted alleyway, but he kept moving. Chances of the vehicle following them were nil since they hadn't been spotted.

"If I'd been more on top of my game," he went on, "I'd have returned to the Bishop so he could make more holy water and consecrated earth, but it never occurred to me a shifter would wear anything crafted with Romani power."

"So there's not enough of whatever's in yours left to create a few more? I can smell it, but a human probably couldn't."

"Any human could smell the garlic if I hadn't masked it with magic. To answer your question, no I don't have more materials. I'll have to go back to the church."

A shudder ran down her back. "Maybe I'll skip that part."

"What?" he teased. "You announced you were going with me. Crucifixes don't go down well?"

"None of it goes down well. Every church considers me an abomination. They've burned us, hung us, and clapped us in irons."

"Yeah, they're not fond of the Romani, either, but their antipathy for us probably doesn't run as hot or as deep." He guided the stallion around several more corners until the group of wagons came into view.

Flame whickered happily at the prospect of his feed bucket and visiting with the other horses. Once they came to the line of hobbled mounts, Elliott jumped down. Tairin tossed a leg over the horse and slipped to the ground. Elliott scooped feed from a barrel and set it in front of the horse, along with a full water bucket.

"Aren't you taking the horse to the church?" she asked.

"No. I'll ride a bicycle, but it's the middle of the night. I'll go early in the morning. Right after matins. The priest was generous. I'll not abuse his kindness by waking him."

Tairin wrapped her arms around him, and he hugged her back. Her face was reflected in moonlight, all exotic angles and delicate lines. He traced the edge of one cheekbone. "You're so lovely. I could look at you forever."

Her lips parted in a soft smile. "You're quite a knockout yourself." She brushed her thumb over his lower lip, and his cock hardened, pressing against her belly.

He'd bent his head, intent on kissing her, when footsteps closed from behind them. "Thought I heard something out here," Michael said, still moving toward them. "Glad you're back. Both of you. Come into my wagon. The elders are gathered. We need to know if the shift—" Michael must have remembered they weren't out of everyone's earshot. "Come inside," he repeated, his voice gruff, and turned back the way he'd come.

Elliott stepped away from Tairin, but took hold of her hand. *"We'll find time for us later,"* he said into her mind.

"Now is for battle," her wolf replied. *"If we do well in battle, all else will follow."*

Tairin gripped his hand tighter and muttered, "Shifters are nothing if not warriors."

"And lovers," the wolf said, sounding smug.

"What are the lot of you nattering about?" Michael turned to face them. Before Elliott could answer, he went on, "From now until we're done with the task before us, that will be all any of us focus on. Tairin will report on what happened with her journey. If you have something to add to her story, do it. Once that's done, the two of you will go to your wagons for what's left of tonight. Separate wagons. Do I make myself clear?"

He lowered his voice to the barest whisper. "I do not want anyone deciding the two of you sleeping together will jinx our efforts. Romani won't trust shifters in the span of an eye blink, nor will they stop believing mating with one brings curses from the gods."

"Got it." Elliott spoke stiffly. Michael's assessment made sense, but it also drove home just how unwelcome he and Tairin would be in Romani circles.

"It's all right," Tairin said into his mind. *"Being unwelcome is a big step up from hiding what I am."*

Admiration for the levelheaded woman standing by his side made his heart swell with longing. *"I love you."*

"The feeling is mutual."

Michael stopped outside his wagon. "Valentin settled down," he said, keeping his voice to a whisper. "I hope to hell seeing you again—" he eyed Tairin "—doesn't set him off."

"I'll make certain it doesn't." The scent of her magic, musk and wooded glens, rose around them.

Elliott recognized a calming spell, designed to charm even the most reluctant of critics. Tairin followed Michael up the steps and into his wagon. Elliott trailed after them. The next few hours would be busy ones, but his main job was visiting the priest again and lending his magic to making more amulets. After the first few, he'd set up an assembly line operation that made things go faster.

"You again!" Valentin's accented voice thundered. "Get that woman out of here."

"If ye canna calm yourself," Stewart said, "ye must needs leave. Choose now, so ye doona disrupt this gathering further."

Elliott took a deep breath. He wanted to drive his fist through Valentin's face, but that would only make things worse. He ducked his head and entered the wagon. Tairin stood at the far end, magic from her calming spell streaming from her.

"I won't trouble you with my presence for long," she began, her voice low and hypnotic. "My shifter kin have accepted me back into their ranks, and they're prepared to fight alongside us to defeat the vampires…"

Elliott listened to her summarize the parts the Rom needed to know. He could have listened to her forever, as captivated by her spell as every other man in the room. Even Valentin was leaning toward her, intent on her words.

So much power, he marveled. She could have wrested leadership of the caravan from Michael anytime she wished, but she'd done nothing of the sort—

"Elliott!" Michael's voice was sharp with command. "This is the third time I've asked if you have anything to add."

He rose from where he'd been crouched near the door, still entranced by Tairin's magic. "Yes, I do. The shifters have requested protective amulets, and I said we'd provide them. I'll go back by the church early tomorrow for more materials. Also, we'll only need three Romani for each group, not five. We might want to send a few additional men to make certain the magical energies mesh well within each group. Those who aren't selected can return to their caravans."

Before Valentin and the others recovered from the effects of Tairin's magic, Elliott bid the group goodnight and left the wagon. Tairin followed him. Once they were outside, he held out his arms, but she shook her head. "We made Michael a promise."

"Bad luck to break promises." He smiled at her, wanting her so intensely all else paled to nothingness.

"Bad luck to break promises," she agreed and headed for the wagon she shared with a few other unmarried women.

He stared after her long after she'd disappeared inside, longing cutting a path through his soul. He'd buried his emotions deep after his parents died, adding layers to the protections he'd built around his heart as years passed. Understanding flared that his magic had suffered because his spells started and stopped with his mind. No heat. No heart. No spirit.

No more.

Tairin offered him a great gift. The ability to be whole again. Even if it meant leaving the Romani world behind forever, they'd make a life together. From the sound of things, they could throw in their lot with her shifter kinfolk. If not, just being by her side would be more than enough.

He headed for his wagon, intent on seeing just how much amulet material remained. And on finding shoes for Jamal.

CHAPTER 12

The following evening, Tairin sat atop a high, flat seat driving a wagon and team. She'd made sure the two women who'd shared it with her back at the caravan had secured other arrangements. They'd moved their things out while she was preparing to leave.

Curfew wouldn't be for an hour, which should give her plenty of time to reach the castle. She'd dressed in colorful, flowing traditional Romani clothing. If anyone stopped her, she'd tell them she was off to tell fortunes for a gadjo's party. The amulets, additional dark clothing, shoes for Jamal, and food stocked the wagon, along with all her things. Forty men, including Elliott, were strung out half a mile behind her on horseback, traveling in groups of twos and threes.

Elliott had been insistent she use telepathy to summon him if she got into trouble, or the Nazis waylaid her. She'd agreed, but whether she'd actually follow through depended on what she ran up against. Her presence wasn't a critical element in the shifter-Romani coalition to deal with the vampires. Elliott's was, and she'd be damned if she'd pull him away from something far more important than rescuing her.

If she ran into trouble, she'd get herself out of it. No need to put Elliott in danger too. A warm place fluttered behind her breastbone when she thought about him. Soon they'd be free to plan a future together. That a Romani could know what she was and love her anyway gave her hope for détente between their two peoples.

"Good woman. I trained you well," her wolf observed, sounding pleased with itself.

"It's the truth, but you needn't brag about it," she replied, smothering a smile.

A group of planes, flying in a tight formation, roared by overhead. Her horses neighed, tossing their heads and making the bells sewn to their halters jangle.

"Get a car," a passing man yelled at her. When she didn't respond, he followed it up with, "Dumb gypsy bitch. Are you deaf as well as stupid?"

Anger flared hot, but she kept her eyes straight ahead. She could flatten the ignorant bastard with a blast of magic, but then everyone else who was out and about would mob her wagon. Nazis weren't the only ones who didn't care for Romani. People had a love-hate relationship with their abilities, using them when it was convenient and maligning them when it wasn't.

A car honked before pulling around her. It cut back in so close it nearly hit her lead horse. That did it. She guided the team down a side street, determined to use alleys to achieve her destination. The acrid stench of urine in the narrow, cobblestone byway burned her nostrils. Apparently, someone—or maybe more than one person—was hiding out back here.

A blast of pure evil turned the air ahead of her dark. The horses reared in their harnesses, shrieking with fear. Tairin set the wagon's brake and jumped down from the box. Whatever this was, she'd place herself between it and her team. Earth magic gushed into her as she summoned power.

"What is it?" she asked the wolf.

"Demon. Maybe the same one Elliott loosed."

"Should we shift?"

"Maybe. Not yet. It'll spook the horses even worse."

She mixed fire and a little air with her earth magic and built a perimeter behind her. Perhaps the horses sensed it because they quieted. Spinning, she faced whatever was moving closer. Light crackled from her fingertips, and she loosed her signature mix of Romani and shifter power. Maybe it would slow the evil down.

Or not since the thing kept right on coming.

Meara and Jamal were supposed to dispatch the demon—if it was the same one. No way of knowing, and it didn't matter. Black flames licked toward her. She feinted sideways, but wasn't quite fast enough and ended up in the center of a circle of fire. Water would help, but that was her weakest element, plus the closest source was the sewer flowing beneath her feet. She had no idea where the nearest gutter cover was located, and drawing water through earth and cobblestones in sufficient quantities to quell the blaze was beyond her ability.

Her belly tightened into a knot of fear, but she ignored it. Panic wouldn't go down well, and it would interfere with her ability to work magic. She eyed the flames surrounding her. They grew closer but very slowly, surging forward and withdrawing. The thing that had summoned black fire was playing with her.

Why?

She changed the timbre and cadence of her chant to draw out the demon. Gradually, an entity formed behind the circle of fire. Tall, with horns, yellow eyes, red scales, and a forked tail, it raised a hand, pointing talon-tipped fingers right at her. Macabre laughter rose from its throat, and a cascade of ice chips froze her from the inside out.

The black flames burned higher, almost to waist level, but their heat didn't chase away the chill. Changing things up, she channeled earth magic by itself, instructing it to smother the fire. Not all of it—she didn't command enough magic for that—only the spot right in front of her. Choking clouds of noxious smelling sulfur fumes billowed, but a gateway formed in the flames.

Tairin hurried through and tossed a wide ward about herself. The demon might try its fire trick again, but this time she'd make certain it couldn't get close enough to harm her. The smell of singed fabric added to the smoke, suggesting how close the fire had come to immolating her where she stood.

Fear thickened her throat. The demon was laughing harder than ever. Bastard wasn't even breathing hard, where she was gasping as if she'd run miles. How could she get rid of the thing? It wasn't possible with the amount of magic she had to squander defending herself.

Probably what it's counting on. If it keeps me busy enough, I'll never be able to leverage enough magic to make a dent in its attack. Eventually it will wear me down, drain my magical well, and then...

She recognized alien enchantment planting bleak seeds in her mind to demoralize her and poured more magic into her warding. She had to do something, but what?

The talismans.

Were they specific to vampires, or would they work on anything evil? No time like now to find out. Never taking her gaze off the demon, who was building another pyre of black flames right in front of it, she skirted back to her wagon and tugged its side door open. Reaching inside, she herded the pile of amulets close. Draping one around her neck, she grabbed a handful in case their power was additive.

Tairin didn't bother to shut the wagon door. Windows above her in the narrow alleyway had been slamming shut ever since the demon showed up. If Munich's citizens had learned anything from the Nazi regime, it was to turn a blind eye to anything unusual. Not to call what passed for law enforcement. And never to offer help to anyone not part of the Master Race.

Bitterness and anger lent her energy. She hurried back to within striking distance, holding half a dozen amulets before her and chanting to boost their power. Maybe. Shifter and Rom magic might not be a good mix with holy water or consecrated earth. Would the whole mess blow up in her face?

A patch of air between them took on a glassy, incandescent quality, and a loud *whoomping* made her ears hurt. Not good. Mixing incompatible magics could backfire badly. She stared at the demon, seeking clues. The smug expression on its face had departed. If it hadn't been for that, she might have chucked the amulets as far away from her as she could.

Scattering the pyre of flames, the demon faced her, its hands raised. A hail of dark magic pounded against her ward, but it held.

"Ha!" Tairin screeched. "Not as easy pickings as you'd figured."

She set up a triangulation where she fed power through the amulets, and thence to the demon. The patch of air looked more and more like stained glass painted in reds and oranges. When it surrounded the demon, enclosing it, Tairin was certain she'd won. All she had to do was keep funneling power through the leather pouches suspended from one hand.

And keep her wards intact. She'd have enough magic for both —if it didn't take too long.

Cawing rained down from above, and Tairin risked a glance upward. Meara! The vulture plummeted to earth right next to her, transforming between the space of two heartbeats.

"Follow my lead," Meara cried. "Not much left to do. You almost had him."

Tairin drew the same power as Meara and repeated her chant. The stained glass shattered in an earsplitting cacophony. When it cleared, the demon was gone.

Tairin bent over, hands on her knees, sucking air. When she could talk, she ground out. "Was it the same one?"

"Yes. Jamal and I drew it, but it slipped away from us. We infuriated it, but I have no idea why it targeted you."

"I do." Harsh knowledge cut deep. "I smell like Elliott. That's what drew it."

"Why not seek out Elliott?" Meara frowned.

"Because he's with a group of forty Rom—and I was alone." Tairin shook her head. "It's all right. At least I discovered these things—" she shook the bunch of amulets until they jangled against one another "—work against everything evil. I also figured out shifters can use them without incompatible magic coming back to bite us. Where's Jamal?"

"Holding down the fort in the castle. In case the demon gave me the slip again, it would be drawn to where it was freed from Hell."

Tairin withdrew power from the perimeter she'd drawn around the team. Stalking back to the wagon, she dropped the amulets inside and pushed the door until it latched. Ready to get moving again, she stared at the spot the demon had been. Nothing remained but a few charred bits. "Is it gone?"

"This one is a he—Grigori to be precise—and he's back in Hell if that's what you're asking. Impossible to kill those things. Mind if I catch a ride with you?"

Tairin rolled her eyes. "Sorry. I should have offered. I need a crash course in shifter magic. I understand the Romani part of me, but maybe there was something I could've done to wrap things up here faster."

"Let's get moving. We can talk as we go." Meara climbed onto the wagon's seat.

Tairin took the place next to her. She didn't need a watch to know it was now past curfew, and they were still a good half hour from the castle. She released the wagon's brake and clucked to the team.

"Hope no one notices us."

"I'll make certain they don't." The scents of clay baked hot by a southern sun, fresh hay, and rosemary rose around them as Meara worked her brand of power. "You asked about shifter magic. You can learn more about it, but integrating it with the Romani side of your blood will be for you to puzzle through."

"Why can't you or Jamal help me?"

Meara sent half a smile scudding toward her. "Because we're not Romani. Magic is unique to the wielder to some extent, even within our own ranks. Blended power is stronger, but you'll have to find your own way to develop it."

Tairin pushed hair out of her face. "I thought about shifting back there."

"Why didn't you?"

"I couldn't see where it would buy me any advantage. The wolf wasn't pushing for a shift, and it would have if it felt we needed its form. Beyond that, I didn't want to abandon the horses and wagon."

Meara laughed softly. "Spoken like a true Romani. No shifter has ever given a good goddamn about either of those things."

Tairin laughed too. "If what you said earlier is true, all that's about to change. We'll become more like them. They'll become more like us."

"And pretty soon, everyone will react to things just like you do?" Meara furled her brows.

"When you say it like that, it sounds like so much flimflam."

"Change is slow, child. It will take generations for trust to reestablish itself among people who are different than one another. What we're doing is a start, but only a start. Don't expect too much too soon."

Tairin mulled it through as she drove the rest of the way to the courtyard, which was tightly packed with automobiles and horses. There was nowhere for the team and wagon, so she drove behind the crumbling structure. At least passersby on the road wouldn't see the wagon. For good measure, she cast a *don't look here* spell once Meara had climbed down.

Elliott loped toward her. "What happened? Where were you? I'd just gathered a group of men to look for you."

"Jamal knew. He and Meara are linked telepathically. You could have asked him," Tairin replied. Happiness to see Elliott beat a path through her, and she smiled. Too many people around for them to embrace, but she wanted to wrap her arms around him and pull him close.

"Never even thought to look for him. Last time I saw him, he was in his wolf form snarling at the demon."

"So? You could've use telepathy."

Elliott drew his dark brows together, face darkening like a thundercloud. "I didn't. You never answered me. Where were you?"

She shrugged sheepishly, but his tone made her wary. She was here, unharmed. Why was he treating her like a miscreant child? "The demon got away. Somehow it found me, no doubt because I smelled like you and it has a score to settle. Anyway, dealing with it slowed me down, but I managed. Meara showed up, and—"

Elliott grabbed her shoulders, his fingers digging in. "Why didn't you call me? You were supposed to let me know if you ran into trouble."

"I—I had things under control. I didn't need—"

"If Meara showed up, you sure as hell needed something." He shook her, not hard, but anger exploded from her belly.

"Goddammit!" She wrenched away from him. "I've been taking care of myself for two hundred years. Maybe sometimes I didn't do that great a job, but I'm still here. I'm not in the habit of calling for help. Not from you or anyone else." Turning on her heel, she stalked away, seething.

"He was worried about us," the wolf spoke up.

"Whose fucking side are you on?" she demanded.

"All of ours." The wolf sounded sad.

"Get over it. Hooking up with a Rom was a bad idea. They hate me, and right now I'm not overly fond of them, either. I'm done talking."

She jumped down the crumbling steps and pelted down the passageway. The place smelled like Elliott and made her heart hurt.

I can't think about this. Not now.

Not ever, a different inner voice inserted. *Move on. It's the only way to get past painful things.*

Hoping it wouldn't take as long as getting over her mother's death and her father's abandonment, she moved inside Elliott's grotto. It was packed with Romani and shifters, and she slunk into a corner wanting nothing more than to be invisible for a while.

Jamal, back in his human form, noticed her immediately. "Did you bring the amulets?"

Tairin nodded. "Yes. They're in my wagon. And two pieces of welcome news. They work against anything evil, and shifters can use them."

"Just because you apparently did, and they didn't go wrong on you, isn't any guarantee for those of us without mixed blood," a shifter grumbled.

She wanted to carp at him that she'd had a bellyful of glass-half-empties for now, but clamped her jaws together. "Is the plan still to attack tomorrow?" she asked.

"Yes," Jamal replied. "All that's left is to form our groups."

"I'm here." Meara's voice rang from the doorway. "I'll take care of ensuring an optimal mix of magics."

"Once that's done, we'll eat and rest," Michael said. "We want to be as strong as possible for this undertaking. Whichever Romani aren't selected will return to their caravans."

Meara moved to the front of the room. "I want everyone in here, and yes it will be a very tight fit. Romani on the left, shifters on the right." She eyed Michael. "Summon the rest of your people. All of mine are here."

Tairin felt Elliott's essence when he entered the room in the midst of several other Romani. She shrank farther back into her corner. Soon, she'd be able to hide out in a corner of the passageway until it was time to launch their attack. If the goddess were good to her, she'd be able to avoid Elliott entirely. No reason to speak with him ever again.

Better to let her heart scab over. Eventually, she'd heal. She had strength, and her path was to be alone. Today proved that.

"You're making a mistake," her wolf observed.

"I didn't ask you."

"No. You didn't, but you needed to hear that. He's a good man, and he loves us."

"Awk. He's a heavy-handed bastard who thinks he owns us. Or me, anyway. Why am I even discussing this with you?"

"Because we discuss everything important. Your feelings got hurt. You'll forgive him."

"In a pig's eye, I will. You're impossible. Quiet now. I don't want to miss which group Meara puts us in."

Tairin focused her attention on the front of the room. Seven groups had already formed and left the grotto to discuss their respective strategies and get to know one another. She took stock of who was left. Elliott was still in the room, but she'd known that because she hadn't felt his energy depart.

Please, she pleaded with whichever goddess watched over mixed-blood mages, *do not let Meara stick us in the same group.*

Finally, she and Jamal were all that remained. Along with Elliott, Stewart, and Michael.

Tairin straightened from her slump against the wall. "Could you please reassign me?" she asked Meara.

"I will not." Meara eyed her imperiously. "This mix of magics is perfectly balanced, and it's exactly where you belong. I will float between groups, offering assistance as required." She clapped her hands together. "Get moving. Experiment with blending your power so you're ready."

Elliott stalked out of the grotto without a backward glance, clearly as done with her as she was with him.

Except I'm not.

Shut up, she told herself. *Get over it. One more day, and I can be free.*

The prospect didn't do anything but make her feel depressed, and she headed toward the doorway, intent on meeting with her group outside in a place that didn't reek of Elliott. His scent made her want him, but she had to find a way past that.

Jamal caught up with her. "Are you all right?" he asked.

No. I'll never be all right again.

"Yeah. Fine. I brought a couple pair of shoes in the wagon. One of them should fit you."

Jamal probed the edges of her mind, but she shook her head. "Don't. You may mean well now, but it's a little late in the game to start making protective father noises."

"I understand. How can I help?"

"Be my friend."

He draped an arm around her shoulders. "It would be an honor. Tell me what happened with the demon. I apologize for letting it get away."

Grateful for something to think about besides Elliott, she began to talk. "I'd just guided the wagon off Munich's central streets. Too much traffic, and a few passersby who didn't like Romani drove me off the main byway…"

CHAPTER 13

*E*lliott tossed and turned on a makeshift mat in a corner of his grotto. Hours had passed since they'd formed their groups, making certain each of them was armed with an amulet. They'd practiced blending their power, with Tairin keeping herself as far from him as possible. And they'd shared a meal with her sticking to her father's side like a shadow. He'd wanted to talk with her, but she'd made certain there wasn't an opportunity, and the conversation he had in mind was a private one.

Regardless of whether he liked it or not, Michael's directive about not making his feelings about Tairin public until after they were done with the vampire attack made sense. Many of the Romani would believe she'd bewitched him and take it as an omen that their effort to eradicate the vampires was doomed from its outset.

Probably more than a few shifters would interpret it that way too. Except they'd think he'd ensorcelled her, probably to get into her bed.

He needed rest to ensure his magic was as fully recharged as possible, but sleep wouldn't come. Every time he shut his eyes, he saw Tairin. Her tawny hair and liquid dark eyes. The smell of her and her magic tantalized him, made him ache with longing for her.

I have to pull my head out of my ass.

Taking on a nest of vampires was as challenging a magical task as he'd ever set for himself. To go into it mooning like a lovesick adolescent was stupid. He'd put the rest of his group in danger if he wasn't functioning at a hundred percent.

Despite his strong intentions, he replayed what had happened with Tairin for the hundredth time. He'd been so worried about her he was almost sick with fear. When she'd shown up, smiling, happy to see him, what had he done? Grilled her. Rebuked her. Dunned her for taking care of her own problems without him by her side.

"Jesus," he mumbled. "I was a total jerk. No wonder she reacted like she did."

He'd wanted to apologize. Tell her he hadn't meant any of what he'd said, but she never gave him a chance. Hadn't even looked at him from what he could ascertain. It was as if she'd withdrawn into the same shell she was in when he'd apprehended her outside Michael's wagon that night.

He'd hurt her. He'd seen the light flicker and die in her eyes when he grabbed her and shook her. Yeah, he'd actually shaken her. How could he have been such a ham-fisted idiot?

It didn't matter. Nothing did. He'd lost her. She wasn't just angry. She was done with him. He saw it in the set of her shoulders and her refusal to engage on any level. He blew out a breath. And then did it again. He had to find a way past this. Soon he'd be in the thick of a serious battle, and he'd be damned if he'd be the weak link in their chain. Having her or any of the others protect him would be the final straw. It was bad enough she'd spurned him—never mind he deserved it. He'd pull his weight when they took on their assigned vampire. Or die trying.

He shut his eyes again and called a trance state, resolved to get some rest. It wasn't as good as sleep, but at least it would be something. If things went awry later today, it wouldn't be his fault.

He must have drifted off because Michael shaking his shoulder brought him around. "Time to go," Michael said. "You looked exhausted, and I let you sleep as long as I could."

"Thanks." Elliott rolled to a sit and thence to his feet.

The groups were all taking vehicles until they got close to their destination. Mostly because cars were faster than horses and less noticeable on the roadway. While everyone else rested last night, Meara had volunteered to find a place large enough to park a dozen cars. From there, they'd go on foot.

Elliott followed Michael to a sleek, black Mercedes 770 sedan. Tairin was in the front seat with Jamal and Stewart, so Elliott crawled into the back with Michael. It was one of the cars the Reich favored, so they wouldn't be overly noticeable. Elliott looked away from where Tairin sat. He focused on gathering his power and girding himself for the task ahead.

"Are we clear about our roles?" Michael asked as the car rolled forward.

"Aye, I believe we are," Stewart replied. "'Twill be good to get to the far side of this."

"The challenge," Jamal spoke up, "will be so many of us getting close to the nest without them realizing we're there."

"We snuck up on them," Tairin said.

"Aye, but 'twas only the two of ye, not sixty with strong magic."

"We won't be able to scope them out like Tairin and I did." Elliott joined the conversation. He had to quell his tumbling emotions fast and get down to business.

"Which means we willna have the luxury of selecting which vampire each group targets," Stewart said.

"I'd already come to that conclusion," Michael agreed. "It will be first come, first served. Once they know we're there, they'll focus the full brunt of their hypnotic abilities on us."

"That's where we come in," Jamal said. "Tairin and I are immune to that part of their magic, so we should be able to break its hold on you—if it subverts the amulets' inherent power."

"So long as ye brought up the amulets, we can hope for the best," Stewart cut in, "but they're an unknown quantity. Just because an ancient lore book proclaimed that particular mix works to fend off vampire mind control isna a guarantee."

"True enough," Jamal replied. "Let's recap here. Tairin will weave and hold the magic to keep the vampire from turning you Romani into their next meal. Michael and I will capture it. Stewart will help us drive it to the ground."

"And I'll pound a silver stake through its heart," Elliott said. "This all sounds nice and neat and clinical here in this car, but we'll be surrounded by eleven other groups. The odds of every single group killing their vampire aren't good, which means we could end up dealing with more than one of those bastards."

"Granted, there are more than a few loose ends." Jamal exchanged glances with him in the rearview mirror. "But we could have accomplished this with only three or four of us on each team. That we brought one extra man was overkill, and it should mean victory for us."

"I hope you're right," Tairin said. "Do you expect we'll have to shift?"

"I'm not thinking we will," Jamal replied. "Unless one of those abominations gets away. They're fast. Far faster than humans. A wolf could run one to ground, though."

He guided the car onto a side road, following the vehicle ahead of them. This wasn't the same track Elliott and Tairin had used with the horse. That one wouldn't have been wide enough for vehicles, but the nest was within easy striking distance.

"We'll have to use magic to get past these farms unnoticed,"

Elliott said, "but not so much we tip the vampires off. I assume they're sensitive to expended power."

"Not as much as ye might believe," Stewart answered. "If they were, they'd have sensed ye and Tairin."

"It isn't that they're not aware," Jamal countered and drew the car to a stop off the road in a wide copse of trees. "They've been at the top of the food chain for so long, they don't bother to be cautious. It's not in their nature. Ward yourselves for as long as it makes sense."

Elliott crawled out of the back of the car and stood with the others, who'd already arrived. No one had much to say. They'd either succeed or not—and everyone knew it.

Once the other cars arrived, disgorging their occupants, shifters and Romani set off for the nest, keeping to their respective groups. Elliott had no idea if the vampires would still be there. Perhaps they moved around. The shifters seemed to know more about vampires than Romani did, and they hadn't expressed doubts about locating the creatures, so Elliott kept his concerns to himself.

As he thought about it, moving the coffins would be a big job. Once vampires settled into a camp, they probably remained there until they left the area. That it was daylight meant they should be exactly where he and Tairin had found them.

What the hell did they even need the coffins for? They might be stronger at night like Meara indicated, but they'd been pretty damned functional when he and Tairin saw them, and it had been daylight then. Words from the lore book slapped him smartly.

While vampire powers are enhanced by darkness, they are perfectly capable of functioning in broad daylight. The idea that light weakens them is nothing more than a myth.

Jamal straightened his spine. They'd do what they'd come for. No choice. Not really. He was part of a horizontal line, flanking one end of it. Michael was to his left, then Jamal, then Stewart, then Tairin at the far end. It was the most effective way to utilize their magic. Far better than bunching up in front and behind each other. Six groups, similarly arrayed, walked ahead of them and five behind.

They intercepted the path he and Tairin had taken the other night. It felt like that had happened several lifetimes ago, but only a scant handful of days had passed. *"Careful,"* he sent to Keenan who was part of the lead group. *"You're close."*

Jamal glanced his way and placed a finger over his mouth in the universal sign for silence. Elliott nodded and focused on keeping the ward shielding his magic and his presence in place. His heart beat faster, and the sharp, metallic taste of adrenaline burned his mouth. Romani weren't warriors. It didn't come naturally to them, but three dozen of his kin had accepted this task, and pride for his people welled in him.

He made himself a promise to live through the battle to come and to make certain Tairin did too. Once it was over, he'd throw himself on her mercy. Tell her how much he loved her and what a terrible mistake he'd made. It might not work, but he had to try. The unsettled place within him receded, making it possible to focus his concentration on what lay ahead. The pungent stench of death and rot reached him, which meant his worries about the vampires not being there had been stupid. They might be entertaining Nazis again, but Elliott wasn't worried about the SS. They were mere men, and men were easy to kill. Even men with guns. Magic was faster than any bullet.

"Ready yourselves." Jamal breathed the words into their minds.

Squawking from overhead sent his heart thudding into overdrive until he recognized Meara's vulture form winging its way ahead of them. She'd been vague about her role, but at the moment she was functioning as a forward scout.

The leading group shot forward. It was part of their plan once vampires came into view. No hesitation. No "I'll take this one, and you take that one." They'd target whichever vampire didn't already have a bunch of them ringed around it. The battle wouldn't last long. An hour from now, they'd either be victorious —or drained of blood and turned. It wasn't ideal. Far better to pit the strongest of them against the older vampires, but they hadn't figured they'd have adequate time to determine such things. Not and remain undetected.

Surprise was a key element in their attack, and so far, it was panning out.

Elliott raced forward with his group. They came to the clearing. The groups ahead of them were fully engaged with vampires, except other vampires had gone to their companions' aid.

"That one," Jamal bellowed and pointed to a vampire with long, blue-black hair, who'd taken on one of their groups as it attacked a different vampire with silvery locks. The evil creatures were garbed in the same heavy, silken robes they'd worn last time Elliott was here. He sprinted in the direction Jamal indicated, but it felt as if he were running through molasses. His limbs didn't want to obey commands from his brain.

The vampire they'd targeted turned liquid, dark eyes with golden centers on them. Magic pulsing from it was so strong, it was all Elliott could do to remain upright. The creature was beautiful in an unearthly way. Stopping in his tracks to stare at it was the right thing to do.

The only thing to do.

Magic crackled around him, and the vampire's spell shattered. Tairin slapped him, Stewart, and Michael across their shoulders. "Come on," she shouted. "Father is by himself up there."

Jamal was indeed facing off against the dusky-haired vampire. At least it had left off trying to help its kinsman with the silver hair. Magic flared from Jamal's raised hands, but it rolled right off the vampire, who opened his mouth and laughed.

"Come on little shifter." He crooked a finger Jamal's way. "If you stop this charade, I'll make you one of us. It's not so different from the power you have now."

"What makes you think I'd be the least bit interested?" Jamal asked.

"Oh come now." Compulsion flowed from the vampire. It had to have snared Jamal, but he didn't seem fazed. "All of us want more power. All the power we can get our hands—or in your case paws—on."

"Make it worth my while." An easy smile crossed Jamal's face.

Elliott understood what the shifter was doing. Flattery could divert the vampire just long enough for them to attack it. *"Go around behind the vampire,"* he told Michael and Stewart. *"Do it while Jamal is keeping him busy."*

He pulled the sharpened silver stake from his coat pocket, keeping it cupped in a hand and hidden, while he readied himself to spring. This was going even faster than he'd anticipated, but things could still go seriously sideways. The crippling inertia hit again as another vampire targeted him, and likely other Romani as well. Tairin intercepted its poison almost immediately.

He glanced her way, but she was already spinning in another direction, magic jetting from her outraised hands. She'd braided her hair tight against her head, and her eyes glowed with delight. She was enjoying this. Battle was part of her birthright, and he loved her fierceness.

And her. If he'd had time, he'd have begged the gods for one more chance to make things right with her.

Around them, the stench of rot and death thickened until his gorge clenched in protest. In his peripheral vision, a vampire with a stake through its heart dissolved into nothing more than bones riddled with holes. So that was what Meara had meant, but at least one vampire was out of the way. Elliott would've liked to move around the battleground and take stock of how they were doing, but that was Meara's job, not his.

Michael and Stewart were in position. They stormed the vampire from behind, knocking it on its belly. The thing bellowed its outrage and writhed beneath the two men. Jamal jumped on the heap, but the vampire was strong enough to throw him off. Undaunted, Jamal leapt back atop the thing, but from a different angle.

Elliott didn't hesitate. Whether he staked it from the front or the back made little difference. Jamal made space for him, chanting like a madman as his power flared, creating a blue-white nimbus.

Elliott straddled the vampire. Lodging the stake midway down its back, he pounded it home with a magical assist. Black blood spattered him, smelling worse than the ripest charnel pit. Small black bugs followed the blood and latched onto his hands, biting deep.

What the hell were they? He hadn't read anything about them in the lore books.

The body beneath his bucked and writhed, but he held fast. More black ichor geysered, coating him in the noxious stuff. The biting insects disappeared into his hands and arms. They burned with an unholy fury, but he couldn't let go of his stake long enough to claw them out of him.

Jamal noticed the bugs—beetle-sized with sharp beaks and hard carapaces. "No!" he screeched and swept the ones that hadn't dug their way through Elliott's skin off him, smashing them one by one.

The vampire's movements ceased abruptly, and its body exploded, leaving nothing but bones beneath Elliott's splayed legs. Bits of flesh and sinew flew through the air, splattering everything within a five-foot radius.

He might be coated with vampire blood and stinking of dead things, but victory was still sweet. "We did it," he crowed, gasping and panting.

"Aye, lad, that we did," Stewart dragged him off the vampire's bones and to his feet.

Elliott surveyed the battleground. Two vampires remained, but gangs of shifters and Romani converged on them, so they'd be dead very soon. "We got lucky," he ground out, still struggling for breath. "No SS. I worried about that, but only when we were almost here."

"Not that lucky." Jamal wound a hand around his arm. "How many of those bugs got inside you?"

Elliott shrugged. "I have no idea. Some. Why?"

Jamal's nostrils flared, and he looked away.

"What?" Michael planted himself in front of the shifter. "What bugs?"

"They're not really bugs," Jamal said. "They're part of a master vampire's essence. This one must have sired the remainder of this nest. The things that looked like beetles are the way vampire lords ensure their survival and the survival of their line—even after death."

Elliott's mouth gaped open. He clawed at his hands and forearms, but the small holes the bugs that weren't bugs had made were already closed. "Noooooo." He moaned and shook his head back and forth. "I can't become a vampire. I won't. I'll kill myself first."

The euphoria from what he'd been sure was victory turned to ashes, bitter in his mouth. Spinning away from them, he doubled over and vomited. Even after his stomach was empty, dry heaves racked him, and he fell to his knees. At least Tairin was still alive. He'd kept her safe. It made his own death palatable.

"Any chance ye're mistaken about this?" Stewart faced off against Jamal.

"None. I've seen it before."

"We'll get him back to the caravan," Michael announced, his face drawn into a mass of grief-torn wrinkles. "Surely if all of us lend our power, we can drive the vampiric essence out."

"Won't work." Jamal spoke flatly. "I've seen this before." He repeated himself. "It's one of the worst journeys a creature that's not evil to begin with can take."

"We can save him," Tairin's wolf sounded frantic, *"but we must begin now."*

Tairin looked from her father to Elliott. Apprehension and guilt streamed from her in bright, pulsing waves. "My wolf and I can fix this," she said.

"No." Jamal made a grab for her, but she sidestepped him neatly and ran to Elliott's side.

"I admire your courage, but it's too dangerous," her father said.

Tairin knelt by Elliott and wrapped her arms around him. She exchanged a pointed look with her father. "I don't want to live without him."

Her embrace laved his soul, but Elliott pulled away from her. "Hang onto your anger from earlier," he said, each word like stabbing a knife into his heart. "I'll take care of my problem—before the vampire grows so strong inside me that I can't."

"I don't think so." She spaced her words out and grasped his face between her hands.

"I love you, Tairin. Live a good life. Find a way to be happy. I'm touched you and your wolf are willing to try to save me, but your father says it's perilous, and I won't risk either of you."

Elliott wrenched away from her and pushed heavily to his feet. He felt dark power rooting within him and understood he had to be quick about his next steps. If he waited too long, the vampire would never let him do away with their shared body.

Spinning, he sprinted into the nearby woods. He knew this country and headed for a waterfall studded with sharp rocks at its bottom, intent on running off the precipice. He was still human enough, the fall was certain to kill him.

It was for the best. He'd told Tairin he loved her. And she still loved him. He'd seen it in her eyes. Nothing more needed to be said.

Elliott cleared his mind as he ran. If he were going to die, he'd do it as himself, not as the insidious presence clawing its way through him. The pounding of a large animal crashing through the underbrush made him run faster. Whatever was back there would not catch him. He'd see to it. He was almost to the cliff over the abyss. Just a few more yards. He could make it.

Something heavy sprang on him, shoving him to the forest floor.

Tairin's wolf.

Before he could roll out from beneath it, tell it he appreciated its efforts, but he was beyond salvage, the wolf sank its fangs into his shoulder. Pain shot through him, and a tortured scream rose from his throat. More agony than he'd ever have imagined possible from an animal bite seared him—and he'd had plenty over the years.

His shoulder caught fire. He could almost smell his flesh burning, but it had to be a magical illusion.

"Fight, goddammit!" the wolf urged and buried its fangs in his other shoulder.

"Fight what? How?"

"Drive out the dark. I've given you shifter blood. Sent a bond animal of your own into you. Find your wolf side and shift. If you waste my gift, you'll drag us—Tairin, me, and your wolf—into night everlasting with you."

CHAPTER 14

airin watched in disbelief as Elliott tore out of the clearing. She'd offered him a chance. Why hadn't he taken it? Other shifters and Romani moved toward them, and the buzz of conversation rose and fell with people wanting to know what happened.

"Come on," her wolf urged. *"We have to do this now. I can't bring him back from the dead. Hurry. I found a bond animal willing to take a chance on him."*

Clothing ripped as she shifted and bounded after Elliott before her paws were fully formed, with her father's cries of, "Stop," ringing in her ears. At first, she figured he'd be easy to catch, but the vampire's supernatural speed was already taking hold. She'd never have caught up to him in her human form.

"Not good news that he's so fast already," the wolf said, mirroring her thoughts.

"Yeah, that vampire we killed must've been hella strong."

"Sire to that nest and maybe several more we don't know about," the wolf replied.

Tairin didn't respond. The thought of facing down more vampires wasn't high on her list, but she'd do it if it meant sabo-

250

taging the Nazi war machine. *"Did you know what those bug things were before Jamal told us?"*

"Yes. I've never seen them, but other bond animals have, including the one who just agreed to bond with Elliott." The wolf hesitated. *"It's why I know what we need to do. It's dangerous. We all might die."*

"I gathered that from Jamal's reaction, but if we don't intervene, Elliott will destroy himself."

"I have your assent to move forward?" The wolf ran faster. A few more leaping bounds and they'd reach Elliott. Not a moment too soon, judging from the deafening noise of an enormous waterfall.

"Yes."

The wolf sprang, using its weight to hold Elliott down while it bit deep, infusing shifter essence into the wound. Tairin felt the new bond animal transit into Elliott. He screamed, a tortured howl as shifter blood battled the vampire inside him. Tairin would've saved him from the agony, but she couldn't. All she could do was hope the four of them would be strong enough to defeat the vampire.

"Fight, goddammit!" the wolf urged and buried its fangs in Elliott's other shoulder.

"Fight what? How?" he asked, shuddering with pain.

"Drive out the dark. I've given you shifter blood. Sent a bond animal of your own into you. Find your wolf side and shift. If you waste my gift, you'll drag us—Tairin, me, and your wolf—into night everlasting with you."

So that was the danger. Nice to have it spelled out.

"Listen to me," Tairin said. *"Latch onto your Romani power and fill yourself with earth magic. As much as you can hold. When you think there's no more space, keep going."*

Elliott pushed his way out from beneath the wolf and rolled into a crouch, hands splayed on the dirt in front of him to maximize his contact with the earth. Power flared blue-white around him, Romani but with dark-tinged edges that had to be the vampire moving into ascendency. His long hair had come out of its leather thong and dragged in the dirt, shrouding his face from view.

"*Hurry,*" Tairin urged.

"*I'm trying. Tell me what to do next.*" His mind voice held a tortured note.

"*There's a wolf within you. Summon it. Don't be gentle. They're not gentle creatures. Command it to transform your shared body.*"

Tairin sat on her haunches, willing Elliott to have the strength for the transformation. Shifters dreamed their animals, got to know them before their first shift. Even with an introduction, the initial transition was a jarring experience. Painful as bones, muscle, and sinew rearranged themselves. Plus, it was unnatural to cede control of your body to another.

Light pulsed around him, and Elliott grunted with effort. At first, the glowing nimbus grew brighter, and hope filled her that they'd pulled this off, cheated the vampire of another few millennia of life. As she watched intently, the glow began to fade.

"*No!*" Tairin shrieked. "*Try harder.*"

"I—I'm trying as hard as I can." Elliott reverted to spoken speech, probably to conserve his magic. "I'm not strong enough. There's a battle raging inside me, and it's draining my power. Every time I try to latch onto more, it slips away."

Footsteps pounded toward them, and Tairin sensed Jamal, Michael, Stewart, and Meara. The group skidded to a halt next to Elliott.

"*Help him,*" Tairin pleaded and rose to stand on all four feet.

"It's exactly what I intend to do. You were brave but foolish." Red light pulsed around the vulture shifter, and she hunkered next to Elliott, placing her hands over the bite wounds on both his shoulders. "Do not fight me," she instructed.

"I won't."

"You have to corral the vampire. Keep it out of the way while I feed power into your wolf."

"Got it," Elliott said through clenched teeth. Lines of strain furrowed into his forehead, and sweat beaded despite the chill of the day.

"What can we do?" Michael asked.

Meara angled her head toward him. "Can you strengthen his Romani magic by touching him?"

Stewart nodded sharply. "Aye."

"Then do it." Meara turned her attention back to Elliott. His body had begun to undulate, rocking where he crouched. The bright light around him had eroded to almost nothing.

Michael knelt behind Elliott on one side, Stewart on the other. Each grabbed one of his arms and began a low chant in Coptic. The scents of their combined magic—earthy and pungent—reminded Tairin of her long years traveling with gypsies.

Meara screeched, "Now!" in Gaelic, and a whirling red vortex formed around the tableau of Romani and her. Her power stung Tairin's nose with its baked clay, hay, and rosemary scents. Jamal joined in with Meara's Gaelic chant.

"What can I do?" Tairin asked her father.

"You and your wolf offered the gift of shifter ability to save his life. Your task is done," Jamal said into her mind as he continued to chant.

Unsettled, frantic with worry, Tairin paced in a tight circle, remaining in her wolf form. She wanted to see what Meara was doing, but the swirling vortex blocked her vision.

"Do you know about castings like this?" she asked her wolf.

"No. Meara is one of the strongest of us, though. Have faith in her. I've never known her to fail."

Elliott shrieked, a feral roar that sounded as if his soul were being torn out by its moorings. He did it again, and again. If Tairin had hands, she'd have covered her ears. For the first time, she doubted the wisdom of what she and her wolf had done. Elliott was suffering the torments of the damned, his screams testimony to his anguish. She loped to the precipice and looked at a hundred-fifty-foot waterfall splattering onto a knifelike constellation of rocks. Elliott had chosen well. It would've been a certain death—if he'd gotten there in time.

He howled again, a mournful agonized wail that shredded her heart. She'd done this to him. Maybe it would have been better to let him leap to the rocks mocking her from below.

"*Come on,*" her wolf urged. "*If he needs us, we must be close.*"

Tairin padded back to the red maelstrom. It looked different than it had when she'd left. Larger and pulsing in a defined rhythm. What did that mean? She stared at her father, but his eyes were shut and his forehead creased in concentration as Gaelic flowed from his throat. She understood the words but hadn't heard the incantation before. The three Romani and Meara were still blocked from her view.

Waiting was hard. She'd never been patient—unless she was in wolf form hunting. Tairin had no idea if she'd make things better or worse, but she pushed her mind voice outward, aiming it at Elliott.

"*Try,*" she urged. "*Please. I can't stand to lose you. Not now. I know I was angry, and I can be a high-handed bitch, but it tore my heart out to walk away from you. I want us to have a life together.*"

Her wolf jumped in. "*Reach for your wolf form. Put your whole heart into calling it. If you can shift, you'll have it. The vampire will vanish. It can't coexist with fully-formed shifter magic.*"

Tairin was panting with anxiety. When Jamal dropped a hand onto her head, she started. She'd been so focused on Elliott, she hadn't heard him walk up to her. She looked at her father, who wasn't chanting anymore. Dread filled her. "*Is he—?*" But she couldn't get the word *turned* out. After all this, had the vampire won out in the end?

"He yet lives as a Romani, but these next few moments will tell the tale." Jamal squatted next to her. "If the vampire takes him, you'll be lost to darkness too. When you bit him, you absorbed some of the vampiric essence. It won't matter if Elliott defeats him." Sorrow bowed his shoulders. "But if he fails, we can't allow either of you to live."

"*I understand.*" Tairin focused all her hopes, dreams, and love on the red whirlwind. Her father had said they were in the endgame. Whatever was going to happen would be over with soon.

The funnel pulsed harder almost as if it were a living, breathing entity. A whooshing noise began from deep in its center. Meara screeched in Gaelic so garbled, Tairin couldn't make it out. Stewart and Michael yelled in Coptic. The red light turned pure, blazing white, so bright she squeezed her eyes shut against its glare.

She felt, rather than saw, the vortex explode. Shock waves pounded against her, and she dug her claws into the earth so she wouldn't be tossed through the air. Wolf scent surrounded her. Had Jamal shifted?

She pried her eyes open, squinting against residual blast waves. A pure black wolf nosed her tentatively. Not Jamal.

"*We did it,*" her wolf crowed. "*We did it.*"

Tairin touched noses with the black wolf, not doubting her wolf, but too scared to believe the nightmare was over. "*Elliott?*"

The black wolf licked her nose. Joy rioted through her. She licked it back, wanting to take off running so they could romp and play, but it was daylight, and wolves were fair game for hunters in their part of Germany. She rubbed her snout against his. Happiness vied with sheer relief at not losing him to darkness and death.

"*We would have died too,*" her wolf reminded her.

"*It was worth it—either way,*" she replied.

Meara, Michael, and Stewart joined them, their weary faces wreathed in smiles. "That was far closer than I would have liked," Meara said. "Until I built the vortex to concentrate my power, I wasn't at all certain we'd prevail."

"Och aye, that vampire was one strong bastard," Stewart said.

"We can hope the Reich will suffer for his permanent absence,"

Michael muttered fiercely. "We have to make certain there aren't any more of those fuckers helping the Nazis."

Tairin smiled to herself. So much for Romani not being warriors. Necessity made for strange bedfellows. Not only had the Rom worked side by side with shifters, it appeared Michael and Stewart had absorbed a corner of their warriors' hearts.

Meara swatted Tairin's rump. "You may as well remain in wolf form. It's easier than explaining why we have a naked woman in the car if the SS stop us for some reason."

"Easier, how?" Tairin asked, adding, *"You're naked."*

"You'll play dead, and we can pretend we were out hunting. As for me, I can create the illusion I'm fully clothed."

Elliott's wolf growled, low and menacing. *"I don't like it."*

"Do you have a better plan?" Meara eyed him. "Seems to me, you haven't enough magic left to kill a fly, let alone launch an attack."

Elliott's wolf subsided into whuffly snarls.

Tairin thought about the shreds of her clothing lying on the ground back at the vampire nest. She might be able to salvage something of them. Maybe, but it probably wasn't worth it. *"Let's at least take my shoes,"* she said. *"I only have one other pair."*

"I would request the same." Elliott's mind voice sounded tired, but he wasn't nearly as out of sorts as his wolf had been. *"What's left of my clothes are saturated with ichor from the vampire when my wolf finally chased it from my body, and Meara killed it again."*

"Some things require killing more than once," Meara muttered. "That vampire was one of them."

Tairin nuzzled his snout again. He must be exhausted. If he wanted to talk about what he'd just gone through, she'd listen. No matter how hard it was to hear.

Aiming for something light and positive, she asked, *"What do you think of your wolf?"*

"It's amazing. The wolf is strong, principled, audacious. Never

could've done this without its help." Elliott hesitated. *"I guess I'm like you now. Romani and shifter."*

Meara clapped her hands together smartly. "Excellent. You two can figure things out together. We need to get moving. So far, we've been lucky not to attract SS attention."

"Only because none of the local farmers reported us," Michael said dourly.

Jamal knelt by Tairin's side and buried a hand in her neck ruff. "I'm grateful your gambit paid off, daughter. You have guts. And it would have been terrible to lose you for a second time."

She locked gazes with him—one lupine, one human. *"I didn't want to lose me, either. If you wish to credit someone with courage, offer it to my wolf. This was its idea, but I've always trusted it. Today was no exception."*

Jamal smiled. "When a shifter and their bondmate have been linked as long as the two of you, there's no longer any difference. You've shared each other's thoughts for so long, you become each other."

Elliott nudged her with his snout. *"We can learn about the fine points of being shifters together. I'm looking forward to it."*

Meara trotted back toward where they'd fought the vampires. The others followed her. The air smelled of smoke, and multiple pyres came into view once Tairin crested a small rise.

"This is why I didn't arrive sooner." Meara swept an arm to one side encompassing the battlefield. "Had to set magic-imbued fires that wouldn't attract too much attention to burn the vampires' remains. I can't hide smoke, so I spelled the place to make it appear someone had burned off a field."

"You've got some hellacious magic." Michael shot her an appraising glance. "No one burns fields this time of year."

"Eh. Details. Seems to have worked. Those fires are damn near out. Everyone else has left. Let's collect our car and get out of here."

Tairin and Elliott curled up on the floorboards beneath the

car's backseat. Jamal drove, with Michael and Stewart next to him in the front. Meara had chosen to fly back in her vulture form. Tairin felt the pulse of her father's magic. He was doing his best to make their car less noticeable.

Sirens sounded from in front of them, strident klaxons blaring discordantly. Jamal pulled the car onto a side road, and the scent of his magic deepened. "Stay down," he warned. "Last thing we need are wolf heads popping up in the backseat."

"What is it?" Tairin asked. *"What's out there?"*

"Shit!" Michael muttered.

"Aye, I feared our luck had been running a mite too strong," Stewart cut in.

"What's going on?" Elliott lifted his head, trying to peer out a window.

"I told you to stay down," Jamal growled. "It's the Fuehrer in one hell of a hurry, with a phalanx of SS surrounding his car. They're almost past us. Ward your power. Make certain nothing leaks out."

"Why?" Elliott's wolf snarled. *"They're our enemy. They must be dealt with. We don't run from confrontations. We fight."*

"Not this time we don't," Jamal's wolf snarled back. *"Fighting for your life drained our power."*

"The motorcade is slowing down," Michael sputtered. "What do we do?"

"Ward your power," Jamal warned again. "All of you. We're not strong enough for a direct confrontation. And two of you are unexplainable. The SS won't bother with prison camp. They'll shoot you on the spot for your pelts."

"I thought we were supposed to play dead," Elliott's wolf growled.

"That wouldn't stop them from taking you for your fur," Jamal retorted. "Do what I say, and do it now."

Tairin felt Elliott's magic recede within him. A sigh of relief rippled past her jaws. She'd forgotten how unmanageable newly bonded animals were. Her wolf had given her fits, and it might've been far worse had they not taken to its form for so many years. She huddled on the floor next to Elliott, barely breathing as minutes dripped by.

"Thanks be to all the gods, the fuckers are speeding back up," Stewart murmured.

No one said anything until Jamal decided enough time had passed and guided the Mercedes back onto the roadway. "No need to wonder if more vampires are out there," Jamal muttered.

"No kidding," Michael agreed. "This pretty much clinches it. Something that could sense magic was riding in one of those cars. The Fuehrer would never allow a Romani or a shifter, let alone witches or mages to get that close to him, so it has to have been a vampire."

"Goddammit!" Jamal pounded the steering wheel with a fist. "I suppose the Fuehrer has his own personal vampire. Makes sense, given that his SS were parlaying with them. He'd never have approved something like that and not wanted the same augmented power for himself."

"Our work may not be done," Tairin spoke up. *"But we can't do anything until we eat and rest and recharge our power. It'll take Elliott a while to recover from the vampire that lodged within him."*

"I'll be fine as soon as the rest of us are ready to launch an attack," he retorted.

If Tairin had been human, she'd have snorted laughter. As it was, a whuffle moved past her open jaws. Men. God forbid anyone suggested even a hint of a weak spot, and they jumped in with both feet—or four paws—denying it.

"Our next skirmish won't be as straightforward as today," Michael said thoughtfully. "Getting close to the Fuehrer will be damn near impossible."

"Aye, but vampires travel in nests—" Stewart began.

A rippling sound of disgust from Jamal cut off Stewart's words. "Don't you see? That's why they were going so fast," Jamal said. "The vampires we killed must have sent out a distress signal, and the ones in the motorcade were on their way to rescue them."

"*I had no idea they had a type of hive mind,*" Tairin cut in, "*but I know very little about them.*"

"How close are we to the castle?" Elliott asked.

"Maybe five minutes," Jamal replied.

"*Can they track us?*"

"Not in cars. If we'd had horses they could," Jamal answered. "Why?"

"*I'm worried about the caravans,*" Elliott said. "*Rom aren't fighters. Those caravans wouldn't know what to do if vampires attacked—or a phalanx of SS showed up.*"

"Being followed isn't a worry, but if our conjecture about Hitler's association with the vampires is accurate, and the nest we destroyed includes more vampires, ones that are part of his personal retinue…" Jamal's words trailed off.

"*We killed the nest's sire. What exactly does that mean?*" Elliott asked.

"That the remainder of the nest will turn the world upside down to exact revenge," Jamal replied. "If there are other old ones in that nest, they may well recognize shifter and Romani magic in the ash piles that are still smoldering."

"*So? We'll stay in our human bodies for a while,*" Tairin said. "*That should solve the problem.*"

"*Not that simple,*" her wolf, who'd been silent for a long time, spoke up.

"Your wolf is correct," Jamal broke in. "Vampires can smell us —even in human form—if they put their minds to it. Which means they can scent Romani as well."

"One problem at a time," Michael muttered. "Let's get out of this car and back to the caravan. I'm going to sequester my people in the mountains between Munich and Dachau. Many deserted farms are tucked away off the main tracks, and it's unlikely we'll be discovered there. Not immediately, anyway."

"What about the other caravans?" Stewart asked. "I'll throw my people's lot in with yours. We'll be stronger that way, but there are ten other groups."

Michael shrugged. "I can't speak for them. We've always operated independently. I'm doing what's best for my people. The other leaders will have to make that decision for theirs."

"Ye must tell them about the vampires and the Fuehrer," Stewart countered.

"I'll take care of that once I instruct my people to finish packing their belongings," Michael agreed.

"Tairin and I will remain in the castle for a few hours," Elliott said. *"It's already warded, and we need rest."*

"What will you do after that?" Michael asked, his tone carefully neutral.

"In truth, I have no idea," Elliott replied. *"It depends on what Tairin wants—and who's comfortable having two mixed blood mages in their midst."*

"We'll sleep on it," Tairin said. The specter of leaving the caravan made her sad, but her wagon and team were behind the crumbling castle. Maybe a part of her had known she'd never return to the caravan to live.

Jamal pulled into the castle's courtyard and killed the ignition. "No one asked, but I shall remain with my daughter and her husband to be—if they'll have me."

"Of course we will," Tairin and Elliott replied almost in unison.

Jamal got out of the car and opened the back door so the wolves could jump down.

Michael pushed the front door open and came around to Elliott. "I'm very glad you're still alive, son. I plan to read up on the infection that passed from the vampire to you. It has to be in the lore books."

Light flared around Elliott's wolf. When it cleared, he was a man again, his torso crisscrossed with a fine network of cuts that hadn't been there before. He wrapped his arms around Michael, and the older man hugged him back. "I still have some of the lore books," Elliott said. "You'll want to take them back with you. Once you figure things out, tell me where you'll be."

"Of course. We'll need our combined power to take on the rest of those vampires." Michael let go, and a grim smile spread across his face. "Nothing like a crash course in warcraft."

Stewart walked into the courtyard, his and Michael's horses in tow. "We should get moving." He pulled himself onto his mount, a tall, sorrel gelding.

"Hang on. I'll be ready soon." Michael detoured into the tunnel, returning with an armload of books. Once he'd tucked them into his saddlebags, he swung astride his mount. "Good day's work. Thanks, Jamal, and please offer Meara our appreciation as well. Without her, my boy would've died."

"Will do." Jamal raised a hand in farewell.

Tairin ran around to where her wagon was tethered, remaining as far from her team as she could. Elliott followed her and opened the wagon's side door. She bounded inside and shed her wolf body for her human one. A quick foray into one of many boxes lining the floor and walls produced clothes, and she wrapped a skirt and tunic around herself. When she came back outside, Elliott held her shoes dangling from one hand.

She wrapped her arms around him, trying out and discarding words to describe the complex array of emotions buffeting her. Gratitude, love, relief, anticipation, and so much else she couldn't name.

"Yeah." He smoothed hair back from her face. "All those things, and more besides. I'm so glad you didn't cut me out of your life. I'm sorry for the way I was last night. I—"

"Hush." She laid a hand over his mouth. "I've always had a hot temper. It got the better of me. My wolf knew I was wrong, and it told me, but that conversation can wait. Right now, I need to sleep. Do you want to share the pallet in my wagon or shall we lie down inside your grotto?"

He smiled at her. "That pallet sounds better than sleeping on the ground. We should tell your father what we're doing."

"Jamal will figure it out. I suspect he's exhausted too. Hell, he could be curled up asleep in the backseat of his car by now." She grinned crookedly. "Keeping you out of evil's clutches was a full-time job—for all of us."

"I have one question. The rest can wait."

Tairin nodded encouragement. "Yes? What is it?"

"From what I know about shifters, your animals come to you in dreams when you're very young. Where did my wolf come from? I asked it, but it told me that wasn't important. What was significant was that it chose to bond with me."

She laced her fingers with his. "That's true enough. The bond animals live in two places. With us and on another plane, maybe another universe. I've never totally understood where my wolf is when it's not with me. I do know they converse with others like them in the other place."

"That doesn't exactly answer how my wolf found me."

"In a way it does," she replied. "Your need was great, and one of the unbound wolves heeded my wolf's call. I'm looking forward to getting to know that side of you better." A soft smile lifted some of the weariness from her features. "I already know your wolf is brave and selfless. It didn't hesitate when it sensed your desperation."

A shadow crossed his face, maybe because she'd just reminded him how close he came to being absorbed by the master vampire. His next words clinched her suspicions.

"I can't think about that now. Not until I have more distance from it. Thanks for your explanation about my wolf, though. I'm going to collect some clothes from my chest. Back very soon."

She wound her arms around his naked body, tracing the many cuts with her fingertips. Had the vampire made those wounds leaving? Her mind recoiled at the thought of how close she'd come to losing the man in her arms.

Elliott kissed her gently before disentangling himself from her embrace. "I love you, Tairin. Go get the bed warm for us. If I don't leave now, I never will, and I'll want clothes after we get up."

She watched him walk away, his tread heavy and resolute, and crawled back inside her wagon. Dragging a rough, woolen blanket off a shelf, she wrapped it around herself and lay on a straw-filled pallet on the floor, making certain to leave space and part of the blanket for Elliott.

Weariness crashed over her as soon as she was prone. She tried to stay awake until Elliott got back, but the combination of stress and draining her magic to bedrock won. Sleep claimed her. She roused slightly when he settled next to her, but was asleep again before she could tell him she loved him.

CHAPTER 15

*E*lliott woke with a sleeping Tairin cradled in his arms. It was still dark outside, but chirping birds signaled morning wasn't far off. He'd wanted to tell her so many things the previous evening. How much she meant to him, the life he hoped they'd share, but he'd been as tapped out as she. It hadn't helped that Jamal waylaid him for a chat when he was pulling clothes out of his chest.

Mostly the shifter had wanted to reassure Elliott that he and Tairin would always have a place in shifter circles. He'd also extended an open offer of assistance as Elliott figured out his new magic. Though he didn't say as much, he'd implied the Romani might be less willing to accept a mixed blood couple. And word about what happened to Elliott would spread like wildfire through the Rom caravans.

Tairin stirred and her eyes flickered open. A sleepy smile formed on her generous mouth. "Morning, handsome."

"Morning, yourself." He smiled back.

"How are you feeling?" She quirked a brow his way.

"Better than I have a right to." He laced his fingers into her hair to move strands away from her face, loving the silky feel of her hair and skin beneath his fingers.

"None of us have a right to much of anything," she said, and her tone turned serious. "Just getting up to fight another day might be the best we can hope for—until the Reich's no longer in power."

"If we can hold out long enough, we should have help."

Tairin narrowed her eyes. "Your seer gift? You saw something?"

"Not really, but I can't imagine the States not joining the Allies. And that pact between Germany and the USSR has more holes than Swiss cheese."

The corners of her mouth twitched into a bigger smile, and she snuggled deeper into his embrace. "Why are we talking politics before the sun's even up?"

"You tell me. What do you want to talk about?"

"Us. I never got a chance to tell you how much you mean to me." She angled her head so she could look at his face. "When Jamal explained the vampire had found a way to keep on living— in your body—I was devastated. I would've done anything to save you. Anything. My wolf agreed."

Elliott's heart cracked wide open and spilled over. "Even though you put your own lives on the line. That was actually a tipping point for me. Meara had me buried in that vortex. I couldn't see beyond it, but I could hear."

"So you heard Jamal?"

He nodded. "Yes. When he said you and your wolf and the wolf I felt within me would be lost to darkness if I failed, that you'd absorbed some of the vampiric essence, I knew I had to try harder. Your wolf said the same thing earlier—and my wolf had been giving me nine kinds of hell—but none of it totally sank in. Your father's words did. My death was one thing, but I couldn't stand the thought of you succumbing because I'd been stupid enough to not pay attention to what looked like garden variety beetles."

Tairin snaked a hand out from beneath the blanket and cupped the side of his face. "That part is behind us. If you ever want to talk about any of it, I'll be here. Goodness and evil, dark and light, waged a battle in your body. It must've been hell playing host to something like that."

"Doesn't matter. The important thing is you're here in my arms. I'm the luckiest man alive."

Tairin scrunched her face into a wistful expression, her eyes reflecting a complex array of emotion. "Let's hope you're still saying that a year from now."

"I'll be saying it a hundred years from now. Or I think I will. One of the sideline benefits of my new shifter status has to be an enhanced lifespan."

"Indeed it is. Look at the positives, eh?"

"Always. Even if most Romani bar us from their caravans, having you by my side is a more than even trade."

Pale, gray light seeped through cracks between the wagon's boards. Morning would be upon them soon. He had no idea what the day would bring, but it would be chockful of things to do. If he left the caravan, he'd need to gather all his things. He and Tairin—and perhaps Jamal and Meara—would have to find a place to stay for at least a few days until they could craft longer-term plans.

Before the day with all its problems rose to meet them, Elliott cradled Tairin's neck in one hand and kissed her gently. He wanted to claim her, make her his, but the choice was hers to make. If it hadn't been wartime, he'd have taken her to the fanciest hotel in Munich and requested the bridal suite. She deserved rose petals and soft linens, not a dusty wagon bed for their first lovemaking.

She also deserved the formality of being his wife. Before he could pull away, ask her to marry him, she wove her arms around his body and kissed him back, opening her mouth to his tongue. His body responded instantly, cock hardening where it pressed against her belly. He nibbled and sucked and bit her lips. She bit back, making little, mewling sounds as she explored his mouth with her tongue and lips.

Her hips bucked against his, and she sandwiched one of his legs between hers, rocking against him. The need to see her naked rushed through him, hot and primitive, but it was nippy inside the wagon. Easy to fix. Magic simmered through him until it enclosed them in warmth. Moving a hand between them, he teased the nearest breast. Delighted by how peaked her nipple was, he rolled it between his fingers, tugging gently.

Elliott didn't want to stop kissing her lush lips, but he had other tasks for his mouth. He licked his way down her chin and neck, pushing her tunic out of the way so he could suckle the breast he'd been toying with. She arched her back, pressing her nipple into his mouth.

He took the other breast in his hand, twirling and teasing the nipple. Because he wanted both breasts, he moved them together and lashed his tongue from one to the other. She raked her nails up his back and tangled her hands in the trailing ends of his hair.

Breath coming fast, throat thick with desire, he let go of her breasts and tugged her tunic over her head. For long moments he gazed at her breasts. They were high and full and perfect. While he was lost in admiring her, she reached between his legs and curved her fingers around his rigid flesh.

"Convenient one of us is naked." She grinned coquettishly. "I got cheated the other night when I didn't get to see your body, but you got an eyeful of mine."

"I plan on an even bigger eyeful. Why do you think I made the space around us warm?" he joked back and unfastened the ties holding her skirt together.

She shimmied out of it and lay beneath his gaze, all flat stomach and long, shapely legs. Tawny curls beaded with moisture framed the vee between her legs. The musk of her arousal made it almost impossible not to plunge between them, but he needed to take this slow. She was a virgin, and he wanted today to be exceptional for her. His cock ached with yearning. So did his heart and mind, but he ignored his body's pleas to hurry.

Tairin ran her fingertips the length of his shaft, and he shuddered, perilously close to release. "I love you touching me," he managed between panting breaths, "but you have to stop or I'll spend."

"This way, I'll get to watch."

Raw hunger in her voice excited him, made him want her eyes on him when semen juddered from his cock. "I'd like that sometime, but not today."

He wasn't sure where he got the discipline, but he uncurled her fingers from him and knelt between her legs. Bending low, he kissed her stomach and then moved his mouth lower still until he fastened it over the sensitive nub between her legs. She writhed beneath him, her back bent like a bow. He slid first one and then two fingers into the tight hotness between her legs, feeling her muscles clench around him.

He nipped and sucked her nub, feeling her arousal build. When she was as close as she could get to release without tumbling over the edge, he withdrew his hand and straightened. Kneeling over her, he seated his harder than hard cock at her entrance and pushed inside, but very slowly.

Her nipples were puckered buds of need, and a beautiful rose color splotched her chest and face. She raised her legs and wrapped them around his hips, drawing him inside her scorching core. She curled her hands around his buttocks and pulled hard until his shaft was fully encased in her body. The sensation was exquisite, unbelievable. The feel of her tantalized him, making it excruciatingly difficult to keep to the slow pace he'd planned.

She thrust her hips upward, rocking her sensitive center

against the base of his cock. "Move," she exhorted. "You didn't hurt me. Move. I'm so close."

Elliott didn't recognize the tortured moan that tore out of him as his voice. He withdrew and drove himself back inside, pounding into her as need overcame him. This was his woman. *His.* Lovemaking would seal their bond for now and always.

Her muscles clenched around him as release took her. He tried, but holding his climax in was as futile as controlling the tides or the rising sun. Semen boiled from him, hot, viscous, as his balls drained themselves. Panting and moaning, they ground their bodies against each other while their passion played itself out.

He let himself down atop her and wove his hands into her hair, cradling her head between his hands as he kissed her mouth, forehead, chin, and eyelids. Words felt inadequate after the wonder they'd shared, so he didn't search for any.

Tairin splayed her hands across his back, holding him tight against her. "That was wonderful," she murmured. "I want to stay here and make love all day, but I suppose we should get moving."

He rolled them onto their sides and tucked her head into the hollow between his neck and shoulder. "Task mistress. In truth, I've been half expecting Jamal to roust us."

She grinned. "He wouldn't have. Shifters have good noses, and he'd know what we were up to."

Elliott thought about his newly acquired magic. "So am I all shifter now? Or is part of me still Romani? How does that work?"

"I'm not certain. If you'd been human, and a wolf shifter bit you, you'd have become a shifter. Not been human at all anymore. That's probably a question for Jamal."

Elliott stumbled over his next question, but he wanted to know. "Our wolves. Will they make love too?"

"No. I had sex with regular wolves during that century I lived with them, but it filled a need for contact. My human side was so deeply buried, my wolf was afraid I'd lose it altogether, so it pushed me to be intimate with some of the wolves in the packs we ran with."

Elliott was heartened by how much her wolf saw and understood. "Your wolf loves you."

"Yes, and I love it. You'll develop the same relationship with yours, but it will take time. Our bondmates are more spirit and mind than physical creatures. They'll talk and play and take comfort from being together, but they won't make love. I believe it has something to do with children. When we have them, they'll be from my human body, not my wolf form."

Children.

Elliott winced. "I'm sorry. I shouldn't have come inside you. I was so swept away by desire, I wasn't thinking. I'll have better control next time."

"It's all right." She shot a pointed glance his way. "You wouldn't know this because we never tell the men. One of the reasons human women visit Romani caravans is to get herbal remedies to eliminate pregnancies. And shifters control when we produce offspring."

"So we're taken care of on all fronts?" He furled his brows. At her nod, he went on. "I do want children with you—"

"—but not until we're out of the middle of a war. I understand. It would be very difficult to have a baby right now. We'll just have to make certain we live through this, so those children waiting in the wings get a chance to grace our lives."

He gathered her close. "I like the sound of that. Tairin. Darling, Tairin. I do love you. Tell me you'll marry me. I wanted to propose after we first woke up, but once you kissed me, you forced everything but loving you out of my mind."

"Of course I'll marry you. I love you too, you know." Her words were garbled against his shoulder.

"I have to approve," Elliott's wolf spoke up.

Elliott waited. When the wolf didn't say anything further, he asked, *"Do you? This is the woman we almost gave up everything for. She means everything to me."*

Whuffling lupine laugher filled his mind. *"Of course I do. Be happy together. You've earned it."*

Elliott gazed at Tairin. "How about your wolf? Is it in agreement?"

She smiled. "Oh my yes. It told me as much days ago."

"So we're covered on all fronts?"

"You bet." She kissed him lightly, and twin howls cascaded through his mind from his wolf and hers.

Footsteps pattered their way along with the feel of Jamal's magic. He tapped softly on the wagon's door. "I know you two are up. I didn't want to disturb you, but Michael and Stewart are on their way here, and I thought you'd want to be up and dressed for them. Meara's back too. She arrived last night."

"Out in a few minutes," Elliott called.

He brushed his lips over hers in one last kiss and then dismantled the magic keeping a hive of warm air around them. "Knew I'd want these clothes." He reached for the pile he'd left the night before and dressed quickly.

Tairin put her skirt and tunic back on. Getting to her feet, she dug a black woolen cloak out of a box and snugged it around herself. "What did you do with my shoes? Last I saw, they were dangling from your hand."

Elliott thought about it for a minute and crawled to the far side of the wagon near the door to retrieve them. He stood, but had to bend his head because of the wagon's low roofline. Tairin could stand, but the top of her head touched the ceiling.

His shoes must still be in Jamal's car. "Meet you in the grotto or wherever Jamal and Meara are," he said. Stockings in hand, he let himself out the door and went in search of the two shifters.

Jamal and Meara stood by the Mercedes. They looked up at his approach wearing worried expressions. Elliott opened one of the car's back doors, rescued his shoes, and balanced from foot to foot as he slid first his stockings and then his shoes on. No one said anything.

"Looks like bad news," he ventured. "Are either of you going to tell me?"

"No worse than we'd imagined," Meara replied tightlipped. "I did a spot of aerial reconnaissance after I left all of you. Convenient being a bird, particularly a vulture when bodies are burning. No one looks twice at you."

"Or checks to see if you're not what you appear," Jamal cut in.

Meara made a chopping motion with one hand. "You already know about Hitler's motorcade. Jamal told me it passed you. And you guessed correctly it was heading for the vampire nest."

"How many more of those bastards are there?" Elliott's muscles clenched into rocks.

"Four," Meara replied. "Furious is an understated word for their reaction to finding the nest gone and their sire and compatriots dead. They ran about like a pack of truffle-sniffing pigs." She shut her jaws with a clack. "It'll be a miracle if they didn't catch all of our scents from that killing field."

"Vampires are exceptional hunters," Jamal said. "They're tireless and will track a scent for years if they're bent on revenge. And they will be. Make no mistake about it."

A deeply sinking sensation cut into Elliott's earlier joy. "Someone has to tell the caravans."

"I already did," Meara snarled. "For all the bonhomie they welcomed me with. You'd think they'd have been grateful. Ach. It doesn't matter. What does is you'll have to go to ground. All of you."

Tairin joined the group. "I heard most of that. It's not any different from what we figured would happen yesterday. We extrapolated at least one vampire was in the motorcade. Four isn't that many more."

"Four now," Jamal corrected. "They can make more far faster

than we can reproduce, but I grant you that newly made ones aren't much of a threat. Not for a good ten years or so."

Elliott exhaled sharply and focused his next words on Jamal. "You said Michael and Stewart were on their way here. Why aren't they seeing to getting their caravans moving?"

"Sorry. I wasn't clear," Jamal replied. "Their caravans are with them, and they'll only stop here long enough to let us know roughly where they'll be. After that, they'll go to ground. I hope to hell Hitler keeps those vampires busy enough they won't have time on their hands to go hunting."

"Ha!" Elliott rolled his eyes. "Hitler only thinks he has the upper hand. Those vampires will do whatever the hell they please."

"I'll keep to my bird form for a while," Meara announced. "If anything happens that you need to know about, I'll find you. While I'm about it, I'll warn our kin to be vigilant."

Elliott turned to Tairin. "Where do you want to go?"

Tairin glanced at Jamal. "Will you be with us?"

"I'd like that."

The noise of distant wagon wheels announced caravans drawing near. At least it eradicated the problem of his personal belongings. They'd be in the wagon he'd shared with two other unattached men. He could catch up with it once they stopped somewhere. Elliott thought about Michael and Stewart and the other Romani who'd fought the vampires. Presumably, traces of all their scents remained on the battlefield.

Traces that could be tracked.

Yesterday proved shifters and Romani working together were a match for vampires. Maybe shifters alone could take down a vampire, but Elliott doubted an entire caravan of Romani would be a match for one. Concern for his people cut deep.

"If it's all right with you—" he looked from Tairin to Jamal "—I'd like to be close to wherever Michael's and Stewart's caravans settle. That way, we could help if one of the vampires tracks them."

Tairin nodded slowly. "We can do that."

"I'm certain there will be shifter dwellings, like the one where Tairin found me, somewhere near the caravans," Jamal said. "We can hunt for them once we know exactly where they'll hole up."

"Shifter dwellings?" Elliott asked.

"Hidden grottos, not unlike yours here," Meara replied. "Shielded by magic, they've existed since close to the beginning of time."

Michael and Stewart rode into the courtyard, their faces set in grim lines. Lines of colorful wagons pulled into view behind them. Michael brought his horse to a stop next to Elliott and Tairin. "Not staying long," he said. "If we're able to make it a few miles out of Munich where we might have a shot at disappearing, I'll be amazed. The roads are crawling with SS vehicles. They stopped us twice driving our wagons across town."

"Och aye," Stewart put in. "Sodding bastards. They were torn. Happy to be rid of Romani scum on the one hand and itching to arrest us on the other."

"What'd they do?" Elliott asked, alarmed.

"Wrote us warnings. Told us we had to register as undesirables in Dachau," Michael replied, making a sour face.

"You told them that was your destination?" Meara asked.

Stewart made a grunting noise. "Aye. Should've picked a place much farther away, but I wasna thinking."

"If you had picked a more distant location," Jamal said, "it might have tipped the balance in favor of arresting both caravans on the spot. What you did worked because they waved you through."

"Eh. Maybe so," Stewart replied, but he didn't sound convinced.

"Look here." Meara squatted in the dirt and drew a diagram. "Take the overgrown track around the castle. Tairin will need to move her wagon. Right now, it's blocking things. The trail meanders a bit, but after a few miles, it will bring you to a heavily wooded glen. Three deserted shepherd's cottages butt up against a steep hillside. There's water and decent hunting. I found it last night, and no one's been there for at least the last fifty years."

Flickers of optimism replaced the despair brimming from Michael's dark eyes. "Even if we don't remain there long, it will at least offer a bit of breathing room."

Meara pushed to her feet and squared her shoulders. "A spot of advice, Romani?"

"What might that be?" Michael met her direct gaze.

"Your wagons are impossible to hide. If you decide to leave the wooded glen, you'll need to find cars to move your people. It's the only way you can possibly blend in enough you might escape notice, but even that's far from certain."

"I understand," Michael said. "Our old ways have to die for my people to survive."

"No space or time for sorrow," Stewart muttered, following it with, "Tairin, if ye could move your wagon."

"I'll take care of it right now." She sprinted toward the back of the castle's ruins.

"We'll be behind you," Elliott told Michael. "And we'll settle nearby, at least for now. Apart from the caravan, but close enough to help if the vampires track you."

"Ye needn't do that—" Stewart began.

"We want to," Jamal cut in, breaking his silence.

"Thank you. We'll talk more, craft our strategy, once the wagons are out of sight and our caravans safer than they are right now," Michael replied.

Elliott followed Tairin to her wagon to help her move it. She released the brake, and he grabbed the lead horse's halter and led it in a broad circle off the track. After setting the brake again, Tairin walked to his side with tears glistening in her eyes.

"What's wrong?" he asked once the wagons had rolled past them.

She squared her shoulders. "All my life, I was certain I was damaged goods from a tarnished legacy. In the past few days, I've discovered a father who never stopped loving me…" She hesitated and brushed tears that had overflowed off her cheeks. "And you. I found a man I care about and respect and love. One who loves me back, who was able to look past my shifter blood."

She turned to face him and grasped his hands in hers. "I'm not angry anymore. Not at the Rom for Mother, and not at Father for what he did. The future is precarious, and it doesn't take your seer ability to see more battles ahead, but I'm grateful for so many things."

"Both of us are," her wolf said.

Elliott gathered her against him, holding her. "I have the best woman in the world. One who risked her life to save mine." He stroked her hair. "Whatever tomorrow brings, we'll be stronger facing it because we're together."

"Don't forget about me," Elliott's wolf spoke up.

Elliott laughed, and Tairin joined in. "I don't think forgetting about you is possible," Elliott said.

"Shift," his wolf suggested. *"Get to know me when death isn't sitting on our shoulders like a gargoyle."*

Jamal joined them. "We must be better hidden than we are," he told Elliott's wolf. "Once it's safe, all three of us will shift and run as a pack."

"I'll hold you to it," Elliott's wolf said, adding a whuffly growl after its words.

Elliott didn't doubt it for a moment. He let go of Tairin. "So long as we have the wagon, I'm going to collect the few things I have in the grotto and take them with us."

"I'll magic it up to obliterate your scent," Jamal said.

"While you two are about that, I'll get Flame," Tairin offered. "Do you want to ride him or hitch him to the wagon?"

"Hitch him," Elliott said. "That way, I'll get to sit next to you on the box."

Tairin flashed him a smile that was full of promise and ran lightly toward where Flame was tethered.

"Are you bringing your Mercedes?" Elliott asked Jamal as they made their way down the tunnel to the grotto.

"Of course. I can't leave it here. Besides, we may need it."

On that sober note, Elliott piled his meager belongings into the carved chest and dragged it into the tunnel and toward the opening. It would probably take two of them to heft it up the steps.

Behind him, magic flashed blue-white.

Endings.

He hadn't expected to remain in the grottos forever, but it had been his magical home for long enough, he'd grown fond of it, returning there each time the caravan went through Munich.

Tairin joined him. "Beginnings too," she observed and helped him hoist the chest up the stairs.

"You were in my head." He joined her in the courtyard and dragged the chest toward her wagon.

"Of course. We're one now."

Despite everything, happiness speared him. He set the chest down and hugged her tight. "Yes," he agreed. "One. Now and forever."

Jamal joined them. "Need help with that chest? We should be gone from here before the feel of my magic draws anyone. The neutralizing spell I cast will take time to eradicate all our scents."

"Nope. No help needed." Tairin wriggled free from Elliott's embrace. "We've got it." She picked up one side of the chest.

Elliott grabbed the other. Together they covered the few feet to the team and wagon and hoisted the trunk through the open side door, latching it securely.

The roar of Jamal's engine filled Elliott's ears, and the car rolled past them. Jamal leaned out the window. "Figured I needed to go first in case I break an axle. Meara said this track was rough."

"Get a wagon," Tairin yelled after him and dissolved into laughter as she clambered onto the wagon's seat.

Elliott joined her. Snapping up the reins, he guided the horses into unknown territory with the woman who meant more than life itself leaning into him. "It feels wrong with everything that's facing us, but I'm happy."

"Me too. Don't begrudge us moments of joy." Her expression turned serious. "One thing I learned after first the Rom, and then the shifters, made it clear I wasn't wanted was that you have to latch onto pockets of happiness where you find them."

He transferred the reins to one hand and draped an arm around her shoulders. "Remind me of that from time to time, please."

"I will. Promise."

Drawing the team to a halt, he gathered Tairin into his arms and kissed her.

THIS IS the end of *Tarnished Legacy*. The next book in the *Soul Dance*, series, *Tarnished Prophecy*, picks up where this one ended. It's Jamal and Ilona's tale. Read on for a sample.

ABOUT THE AUTHOR

Ann Gimpel is a USA Today bestselling author. A lifelong aficionado of the unusual, she began writing speculative fiction a few years ago. Since then her short fiction has appeared in many webzines, magazines, and anthologies. Her longer books run the gamut from urban fantasy to paranormal romance to science fiction. Once upon a time, she nurtured clients. Now she nurtures dark, gritty fantasy stories that push hard against reality. When she's not writing, she's in the backcountry getting down and dirty with her camera. She's published more than 50 books to date, with several more planned for 2017 and beyond. A husband, grown children, grandchildren, and wolf hybrids round out her family.

Keep up with Ann at:

www.anngimpel.com or

http://anngimpelaudiobooks.com

If you enjoyed what you read, sign up for special offers and pre-release special reads featured in Ann's newsletter. The link is at the top of the page in both of Ann's websites.

TARNISHED PROPHECY DESCRIPTION AND SAMPLE

Tarnished Prophecy

Germany 1940

Magic runs strong in Ilona, a gypsy seer. Powerful ability isn't valued in Romani women, so she focuses her fortunetelling on inconsequential details. Nothing that could come back to haunt her caravan if a prediction went bad. Rounded up and dumped in Dachau prison camp, she has plenty of time to rue her decision to downplay her ability. If she'd taken the time to scry her own future, she'd still be free.

A wolf shifter, Jamal made the mistake of falling for a Romani woman centuries ago. His arrogance caused both death and heartache, and he's been alone ever since. Meanwhile, the recent threat of vampires joining the Third Reich provided ample reason for shifters and Rom to lay ancient enmity aside and work together, but their détente is fragile.

Jamal and a group of shifters come across Ilona after her escape from Dachau. Vulnerable, terrified, she's fully prepared to fight. Her courage and mettle touch places in him that he'd thought were dead, but she's Romani. His last relationship ended so badly, the last thing he needs is to fall for another gypsy woman. He wrestles his tumbling emotions into submission, but when she trains her enigmatic, gray gaze on him, his resolve fritters away like so much fairy dust.

TARNISHED PROPHECY, CHAPTER 1

$\mathcal{I}$lona Lovas pressed into the shadowed place her bunk attached to the wall, wishing night would last forever. At least at night, she could lie down and no one bothered her. Stacked in three layers on both sides of a drafty barrack building, the beds consisted of wooden slats. Nothing to cushion them and no blankets unless you were one of the lucky ones who hadn't been stripped of every single possession on your way into Dachau. She'd been told she was on her way to a work camp, but it was really a prison.

The fine, old medieval village of Dachau sprawled around the camp. There had to be gypsies left who hadn't been imprisoned, but efforts at telepathic communication failed to raise anyone at all. Ilona thinned her lips into a harsh line. Everyone was running scared. If any Romani remained, they were keeping a very low profile. Help wouldn't come from any but her own efforts. Tears threatened—hot and bitter—but she blinked them back. No energy to do anything that wasn't essential, and crying was an indulgence.

Barely three weeks had passed since she'd been plucked from the streets of Augsburg for the high crime of being a gypsy. All she'd been doing was shopping in the open-air market. For once, she hadn't even stolen so much as a sweetmeat. Three weeks, but it may as well have been three years. Life in Valentin's caravan had been difficult, but it was paradise compared with where she was now. At first, she'd nurtured the hope Valentin would show up to claim her. It would be easy enough to figure out where she was, but for all his bluff and bravado, he was a coward underneath. Besides, even if he'd risked himself, like as not he'd have ended up an inmate.

No one who wasn't Aryan had any rights in Hitler's Germany. Maybe someday the war would be over and…

Who am I kidding? At this rate, I'll be dead before three months are out. Waiting out a multi-year war isn't even a remote possibility.

Her stomach cramped from hunger and she wrapped her arms around her middle, trying to think about something other than food. She'd attempted to wrangle an assignment in the kitchen where she could steal more to eat, but so far the Nazi officers marched her—and every other woman in this building—through the streets of Dachau each morning to a garment factory where they sewed Nazi uniforms twelve to fourteen hours a day.

No food. No water. Not even a bathroom break. Some of the women soiled themselves and were forced to sit in their own filth as tears of humiliation mingled with the thread and fabric.

Fury washed through her, and she curled her hands into fists. No one should be treated this way. None of them were guilty of anything—except being gypsies or Jews or immigrants or malformed or mentally deficient.

Her little brother, Aron, had been with her the day she'd been taken prisoner. They'd been separated at Dachau's gates where she'd been forced to stand with other women, and he'd been prodded into a group of teenaged boys. He'd slipped away from them, though, and made a run for it with three guards hot on his heels. Heedless of punishment, she'd sent magic zinging after him to add speed to his feet, but something dark and malevolent stepped between them, halting the flow of her power.

A strikingly beautiful man robed in scarlet with waist-length dark hair and eyes the shade of a turbulent ocean stared at her as he probed her mind. A predatory smile revealed elongated fangs.

Breath whooshed from her, and her throat thickened in horror.

A vampire. It had to be a vampire. Nothing else could feel so profane.

Who would've thought they even still existed? She'd read about them, but from all accounts, they'd never moved out of Egypt where they'd been a true scourge in ancient times.

The vampire was still focused intently on her. Waves of sexual heat poured from him, snaring her in their net. The lust felt perverse, wrong, but she was rooted in place. She didn't have enough magic at her disposal to both keep him out of her mind and move away from his leering gaze. Even placing herself behind the other women wasn't possible. She tugged at a foot, but it refused to budge.

Damn but he was strong. Far stronger than any Romani. Stronger than the occasional shifter she'd run across as well.

The Nazis who'd taken off after Aron trotted to the vampire, pointing in the direction they'd just come from. Her brother— always a fast runner—had clearly given them the slip, but his chances against a vampire wouldn't be good. At least the SS officers had refocused the creature's attention away from her. She felt dirty, like she'd taken a bath in smut, but her body was hers to command again.

She had to warn Aron, so she risked telepathy, doing her damnedest to shield it from the vampire still deep in conversation with the Nazis.

"Aron! They just sicced a vampire on you. Go to ground. Wind power around you. Remain there until tonight."

Her brother didn't answer, which probably meant his full

magical ability was focused on flight. The vampire didn't even look up. Ilona inhaled raggedly. Good. Maybe the fell creature hadn't noticed.

A club landed on the backs of her legs, and she yelped.

"Gypsy bitch!" a guard snarled. "Get moving. Next time, the club lands on your head."

She'd staggered into the camp, her calves on fire, and her stint in Hell had officially begun. At least so far she hadn't been forced to entertain the German officers, but it was only a matter of time. They grabbed women at random each night. When the women returned at dawn, their faces held a resigned, drawn look and they shook their heads sadly, refusing to talk about how they'd been used.

Soon, her half-starved state would erode her magic. When that happened, her ability to make herself invisible to the Nazis trolling through the women's barracks each night wouldn't be there anymore. It was probably the only reason she'd escaped their net so far.

Yeah. When that happens, I'll be fair game for any ass with a hard on.

Dead was better than raped, and an idea took form. Later this morning when her group was on its way to the garment factory, she'd summon power—while she still had some—create an invisibility illusion, and run. Better not to go far. She'd go to ground the first opportunity she found and wait out the day. When night fell, she'd make her way out of Dachau.

Saliva flooded her mouth, and her gut clenched from nausea. She might have vomited from nerves if she'd had anything in her stomach. Could she pull this off? Why hadn't she done something before? When the answer came, she felt ashamed. She'd been waiting for Valentin—or someone—to rescue her. Or for the Nazis to announce they'd made a mistake. She was innocent, and they were releasing her.

Except that hadn't happened to anyone during her brief tenure in Dachau. The only way out of this place would be in a box if she didn't take matters into her own hands. Soon, she'd be too weak to leverage the amount of power required to vanish from prying eyes. It wasn't just cloaking herself. She also had to plant a suggestion in the guards' minds that they'd never seen her.

Hard to raise an alarm for someone no longer on your mental roster of prisoners. They might have a paper list, but she'd never seen them use one.

Ilona scrunched her eyes shut. They felt hot and gritty, and a headache pounded behind one temple. Where would she go—assuming she pulled off her escape? Not back to the caravan. Associating with gypsies wasn't safe. The guards had stolen her rings and bracelets and hoop earrings, so nothing marked her as Romani. Her hair was dark and curly, but she had gray eyes, and lacked the sharp facial features common to her people. She couldn't pass as Aryan, but at least she might not be pegged as Rom absent her jewelry and colorful, flowing skirts.

Her prison clothes would have to go...

Stop! One thing at a time. My first focus has to be escape. Once I'm hidden somewhere, I can work out the rest of it.

She relaxed her muscles, which had tightened into rocks, but sleep was out of the question. Dawn couldn't be far off. She had a plan. One she'd put into action because it was better than fading away and dying in Dachau. The guards dragged dead bodies out of her barracks each morning. If she waited too long, she'd meet the same fate. She'd been young and strong when the Nazis captured her, but those resources were dwindling.

Fear—the same terror that turned all of them into mewling ninnies dancing to a malevolent Pied Piper—lodged behind her breastbone and accentuated every beat of her heart. She pushed it back. She'd need its energy for her flight, and only a fool frittered away resources.

∼

289

Ilona walked at the tail end of the line of women plodding to the garment factory. Dawn was just breaking, and the gunmetal sky spit sleet. She knew better than to talk, and she kept her hands clasped in front of her. With downcast eyes, the human queue moved like an undulating snake through deserted streets. Dachau might always have been quiet at this hour, but she bet it had never been this quiet. Everyone avoided the Nazis for the best of reasons. They no longer needed a reason to imprison you in a world that had turned upside down. A world where no one asked questions anymore.

Sleep had continued to elude her for what was left of the night, but she'd traded her ambivalence for acceptance. She'd try her best. If it worked, she'd be on her way to freedom. If it failed, death would end her misery.

The woman in front of her stumbled but recovered and kept moving before a guard could swat her with a baton—or shoot her outright. Prisoners were a commodity. Nothing more, nothing less. Easier to kill the weak and move on. New prisoners arrived daily. So many, some of the barracks stuffed them two to a narrow bunk. At least it was warmer that way.

Ilona girded herself and tapped into her magic. One more block and she'd have to do this. If she waited much longer, they'd be at the factory, and escape would be much harder.

Impossible after the women were herded inside.

Once she began, she'd have to be quick. If any of the guards felt her magic—and they might if they were gypsies hiding what they were—the jig would be up. Of course, it would be all over for them too because she'd finger them for being just like her.

Takes one to know one.

A grim smile parted her lips, but her head was down so no one saw it. Her hands shook where they were clutched in front of her, so she gripped them hard enough to hurt. Casting spells was easier if she had the use of her hands, but that part would have to wait until no one could see her.

She inhaled deep, blew it out, and did it again aiming for a calm, clear center. Her power had always been strong for a Romani. Her fortunes smacking of clairvoyance rather than pretense. Ilona let her power build. She wouldn't get to do this again if it turned to shit.

Means I have to get it right the first time.

Magic spilled through her. So much, she feared luminance dancing around her might give her away. Working fast, she reached into the minds of the half dozen guards flanking them.

"You have never seen me. You will not miss me."

Ilona repeated the suggestion twice more. Three was a power number, and she wasn't leaving anything to chance. No sooner had the third iteration left her mind than she drew invisibility from the crown of her head to the soles of her feet and stepped out of the line.

She'd planned to wait long enough to see if any of the guards raised an alarm, but the specter of freedom was heady, and she couldn't force herself to turn as she'd planned to watch the line move away without her.

Heart pounding and throat clotted nearly shut with anxiety, she ran as fast as she could down a side street, and then another one, angling toward the road out of town. After the first few minutes where she'd expected bullets to rip through her spine, her breathing eased a little.

She'd pulled it off—at least for now. Maybe going to ground wasn't such a good idea. She had no idea if she'd eradicated herself permanently from the guards' memories, or if her magical intervention would fade. She'd employed subliminal suggestion before, but always when her caravan was within hours of leaving a town. By the time a gadjo discovered she'd hoodwinked him, it would be too late to do anything about it.

Not that no one ever drove after caravans demanding the head of the gypsy who'd cheated them, but Valentin always dealt with them. She didn't know if anyone had ever come after her, claiming she'd played them false.

She took stock of her magic. It was weakening, but she had enough left to clear the ancient town's walls. Once she was outside Dachau, she could take to back ways, and she wouldn't need to be invisible.

Clothes. She'd need something other than her prison garb.

Ilona scanned the street. Nothing here. She'd been to Dachau with the caravan numerous times, and she tried to remember where shops that sold clothing were located. And then she rolled her eyes. She had no money, and all the shops were still closed.

Probably better. I can break in.

She winced. Stealing a few Reichsmarks from the gadjo paled in comparison with what she had in mind, but she had no choice. Her striped prison suit had to go, and it was too cold to be naked. Never mind the type of attention that would garner.

A quarter mile to the east brought her to a lane of shuttered women's dress shops. Most were multi-story, which no doubt meant the proprietors slept upstairs. Toward the end of the street, a door opened, and a buxom, blonde woman swathed in gingham and a white apron bustled out, leaving the door ajar behind her.

If it wasn't an opportunity, Ilona had never seen one. She hurried up the steps and inside a cozy room lined with samples. Except they were one of a kind. The sharp-eyed woman who'd just left—maybe to go to market—would notice if anything hanging from the hooks adorning the room were missing.

A curtained alcove was inset on the rear wall. She hustled through it, hoping to find more clothing. After all, this place had to have stock to sell beyond the display samples. Her heart pounded so hard, she expected to hear footsteps clattering down the stairs demanding to know what was going on, but silence reigned from the house's upper levels. Piles of clothing scattered through the back room. Exactly what she needed.

Without stopping to check sizes, she scooped a woolen skirt, wool tunic, cotton shirt, and thick jacket beneath one arm. A stack of sturdy socks beckoned, so she took a pair of them too and extended her invisibility illusion to cover everything.

She'd just moved beyond the curtain, intent on the door, when the woman returned carting a bucket that smelled heavenly. Fresh milk. Meant a cow was nearby. Her mouth watered, but she froze in place willing the woman to move back upstairs with her pail. She'd obviously procured the milk for breakfast.

So far, the goddess had shielded Ilona from harm, but she wasn't under any illusions. The Nazis offered bounties for the return of escaped prisoners. This shop didn't look prosperous enough for its owner to turn down a hundred reichsmarks.

The woman crossed the shop, moving carefully to keep milk from sloshing onto her shiny, wooden floor. Ilona would have employed a small spell to speed her on her way, but she needed to conserve her magic. It wouldn't last forever.

The woman stopped near the curtain, nostrils flaring. She made a face, as if she'd smelled something putrid. Ilona clamped her teeth together to keep them from clanking against each other and giving her away. She could shield her visual presence, but not her stench. She hadn't had a bath since the Nazis captured her. Her nose had adapted, but she must be ripe as rotten cheese.

"Piotr," the woman yelled.

"Yes, Momma," a child's voice floated down the stairs.

"Get the mop, bucket, and lye soap. It stinks in here. Must be that smelly customer we had yesterday, although she didn't seem to be quite that rank while she was in here."

"Before breakfast?" the child inquired.

"Yes, before breakfast." The woman sounded annoyed. "It will take me time to cook something and time for the floor to dry. No reason they can't happen together."

Ilona edged toward the door, taking care to be silent and praying a squeaky floorboard wouldn't give her away. The woman had closed the door, but if she'd just start up the stairs, her heavy tread would hide the snick of the latch when Ilona let herself out.

Sighing and muttering in German, the woman disappeared behind the curtain, pail still in hand. Before her son could appear with the mop and bucket, Ilona let herself out deploying still more magic to dampen the noise of the latch. Milk would have been wonderful, but she didn't have time to hunt down the cow.

She felt lightheaded from all the power sluicing through her, but ran anyway, picking a direct route that would lead out of town. A quarter hour later, staggering and panting, she cleared Dachau and hunted for something, anything, that would hide her from prying eyes for long enough to change clothes.

A small stream cascaded down a muddy hillside before vanishing into a thicket of bushes and trees. With the last of her fading energy, Ilona staggered up the hill choked with a blanket of leaves and crisscrossing tree limbs. Her feet ached in their ill-fitting prison shoes, and her arm still clutching the stolen clothing cramped.

Once she moved beyond sight of the road, she loosed her magic. Not having to maintain invisibility shored up her flagging strength, but not by much. Ilona worked her way through a slight opening in the vegetation and stopped in a grove of oak trees. The stream cut through them, which meant she could bathe. Maybe next time she stole something, her reek wouldn't almost be her undoing.

If she hadn't been so exhausted, she'd have whooped aloud. She was free. She'd pulled it off against what felt like daunting odds. Locating a dry spot, she piled her new clothing atop it and stripped off her stinking prison suit. It would be better if she could find a place to hide it, but that wasn't likely. When she was ready to leave, she'd wad it up and bury it beneath the thick carpet of leaves and debris.

Unbuckling her shoes, she waded into the creek. Her teeth chattered from the cold, but she squatted in the water and washed weeks of grit and grime from her body. Even though she was beyond cold, she tilted her head until her hair was immersed and scrubbed her scalp with sand from the creek bottom, rinsing it well. Once she was as clean as she could get absent soap and shampoo, she moved upstream and drank her fill. Food would have to wait until her power wasn't as depleted. She could lure small game—mice and suchlike—but not until she'd rested.

She should have escaped right after they'd captured her. Today proved she could have, but fear had held her back. No more. She couldn't eradicate her fears, but she was done giving in to them.

Ilona made her way to where she'd left her clothes, gratified no one had come anywhere close while she bathed. She hadn't seen any human tracks on her way up the hill, but it paid to be cautious.

She aimed to remain free. Not an easy task, but one she was prepared to die for. As she wrapped herself in the clothing, she savored the finely woven fabrics next to her skin. The socks had been an indulgence, but they padded her feet, making the prison shoes less painful. It would be lovely to replace them, but she wasn't about to return to Dachau. Maybe she'd risk a cobbler's shop in another town, but not this one.

Ilona eyed her discarded prison attire and stopped worrying about it. Surely, she wasn't the first to escape Dachau. No one would associate the shapeless mass of sackcloth with her, and she'd left before they'd gotten around to stenciling a number into her forearm. By the time anyone found her prison clothing, she'd be long gone.

Sleep beckoned, but she had to put some miles between her and her current location. As many as possible. She'd taken the southern route out of town—the opposite way from Augsburg. Munich was ten miles away. It might be a good place to lose herself. Maybe even a good place to find work. She couldn't walk that far without rest, but she could maybe make half that.

There were probably Rom caravans in Munich, but if she'd

wanted a caravan, she'd have headed back to Augsburg. She wasn't exactly done with being a gypsy, but she was done associating with them. Guilt nagged. The Rom were her people, but she couldn't do much to save them from Nazi persecution. Hell, she was having the devil's own time saving herself.

Ilona made her way along the steep side hill until she came to a dirt track leading roughly where she wanted to go. She pulled the hood of her jacket over her head to hide her dark hair and made as good a time as she could.

Where was Aron? Had he made it out of Dachau too?

She started to raise her mind voice, and then remembered the vampire. If they were in league with the Nazis—and it certainly appeared that way—the one she'd seen that day could scarcely be the only one. Magic to hide herself was one thing. Projected power quite another. The last thing she needed was undue attention—or any attention at all.

She'd been worse than a fool to deploy power standing in the yard outside Dachau's gates. If she wanted to remain alive, she'd have to do a better job checking for who might be sensitive to magic before she deployed any.

Ilona murmured a quick prayer thanking Isis for her escape and asking her to watch over Aron. Today had gone surprisingly well. Maybe it boded well for both their futures.

Do not grow complacent, her inner voice cautioned.

All it takes is one vampire—or a car full of Nazis—for my carefully balanced world to shatter.